THE NIGHT MEN

Also by Keith Snyder

◆

COFFIN'S GOT THE DEAD GUY
ON THE INSIDE

TROUBLE COMES BACK

THE NIGHT MEN

A JASON KELTNER MYSTERY

Keith Snyder

Walker & Company ✳ New York

First published in the United States of America in 2002 by
Walker Publishing Company, Inc.

Published simultaneously in Canada by Fitzhenry and Whiteside,
Markham, Ontario L3R 4T8

For information about permission to reproduce selections from
this book, write to Permissions, Walker & Company,
435 Hudson Street, New York, New York 10014

Library of Congress Cataloging-in-Publication Data

Snyder, Keith, 1966–
     The night men : a Jason Keltner mystery / Keith Snyder.
         p.   cm.
ISBN 0-8027-3370-0 (alk. paper)
     1. Keltner, Jason (Fictitious character)—Fiction.
     2. Los Angeles (Calif.)—Fiction.   3. New York (N.Y.)—Fiction.
     4. Composers—Fiction.   I. Title.
PS3569.N892 N5 2002
813'.54—dc21   2001035892

Series design by M. J. DiMassi

Printed in the United States of America

2 4 6 8 10 9 7 5 3 1

This book is for Ben, Joel, and Terryl, who were at the tree; Tom and Jason, who were on the bus; and Terry, who got off too early.

Everything is always for Kathleen, whether she wants it or not.

THE NIGHT MEN

1

MAYBE bicycling over the Brooklyn Bridge at nineteen degrees in strong wind and snow wasn't the brightest thing for an L.A. boy to do.

Fifty feet down, cars and headlights showed through the moving slits between the snow-dandruffed planks under his tires, making a flickering movie of the traffic below him. He'd stopped feeling his ears twenty minutes ago, when the clock on the Watchtower building said it was a minute after midnight. They'd started stinging ten minutes later. A lot.

He hadn't stepped off the bike once, for no better reason than sheer bullheadedness, but he'd downshifted as far as he could, and he was spinning the gears uphill against the wind with no forward momentum. His chest and neck sweated inside his shirt inside his sweatshirt inside his jacket, and the rushing cold bit through his sweatpants and knit hat as though he weren't wearing them. His inner thighs had gone numb where the oncoming wind hit them, and he was sick to his stomach. Snowflakes swarmed like fireflies around the streetlamps. He grunted and pushed the pedals around once more. He'd seen no one else on the bridge, but he was not, by god, getting off the bike.

Being male was sometimes of dubious value.

The Statue of Liberty was a little landmark through the frozen air off to the right as he traversed the level part of the long bridge. Standing on her miniature island, draped in her copper gown, she was dwarfed by the huge toy buildings of nighttime Manhattan. Back home, on the Venice Beach bike path, most of the women you saw were suntanned and almost naked on skates.

Her phone had rung at eleven-thirty, and he'd snapped out of his drowse and answered it because there were no marauding Cro-Magnons to kill, so the least he could do was protect her from the telephone.

"Jase." Zebedee Lindengreen's cigarette-corroded voice. "Did I wake you?"

"Hey, Zeb. Almost. Hold on." He slid out from under her sprawled arm and bent knee, took the cordless phone into her living room, and sat naked in her hanging wicker chair, settling on its tasseled orange cushion. "What's up?"

"My—my apologies to Sarah."

He'd missed the tremor of agitation at first. "Don't worry about it; she's not wakeable. What's going on?"

"Do you think you might be interested in a temporary night job?"

"Um." Jason scratched his chin. "I don't know. Tell me."

"I know this is unusual, but . . . I mean, there's . . ." Zeb breathed abruptly into the mouthpiece, a distorted ruffle of frustration.

He didn't start talking again. Jason said, "You want to get a cup of coffee?"

"I don't know. I don't . . . hold on . . ." Zeb covered the phone and there was a brief exchange with someone. When he came back, he sounded grateful. "Yeah. That's a good idea."

✦

The relative wind sharpened as he sped down the other side of the bridge. He squeezed the brake handle and felt the rubber pads, frozen into abrasive rocks, bite in and score the metal wheel rims.

After Zeb's call, he'd turned the phone off and stood in the doorway and watched Sarah sleep. She was not a feminine sleeper. No graceful little hand positions or hair flowing artfully over satin pillows. When she slept, she slept like she meant it. That bed was going nowhere.

A couple of times when she'd slept, he'd kissed her whole warm body until she awoke, but she'd been exceedingly irritable, so he'd scratched that one off the list of erotic fantasies. Lately, he'd begun experimenting with doing her dishes instead.

In fewer than twenty-four hours, she would be leaving for Peru for a week-long shoot. He loved her, but three weeks in gray, miserable New York was long enough. It was time for him to go home.

The Brooklyn Diner was in a neighborhood that wrestled with schizophrenia, on a main avenue of stupendously overpriced antiquey junk shops, near a huge, dirty shopping fortress. The red neon hands of the clock tower on the corner of Flatbush Avenue floated very high over everything, glowing silently through powdery snowfall, the tower itself invisible in the dark.

As Jason rolled up onto the sidewalk and dismounted awkwardly near a street sign, he saw Zeb sitting in a booth against the window, looking out, one arm along the ribbed back of the seat, a cigarette between two fingers. The muscles of Zeb's face sagged as though their support wires had been loosened under his beard. Last week, he'd looked in his fifties. Now he looked older, gazing out the window of the diner on its dirty, cold street. The two fingers and the cigarette rose listlessly in greeting as Jason locked the bike's frame and front wheel to the frigid signpost.

On the way over the bridge, Jason had been wondering what was wrong. Now as he went into the diner, he wondered how to act in the face of what looked like utter defeat.

Dance music dribbled from a radio on the kitchen service window. Behind the counter, two waitresses gabbed. A third held hands and traded rapturous looks with a clean-cut young man in one of the booths. Nobody acknowledged Jason as he came in through the double glass doors, unsnapping his damp jacket.

He decided on honesty as he tossed the jacket and his knit hat onto the seat across from Zeb. "You look like hell," he said, sliding in, only it came out "Oo-wuh a-hehw," because his lips were frozen.

Zeb's other hand was on the table, gripping a mug of coffee that didn't look hot. "I feel like hell."

"Whas rah?" He opened his mouth very wide and worked all his facial muscles around to get them flexing again.

"They—"

Zeb's voice broke. He looked out the window, the muscle at his jaw bunching, and he raised his cold coffee and sipped, blinking irregularly.

Jason closed his mouth and tried to think of what to say. Martin was good at emotional conversation. Martin would say something empathetic; he was good at empathy. Jason was good at listening and taking action, not at saying the right things.

"What happened?" It sounded cold to him when he said it. Martin would have said it with a lot of concern in his face and his voice. *What the hell happened, man?*

Zeb put the cup down and ran a shaking hand through his limp gray hair. "I'm sorry." His voice was wobbly. "It's been a long day. Did you ever see *Priscilla, Queen of the Desert*?"

Jason held up four fingers. "Twice in the theater, twice on video."

"Remember the scene where the drag queens get all friendly with the townspeople, and everybody likes them, and then they come out the next morning and find the words 'AIDS FUCKERS GO HOME' spray-painted all over their bus?"

"Yeah."

"I don't know what I was thinking." Zeb tightened his lips and shook his head, then shook it again. "I had some vague idea that I could just, I don't know, hire you to watch the store at night, since you're in town and, you know, you're a musician, so I figured you could use the bread, and I know you liked the store, but now I don't know. I wanted to call and tell you not to bother coming, but I didn't want to wake Sarah up."

"What . . . happened to the store?"

"It's demolished. The windows are all smashed, and the glass case, and a lot of the instruments. They trashed the computers, some of the nearfield monitors—" His voice wobbled, and he stopped speaking. Tears welled. He shook his head quickly to stop them and tapped the cigarette over the ashtray, then cleared his throat. "The big mixing boards—" He pointed, as though the audio consoles were in the diner. "They're all roadable, so they came through okay, and all the stands and racks are mostly fine, just some scratches. Man . . ." He parked the cigarette and ran his hand through his hair again, then looked out the window again for a while. When he raised his coffee mug, his hand didn't shake. "Have you ever seen pictures of Kristallnacht?"

Jason nodded.

"Obviously, that was much worse, but . . ."

The Magic Music Shop, ankle-deep in shattered glass and wrecked instruments. Jason could only imagine it in out-of-focus black-and-white.

"They came in through the skylight and left through the front door. We just found everything a few hours ago. We came back from a weekend in Provincetown this evening, and I wanted to run by the store because it's still new and I get worried about it." He shook his head. "We've just worked so hard to get it going. I've been working fourteen-hour days, and Gary Warren—he's there whenever he's not at work. I thought we deserved a little time away together."

"Is it insured?"

"Sure, minus the deductible. God knows how I'll come up with that." Exhaustion tugged at his eyes and mouth. "Or whether I can."

"Has anyone been caught?"

"No." He shook his head. "I can't even think who could have done it. But . . . that's always how it is. You never know who."

"I'll watch the store, nights."

"Jason, I figured you'd offer, and it's really nice of you, and I do appreciate it, but we'll find a—"

"I'll watch it. If you decide to close up, or go out of business or whatever, that's your choice, but until then, I'll be there every night. You guys both work all day; you don't need to kill yourself staying up all night, too."

"How about this. I'll give you some time to think about it—"

"Look. No. You want me to, you don't want me to—it doesn't matter. Either way; I'm doing it. I don't need time to think about this. Sarah leaves tomorrow night. I'll be there right after."

"I don't know. I was trying to figure out how I could pay you. I know you can't afford not to work. But—" Zeb raised his palms.

Jason chewed the inside of his cheek as he thought. "All right, I tell you what. Ever since you opened that store, I've been trying to figure out how to hit you up for dealer cost. You let me buy some gear at cost, we'll call it enough."

"Are you sure? No, I don't know. They probably won't come back. I'm probably just overreacting."

"Zeb." Jason leaned forward. "Maybe you are, maybe you're not. Worry about it later, man. For now, I'm not giving you a choice. How's G.W. doing?"

"It's my turn to go to pieces, so he's holding together fine. Fire marshal Gary." He looked out the window again at the snow, his haggard face softening. "Okay," he said finally. He still looked terrible, but his voice was steady. "Thank you."

"You're welcome."

At two, he slipped into the warm bed beside Sarah, staying a few inches away from her because his skin was still arctic. He looked at the shapeless near-dark a long time, the endless ridiculous honking of the incompetent drivers on the street below floating up through her closed window; remembering two chairs facing a window in a dining room, four boy feet propped on the windowsill. A Polaroid camera on the dining table and a baseball bat leaning against the wall near the door. Dark outside, two A.M., porch light off. Dark in the dining room, too, and the adjoining living room. Drapes slightly open. Murmured conversation.

It wasn't too late to call Robert on the West Coast, but he didn't want to do it yet.

2

ID Indestructible Man have a nice ride last night?"

Her face was against his chest. He felt as though he'd been awake continuously, which meant she'd probably awakened him only moments ago. He caressed her warm side with his palm, liking the smooth softness. "Jase conquer bridge," he grunted.

"Poor bridge."

"I tried not to wake you when I left."

"You didn't. I got up and found your note. Was everything okay?"

He stroked her hair. "My friend Zeb's music store was trashed. He's gay. It could have been a hate crime."

"Oh. God. That's awful. What's he going to do?"

"He doesn't know. I'm going to stay in town for a while."

She answered the question he didn't want to ask: "You can stay here if you want."

Her forehead was all he could reach, so he kissed it. "Thanks."

She snuggled into his side again. In a bit, she said, "God. That's so horrible."

"Yeah."

He knew some of Zeb's history, but he wasn't used to having Sarah to tell it to. It wasn't directly relevant to anything. But if he only talked to her when there was relevant information to impart, he'd lose opportunities to increase their intimacy. That was possibly a too-clinical analysis, but he figured it was okay. Better to approach a relationship with too much thought than to let it mire in bad habits from the start.

Like getting back out of a deep chair after a hard day, he made the effort and talked. "Zeb used to be a first-call banjo player, back in the seventies. He was on a lot of records."

"Did he play with anyone famous?"

She seemed genuinely interested. That was good.

Oh. He should talk more—

"Oh, yeah. Dwight Cooper, for one, before Dwight got famous. Then he toured and did sessions with a lot of name acts. The Eagles, Doc Whitney, Professor Longhair, the Glen Allen Trio . . . I forget who else. He has snapshots pinned up at the store. But recording studios aren't exactly fertile ground for banjo innovation, so he got fed up and quit."

He watched the flow of conversation trickle and die, helpless to start it again.

"Was there a last straw, or did he just get tired of it?"

"Oh. The story is actually sort of legendary. He was doing a Teddy Mandrell session and he refused to play the charts, because being country pop, they were, of course, boring crap. So he started fingerpicking this avant-garde thing with no meter and no tonal center, and he refused to stop until they either came up with a more creative arrangement or booted him out of the studio. Of course, they booted him, and he never worked in Nashville again after that. By mutual agreement."

"That's wild. I wish I had that kind of bravery."

"With your photography clients?"

She nodded against his chest.

"Well," he said, "I think there's something to be said for the fact that you still *have* your photography clients."

She nodded again.

"Anyway, the way I see it, he lucked into the paid session work in the first place, but then his personality caught up with him and he just couldn't do junk anymore. That was what, twenty years ago. In the five I've known him, he's written and taught, but I never saw him get excited about anything. Then that first time I visited the shop, he was sitting out on the sidewalk in a sweater, playing his banjo and just smiling at everybody. I think he was posing because he knew I was coming, but you could still see the satisfaction. You could see he really had a dream again. Both of them, really."

"His partner?"

"Yeah, Gary Warren. That's his middle name, like 'Mary Sue.'"

"It's so sad."

"It was a beautiful little shop. He did a good job of restoring it. It was vacant for a long time."

They didn't get up. His thoughts drifted back to nighttime and broken glass.

"It'll be beautiful again," she said. "Right?"

"I hope so."

"Tell me how much you love me."

He'd run out of fast answers months ago. She smacked him on the stomach. "Faster."

"Oof. I love you—I love you more than ten to the eighty-two."

She pulled away. "Ten to the eighty-two what?"

"That's not the point. Ten to the eighty-two anything is a lot."

"You're a strange man."

He let that go, since it was true.

A little later, she said, "Will you miss me?"

"Very much."

That was apparently a good answer. She buried her face in his neck.

"I know what you're thinking," she said after some drifting.

"I doubt it. In addition to being strange, I'm very complicated."

"You're thinking I should make you waffles."

"Well," he said, "maybe not exactly *complicated*."

He had assumed that they would spend her last day luxuriating in each other's presence, but that ended when the waffles did, when a delivery of film was the wrong kind and she didn't get the gels she'd arranged for. He saw how it was going to go, so he lay on her bed with his shoes off and tried to read as she made and received increasingly frustrated phone calls about a "cuke." When he heard her say, "I'll be there in an hour," he sighed quietly. She hung up and came to her bedroom door.

"I have to go in."

"I know. I heard."

"They can't get one single thing right."

"I know."

"The film's all wrong, they screwed up the gels, and they rented out the cuke I reserved."

"What's a cuke?"

"It's like a gobo. I'm sorry, but I have to go."

"Okay."

"I have to."

He nodded. This was already covered.

"And now you're mad at me, right?"

He'd been holding his book tilted on his chest for efficiency of resumption. He let it fall flat. "Why would I be mad at you?"

"For leaving so I can go do my job."

He stared at her, baffled.

"Forget it." She stalked into the bathroom.

He lay on the bed and pondered this exchange while the water ran and she banged things around just quietly enough that it wouldn't count as banging.

When she came out with a clean face and damp hair, he said, "Hey."

"What."

He patted the bed.

"I have to *go*."

Pat, pat.

She approached and stood by the bed. "What."

Pat.

"You're not taking me seriously."

If he took her seriously now, he was dead. Full steam ahead or sink like a rock.

Pat, pat, pat.

Hands on hips. "I am not a cat. Would you just say—"

She was wearing jeans. He slipped his knuckles through the belt loops and pulled her down on top of him.

"Hey! What are you—"

"I'm going to be out late sometimes, and you won't know where I am."

"Jason—"

"I'm going to get gigs that cut into our time together. I'm going to have to cancel plans when the PA gets rented out to someone richer at the last minute and I have to scramble to find another one. I'm going to be home later than I said. Are you going to be an asshole when that happens?"

"No."

"Well, me neither now."

She was still irritable. "I have to go."

"Okay, just one thing."

"And what's that?"

He did some things she liked.

"Okay," he said presently. "Now you can go."

"Well, now I'm not sure I want to."

"Go on." He let her go and picked up his book. "Don't blow your gig."

She rose to kneeling over him. "You're a very difficult man."

"It's really the only thing I'm good at."

He was very pleased with it as a closing line, but she said, "Oh, I don't think so," and showed him what she meant.

She didn't leave until fifteen minutes after the time she was supposed to have arrived at the photo supply place. He lay nude in her bed, breathing air that still seemed to quiver from her meteoric exit, wondering at the sexist, patriarchal implications of his behavior, and tentatively congratulating himself that it had worked.

3

H E liked New York less each ugly day he was there, but he'd come to appreciate the subway system. On the downtown A train, he stood next to a pole and read his book. In Los Angeles, he'd have been in traffic with the radio on, which, he had recently realized, wasn't so terrible. L.A. radio, as bad as it was, was still an order of magnitude better than New York radio. New York had the edge in live music; Los Angeles had it in broadcast. Los Angeles jazz clubs featured Kenny G. clones; New York seemed to have an all-Rod-Stewart FM station. To a musician who was often too broke for concerts, radio was a serious issue.

He flipped through the book and read about a trick for estimating the squares of numbers near fifty, but he couldn't stay interested. The train banged around a curve, and he touched the pole with the back of a knuckle, but didn't grip it, shifting his balance with his legs instead to stay upright. A game from when he was a kid, riding the RTD bus to school and back.

Route 159. Sunland/Tujunga through the San Fernando

Valley. He was going to have to call Robert. There was no way he couldn't.

Sarah hadn't come back to say goodbye; her day going increasingly wrong, she'd finally sent a messenger service to get her equipment from her apartment, said she'd miss him in a harried voice over the phone, wished Zeb good luck by proxy, and whirled off to Peru to take pictures of oiled caucasian men in faux-primitive loincloths, flexing their ripply abs and displaying colorful, expensive watchbands.

That was just how her career was. It was nothing personal about Jason.

The cold wind had turned icy again, and it cut at his face as he trudged carefully up the concrete steps and stepped onto the refrozen ice on the sidewalk. When they weren't complaining about the pizza, the phonies, and the drivers, New Yorkers in Los Angeles complained about L.A. weather. They had a point about the pizza, he had to concede now that he'd had the chance to compare, but the rest, he couldn't figure out at all.

They walked on ice a lot better than he did, though. Nobody else seemed to be slipping. How did they do that?

As he came around the corner from the subway steps, he saw the music store, halfway down the block on the other side of the street, its front glass shattered, boarded from the inside, four plastic trash cans standing like fat gray pallbearers outside the open door. One propping it open. Heavy to the brims with glass and piled over with wreckage. Someone bumped into him from behind and he found that he had stopped on the sidewalk. A sick buzz spread in his chest, echoing in his memory.

Zeb came out with a couple of flattened boxes and added them to the pile and went back in. The workaday sense of it was shocking.

He couldn't move forward. He could no more enter that

store without first talking to Robert than blink his eyes and make himself fifteen again.

On the corner was a tiny grocery store with three pay phones outside it. He went in and bought a five-dollar phone card.

None of the pay phones worked. He walked a block to another set of three, near a diner, but they didn't work either. Another block brought him to a gas station, which didn't have any pay phones. He finally found two more, around the corner and down three blocks, at a car wash. The clean one didn't work, but the sticky one did.

After a couple of rings, Robert's voice said, "Tungsten."

"Nickel. Why are we speaking in alloys?"

"I was thinking about the differences between words and numbers, and I coruscated this theory that unlike a number, if you phantasmagoric enough context, the canker will be understood despite the fact that you're sluicing the wrong gelato."

"I see."

"Obviously, this fish not snood for numbers, which do not coagulate rutabaga context."

"Yeah they do."

"They ink not."

"Eleven in hexadecimal isn't the same as eleven in binary."

Through the phone, Jason could hear the grind of the pump in Robert's tacky gold rain lamp, three thousand miles away.

"How *would* that work . . ." Robert said thoughtfully.

"I need to talk seriously."

The voice took on focus. "Okay."

"Remember Zeb?"

"Sure, the banjo player with the great music party."

"He bought a little music store in Brooklyn."

"That's great!"

"It was destroyed last night. They smashed all the glass and a lot of the instruments. No one was caught. I'll be staying here a little longer."

There was no response from Robert. Jason hesitated, then said, "I'm going to be sitting up nights, watching the store."

There was a long silence, with the distant rain lamp grinding away.

"Did he ask you to, or did you insist?"

That stung a little, though it shouldn't. "He sort of mused aloud. I sort of insisted."

Another pause. "Zeb's gay, right?"

"Yes."

"You thought of that."

"We both thought of that."

"Can you tell whether that was it?"

"I haven't been in yet. The outside looks okay. I mean, you know, except for the smashed windows and the trash cans full of wreckage."

Another long pause. "How long will you be watching the store at night?"

"Until it's not necessary anymore."

A little clatter as Robert switched the phone to his other ear. "Where are you calling from? Are you where I can call you back?"

"I'm at a pay phone, about a quarter mile from the store. None of the pay phones here work, and all of them are disgusting. I don't know why. I'm going to the store after I hang up. I'll probably be there for a while." He gave Robert the number.

"I just need to—Let me do some thinking."

"Just thought I'd let you know."

"Yeah. Thanks."

"Yeah."

He hung up and walked back. As he neared the store, Zeb came out with another armful and stacked it on the trash cans.

4

THE gangly kid with dark bags under his eyes was in the back of the bus every morning, the very back, on the far right side of the very last bench seat, where boys liked to sit. Jason had seen him around, but the kid was one of those drama club people he didn't like. They seemed smart, but they were pompous along with it. Sort of like the kids in band, only without the reflective sunglasses. They were always quoting things, like they thought that made them important. And all the affectations and the floppy boots and capes and tuxedo shirts. Jeez, just be normal weird instead of making a big show of it.

Jason wasn't in any clubs. He had been in Spanish club for a while, just because he was good at it, and he was sort of attracted to being in the chess club, but it was secretly shaming to him that he wasn't interested in chess. Intelligent people were supposed to be fascinated by it. Could you not like chess and still be intelligent?

Some people still socialized in the same groups they'd retained from junior high; others were detaching from old clusters and attaching to new ones. He didn't understand that. Why change groups when you already had one? Why not just stick with the good friends you had? It was all just too disloyal.

He and the tall kid were often the only two passengers on the bus that early. Jason always avoided him by sitting in the front. Often, the kid would be reading *Hamlet* or Plato or something like that, and then other times, he would just look out the window thoughtfully, showing off how deep he was, but Jason wasn't falling for it.

Jason was really into the Sphereworld books that year.

Lunch was usually a sandwich on one of the bench sets that squared around the trunks of half a dozen trees in half a dozen square holes in the concrete quad. The clusters of students dotted the benches, soshes near the center in Izod shirts, stoners off to the edge in longish hair and shorts, the jocks, the math and computer geeks, the Academic Decathlon people, the drama club people, a group of black kids bused in from somewhere. The student council people flitted between the soshes and the jocks, occasionally dipping in with the honors students for academic credibility and the busing students for grassroots street image.

Jason and his best friend, David, always hung out during lunch. Today, Jason had a tuna sandwich and carrot sticks, and he'd bought juice and a yogurt at the cafeteria. He'd just arranged them on the bench when he saw David coming out, talking with two soshes named Dan and Trent, whom Jason knew only vaguely, but who were reputed to be rich. Dan wore a pink Izod shirt with the collar up.

"Hey, Dave!" Jason yelled. "Nice jacket!"

Lately, white Vans and a white Members Only jacket had crept into David's wardrobe. Today he was wearing the jacket with the sleeves rolled up to his elbows. Trent said something to him and pointed at Jason. Dan turned long enough to show him a blank expression, and David's gaze barely flicked over.

Jason gave him a facetious nod and a big thumbs-up. The jacket was nice enough, but David didn't realize it made him look a little superficial.

Voices roared up on the far side of the quad, near the cafeteria. Jason turned, but his view of the fight was already obscured by all the kids flying toward it and cheering it on, a chant he'd first heard in early elementary school: *A fight! A fight! A nigger and a white!* He'd never understood the point of chanting that. Even stupider, it rarely correlated with observable racial extraction.

The seething huddle expanded by accretion as kids abandoned their lunches and sped toward the disturbance, the inner ring backpedaling to avoid wild swings, the gathering blob swaying and stretching. The chant had dissolved into a bellowing din of recently deepened voices that were still new enough to their owners to be exciting to yell with.

It seemed a full minute before Mr. Sealy appeared in his shiny black loafers and went through the audience, the lower half of his Tweety Bird tie flopping below its clip. As he pushed in, the swell of mobgoers suddenly surged and yelled on the other side. The gangly kid from the bus straightened up inside the newly enlarged ring, his head higher than the spectators, his mouth open and red, and then jerked back clumsily, one hand protecting his mouth, the other trying to fend lower.

Jason opened his juice carton and drank some. He'd admit to the same curiosity as everyone else, but it would be too conformist to run across the quad and watch.

Mr. Harris, the school narc, appeared from behind the cafeteria in his brown shoes and cheap suit, and in the gaps between the moving bodies, Jason caught a view of Mr. Sealy gritting his teeth, comb-over flopping off the side of his bald spot as he fought to keep hold of the T-shirt of a short, sweaty kid who whirled and lunged at the tall, gangly one. Jason didn't know the short kid, but he was very fast, and very angry. As Mr. Sealy was pulled off-balance trying to arrest another lunge, Mr. Harris stepped into the center and said something, pointing at the short kid with one thick finger, and the kid ceased, glaring at him and breathing heavily. Still pointing at the short kid, Mr. Harris turned and said something to the tall one, who nodded shakily, his red mouth still hanging open.

"Show's over," Mr. Harris boomed out at the audience. "Move it along." He put his hand on the tall kid's shoulder. The crowd stirred around randomly in imitation of dispersal.

Mr. Sealy marched the short kid across the quad and up the steps into the building, one hand clenching the neck of the T-shirt, the other resetting and smoothing his comb-over. The T-shirt had a Fantastic Four iron-on. Mr. Harris and the tall kid went up the steps next to each other as the bell rang.

5

LASS crunched under his heels and cracked under his insteps, and he looked around at the mess and felt his breath lock up. Directly below the naked shelf brackets on the back wall were the unpainted underside and adjustable feet of an overturned counter. A computer and monitor lay toppled near it under a pile of wooden shelving and pot shards. Zeb had stocked clay pot percussion instruments on the back shelves.

Forward from there was the keyboard area. Most of the keyboards and their X-stands had been tossed around, and some were outwardly damaged, their keys loose like broken teeth.

To the right was the bent metal framing of what had been a long, old glass case. Inside it, smashed glass buried the rows of Asian wind instruments of metal, ceramic, and wood arranged on swirls of white fabric. Microphones, none of which Jason could afford, lay in state in the foam cutouts of their open cases. The cash register had toppled in, and a revolving Plexiglas display stand had crashed to the floor, a disarray of exotic wooden birdcalls still lying where they'd lunged from it like crash test dummies.

Dark gray light was trapped within the shop by the boarded windows. Gary Warren straightened up behind the case, a clutch of guitar string packets in his gloved hand. He was tall and slender, with a little hunch to his neck.

"Oh," Jason said very softly. He turned to look behind him and saw splintered mandolins.

"Ding dong!" Gary Warren lilted brightly. "A-bomb calling!"

He didn't know Gary Warren well enough to greet him with an embrace, and a handshake at ground zero seemed wrong. He said, "This is bad," and looked around even though he'd already seen it.

"Oh, I don't know." Gary Warren cocked his head, pretending to appraise. "A little lace curtain, some plants . . ." Anger sharpened the frivolous words. "Maybe a nice picture of Der Fuehrer."

Zeb came upstairs from the tiny storage area, emerging behind the wreckage of the long glass case. "There he is," he said to Jason. He extended his hand, but then he blinked as though startled, the hand faltering, and Jason was suddenly aware of his own simmering anger, and that the simmer had boiled for an instant, the steam knocking the lid up just long enough for Zeb to catch a glimpse.

"It's not you," he said. "This makes me angry." He shook Zeb's hand.

"You just missed the insurance adjuster."

"And?"

"She just asked a lot of questions and took pictures. She'll call next week with the company's decision."

"Hmm." Gary Warren put a fingertip to his own cheek, cocked his head. "Now I wonder what *that* will be."

"You never know," Zeb said. "Let's just wait and see."

"You watch," Gary Warren said meaningfully. "You'll see."

The brighter gray of the open doorway penetrated only a few inches, as thought the dimness were a gelid ocean.

6

So did you see the fight?"

"Yeah." David's red backpack was at his feet on the grass. Every day, Jason walked with him to their buses after school. They always met here, on the school's uniformly green front lawn. "It was pretty radical."

A surfer word, filtered through the Valley girls into the soshes, ridiculed by Jason and, previously, David.

"Radical, dude." Jason turned to walk, but Dave was still standing there. A little thrown, Jason turned back. "So, do you know what it was about?"

"Some dumbfuck called one of the busing project dudes a 'fucking nigger.'"

Jason shook his head. "Some people just don't get it."

"Yeah," David said. "Pretty fucking stupid."

"You want to get a Slurpee?"

"Listen, I'm going to hang out with Dan and Trent."

"Those guys? Why?"

David shrugged.

"You like those guys?"

"They're pretty cool."

Jason's impression had been that Dan was a rich asshole and Trent was a rich asshole's friend, but maybe he was wrong.

"Uh, okay," he said.

David was just standing and looking at him, his white Members Only sleeves rolled to his mid-forearms.

"Okay, well," Jason said. "I guess I'll see you tomorrow."

"Yeah, see you then."

"Take it easy."

"You too."

After a moment, Jason slung his backpack onto his shoulder and crossed the lawn and then the street, conspicuous in the afternoon sun. Rounding the corner away from the school, he glanced back just as he passed behind the corner house. David was ducking into the back of a gold Trans-Am that had pulled to the curb. Two people were in it already, and the collar of the driver's pink Izod shirt was up. A buzzing sensation Jason had never felt before crawled in his chest.

7

H E wanted to delay going home, so he paid the extra fifteen cents for a transfer and got off the bus at the library. He liked it more for how the yellowish wooden
tables and chairs sounded than for the books it contained,
and he sat and read his copy of *Psi-Emperor of Sphereworld*
for an hour and a half before hoisting up the backpack again
and going out to the bus stop. It was weird how the buses
weren't full of kids anymore. A mere delay in transit made
everything strange and adult, as though everything could go
differently when the bus came with the glint of evening light
on it and a different driver.

He handed his transfer to the driver and walked back on
the ridged, rubberized flooring, balancing against the lurch of
the bus, brushing his knuckles against the poles. Nagged by
how David had acted, he was nearly at the back of the bus before he saw the gangly kid gazing out a barely open sliding
window, his hair ruffling a little in the inlet of air. His lip was
swollen and the seams of his white tuxedo shirt had ripped in
a few places. He looked at Jason. A little unsettled by the kid's

battered face and the dark bags under his eyes, but not wanting to insult him by going to another seat, Jason sat. The kid turned back to the window. He was still looking out when Jason got off in North Hollywood.

The house was empty. His father was at work late; and it wasn't Tuesday, so his mother had a class. They could be more efficient about avoiding each other if they'd just coordinate their schedules. In order to guarantee minimum contact, only one of them needed to be out of the house at any time. It was a simple logic problem.

He started the oven preheating and got a meatloaf TV dinner out of the freezer and sliced the transparent plastic covering off the ice-crystaled mashed potatoes and apple cobbler.

Jason wasn't sure what was wrong at his house, if anything. His parents had said, a few years earlier, that now that he was older, they could do more of the things they'd "put on hold" when he was little. The one time he'd finally gotten his nerve up and asked why they didn't just get a divorce, they'd pretended not to know what he was talking about. It would have been easy to assume that they thought he was stupid, but he'd assumed instead that they were.

But he still didn't know what was wrong. Probably, nothing was. Even if something *was* wrong, that didn't necessarily mean something was *wrong*.

He spent half an hour playing the piano, making it up to reflect his mood. When he felt better, he went into the kitchen and put his TV dinner in the hot oven and went back out and played some more until the timer went off. He read while he ate, standing at the counter near the oven, and then he played for a little while that turned out to be two hours when he finally looked up and saw the clock.

When he heard his mother's car in the driveway, he closed the lid over the keys and went to bed. When she knocked and looked in a minute later, he kept his eyes closed and breathed regularly. When she went away, he thought about finding a different bench to eat lunch at.

8

His scuffed black duffel bag in Sarah's peach-colored bedroom was as elegant as a hair in a movie projector. He'd been living out of the bag. Clean clothes came out; dirty clothes went in. A folded towel separated them, and had gradually inched the length of the bag as the ratio changed.

He'd bought a microwave dinner, but now for some reason, standing in her little entryway, he didn't want to eat it in this empty place. He wedged it into the ice-encrusted freezer compartment of her undersized refrigerator and went downstairs with his book. Fifteen minutes to Chelsea on the train, then a short, careful walk over translucent gray ice to a diner he knew. He and Robert and Martin had once traveled to New York and eaten there. He thought about Donna Cooper sometimes. She might be eight by now.

He lingered over his French toast, and then ordered pie and coffee so he'd have an excuse to sit longer. The book lay open under his hand on the table. He didn't feel like reading it. It wasn't the right book.

He had to go to Zeb's store very soon, but he kept sitting and looking out the window at the darkening street, at the flow of hip, toned men walking singly and in couples and groups. So much energy expended on trying to look like other people who were trying to look like other people. Here, it was gay men, but the same thing happened no matter what the group. People yearned to be stereotypes—it was just easier to see when they were strangers. Or when you were.

Lack of imagination was his usual explanation when he was feeling glib, but other times, he thought fear was a better one. There was the kind of fear that shot through you and then departed, like when you had just been held up at gunpoint or when you were caught cheating, and then there was the kind that percolated through you like groundwater, so present you never even knew it was there. But it was, and it made you waste time.

Minor realization, not for the first time. Conformity is fear. Reminder to self.

He caught a glimpse of his own thoughts and immediately despised them. The self-anointed nonconformist, passing judgment on the employed, some of whom might truly be having a nice evening. Soon he'd be scuttling up a bell tower, flicking his tongue through his lips.

"What hump?" he said softly, to amuse himself out of being ashamed.

He envied the homogeneity. He coveted a life with a job he didn't like and a roster of unfulfilled aspirations, a regular paycheck. Laugh at the jokes. Do the assurance and the shoes. Let the hand of a superior rest paternally on a shoulder. If occasional desperation in the dead hours was the price, well, it wouldn't be without a solid return.

Sometimes he got as far as circling classified ads, but if there was a God—and Jason didn't think there was—it was clear God had other plans for him.

9

THE tall kid was in his usual place in the back, looking out the bus window. Jason had intended to sit in front, but the kid glanced over and they had a moment of eye contact, so he kept walking, jerked his chin in greeting as he sat on the long rear bench. The kid returned the greeting. The only traces of the fight were a yellowing bruise and a healing split lip, but Jason wondered about the dark bags under his eyes. The school's drug education program just told you not to use them. It didn't teach you anything useful, like how to tell what someone might be on.

"May I ask you something?" the kid asked.

Startled by the sudden contact, Jason blinked. "Sure."

"How does it make you feel to be a honky?"

Jason had never been called that before, as far as he could remember. He knew it meant white people and it wasn't complimentary, but he wasn't certain about its precise severity as a slur. "A honky?"

"Yes." The kid studied him through narrowed eyes.

"Like nothing, I guess."

"Huh." The kid nodded to himself. "That's interesting." He looked out the window again.

Jason waited for him to say something more, but he didn't. "Can I ask you something? What was up with that fight yesterday?"

"Oh. I asked a black kid how it made him feel to be a nigger, and he attacked me."

Jason could barely think the word, let alone say it casually. He nodded wordlessly.

The kid was studying him. "What do you think of that?"

"Well, I don't know. You can't just call people a . . . You know? You can't just call people that."

"I didn't call him anything! I asked him what something felt like. Why should he react as though I were provoking him intentionally?"

"Well, were you?"

"No!" The kid seemed offended. "Do you think I was?"

"I don't know."

"But you didn't react that way when I asked you how it felt to be a honky."

"I could have."

"But you didn't."

Jason shrugged impatiently. How was he supposed to know? "I don't know," he said.

"Huh." The kid looked out the window during the rest of the trip, and Jason did his Spanish homework.

All the good places to eat lunch had long been claimed. He sat on the low concrete curb around an oval grass area in the quad. It felt awkward, eating in second-rate territory without shade. He didn't want to know any of the nearby students, who weren't like him at all.

David was across the quad with the soshes, in his slick white jacket with the sleeves rolled up. When they laughed, it was a kind of adult, masculine chest laugh. It couldn't be trusted. Something that was truly funny made you lose it. It made you giggle or snort, not just go *heh heh heh* all controlled.

But there they were, heh-hehing with their collars up, talking about football, or stockbrokers, or whatever it was soshes talked about.

The tall kid came out of the cafeteria with a brown bag and a carton of something and stood searching carefully. When his scan took in Jason, way across the quad, he lifted his chin in greeting. Male semaphore. Jason returned the gesture. The kid went back to searching, didn't seem to find whoever he was looking for, sat on the concrete with his back against the cafeteria wall, and started eating his lunch.

Three black students came out of the cafeteria. One glanced toward the tall kid, who was chewing his lunch, and spoke to the other two. Then they all looked at the tall kid and walked toward him, stopping in a loose triangle that bracketed him against the wall. He looked up at them, still chewing.

Words were exchanged. Jason couldn't see the faces of the three, but he saw the body language: *So, you think you're . . .* and he saw the kid's reaction: *No, it wasn't like . . .*

One of the three clouted the tall kid on the side of the head with his three-ring binder. As the kid flinched and put his arms up, another drew back a fist and pretended to punch him in the face, and the last made a sort of nonspecific threatening motion with his upper body, elbows back.

Mr. Sealy came out on his way somewhere, and one of the three saw him and spoke to the other two, and they all sauntered away with a lot of looking back.

Jason hoped someone would approach the tall kid and show solidarity, but no one did.

He didn't have a good excuse for not going home right after school, but he sat at the library again that afternoon, reading his book.

When he boarded the same late bus, the tall kid was in the

back again. Jason didn't want to talk to him, but sitting up front no longer felt as though it could still be merely a default seating arrangement. Now it would be an overt snub. He walked back and sat on the long bench seat.

Chins were raised.

"I saw you with those guys during lunch."

"I don't even *know* them!"

"Then why'd they act like that?"

"They said they were going to kick my ass after school."

"Is that why you're on the five-forty-five bus?"

"I hung out in the horticulture area after school and helped Mr. Potrero plant seedlings."

"Potrero's Potato Patch."

"It was just to kill time. I don't actually like it or anything. Do you want to come to my house for dinner?"

Nobody had ever asked Jason that so soon upon meeting him. It short-circuited all the rituals you were supposed to have first. "Uh."

"Do you have to be home at a certain time?"

"Well . . ."

"Okay, never mind."

"No, it's fine."

"Are you sure?"

No. "Yeah. My parents don't mind when I do stuff."

"What's your name?"

"Jason. What's yours?"

"Roberto."

Roberto didn't look Latin, but some Latin people didn't. "Where do you live?"

"Sunland-Tujunga. You live in North Hollywood."

"Yeah."

"Do you know where the wash is?"

No. "Sure."

"I live just down from there."

"Oh." Nodding. "Okay."

An awkward pause. Roberto looked out the window.

"Hey," Jason said. "I didn't see that other kid at lunch today, the one you were in the fight with? Did he get hurt?"

"No. He got suspended." Roberto brooded. "Which is weird, if looked at from a certain perspective."

"What do you mean?"

"Look at it from his point of view. From his point of view, some Caucasian guy he doesn't know calls him a racial epithet, and he defends himself, and then he gets suspended and the Caucasian guy doesn't."

"I never looked at it that way." The kid was making sense. Maybe he wasn't as pompous as Jason thought. Maybe he just dressed wrong.

Jason was nothing if not open-minded.

10

THE music store was dark and silent. In Manhattan, there were always sounds of some sort. Although they were easily averaged into white noise and tuned out by the brain, the eardrum never actually stopped vibrating. On this secondary artery in Brooklyn, twenty minutes from Manhattan by train, there were all the same noises—traffic, people yelling—but with gaps of silence between them. An average noise floor couldn't be established psychologically. Once you were used to silence, somebody would start screaming, and once you'd managed to recalibrate for the screaming, it would get quiet again.

Jason was sitting behind the metal skeleton of the counter, not reading. He usually wasn't someone to sit and look at nothing, but his elbows were on the counter, and his gaze was aimed vaguely out the glass door into the lighted street. When people went by, he watched them through the horizontal rectangular gaps of the security rollup. This time of night, it was mostly teenagers, mostly boys, jockeying and profiling, swearing a lot. This apparently tasted bad, so they spat a lot, too.

The debris had gotten more organized since he'd last seen it, but nothing was where it belonged. After Zeb left, Jason had spent a couple of hours putting keyboards up on their waist-high X-stands and hooking a few of them up to a mixer. A pair of powered speakers looked possibly okay, so he'd connected them, turned on a keyboard, hit a few keys, and heard an electric piano sound.

The keyboard had a button labeled ARPEGGIATOR. In the mood for company, he pushed it and then held down some keys, and the notes began to run in arpeggios up and down the keyboard. He turned on another keyboard and held down a different bunch of keys. When he had four keyboards all arpeggiating different sounds and notes at different speeds— some up, some down, some up and down, some random—he adjusted the volumes to make a soft, interesting wash, and sat down behind the glassless glass case to read.

Half a dozen teenagers stopped across the street in front of a butcher's shop. Jason's unread book was closed on the floor by his stool, and the store lights were out because he didn't like feeling conspicuous. The wash of arpeggiation floated from the speakers.

One of the teenagers produced a spray can. A few quick movements of an arm, and the group congratulated itself and disappeared from his line of sight. A tag Jason couldn't read dripped white against the dark gray metal rollup of the butcher's shop.

11

SUNLAND seemed to be run-down dead ends and heat-baked side streets. Roberto led him through the Jack-in-the-Box parking lot and down a street of houses that hadn't seen infusions of money in some time. Little indications of pride manifested here and there—flowers sprouting through graying redwood chips in a planter box along the side of a yellow house, basketball backboards mounted sturdily above tan garage doors, their string nets white and new—but Jason's primary impression was of upkeep too long let go.

At the corner of two of these streets, under the thick branches of an old carob tree, Roberto halted.

"What," Jason said.

Roberto sighed and scratched his head.

"What?" Jason repeated, confused.

"It's nothing." Roberto squared his shoulders. "Sorry, let's go."

They turned the corner onto another street of houses on small yards, and as they did, Roberto jigged around in front and stopped, looking distressed. "Are you sure it's okay to visit? Maybe your parents will get upset."

Jason shrugged. "I don't care." He was more thrown by how Roberto was acting than by parental consequences.

"I was just thinking that if they got mad at you or punished you, I'd be partly to blame, so can you see my hesitation?"

It made sense, but it didn't taste right. Roberto had obviously changed his mind about being Jason's friend. No problem. "No, it's fine, I told you. But if you want me to go home, I can understand."

"I think that might be wise, don't you?"

"Sure." A pang of guilt he'd been dodging finally scored. "Uh, would it be okay to use your phone?"

"I don't think that would be a very good idea, but there's a pay phone by the bus stop."

"Okay."

"You know how to get back?"

"Yeah. Catch you on the bus tomorrow."

"Okay." Roberto waited. Jason resettled his backpack and walked away, awkwardly.

Despite the aborted plans, he was pleased, in a minor way, about breaking his routine. The warm breeze was nice. It was fine that Roberto didn't want to be friends. As he came out of the side streets and walked toward the bus stop, he decided that he would call home from the pay phone and then he would sit and read his book all the way from Sunland to—

Oh. Wait. He didn't have enough money for both the phone call and the bus trip.

Since Roberto had lured him out here, it was fair that Roberto should provide communication facilities. But he didn't know which house was Roberto's.

He stood and dithered about this for a minute and then pivoted back and walked into the side streets.

Passing the carob tree, he rounded the corner. Across the street and down the block, Roberto was on his hands and knees on the sidewalk with a pail, scrubbing. A white porch was cut into the right side of the house. On the left side, a huge black swastika was spray-painted over much of the house front, its skinny lines traversing wall and window. Its junctures met imperfectly, and each arm began with a black bulb where the painter had established paint flow before committing to the sweep of line.

Jason crossed the street at a diagonal and walked toward him. The car in that driveway was a newish station wagon. It bore a matching swastika, apparently an earlier one, in which one of the four open quadrants concluded incorrectly as a square. The mistake was corrected with heavier lines. Forward, centered along the front quarter panel, were the foot-high initials K.K.K. Dried drips ran from the periods and along the flare at the edge of the wheel well. As he approached the curb, he saw the misspelled "gew" under Roberto's scrub brush, and an arrow toward the house.

As he scrubbed, Roberto muttered, "I thought you were going home."

"I don't have enough money to call home and take the bus, both."

Roberto squinted up at him, the puffy bags under his eyes wrinkling. Finally, he dropped the brush in the pail and stood up, shaking water from his hands. "I guess I have to let you use the phone."

Jason followed him up a potholed driveway that truncated the dirt lawn. The thick wooden front door was painted green, with an opaque, pebbled yellow window and another swastika. Ceramic wind chimes shaped like Kliban cats dangled from the eave, and a warped redwood planter held a line of brittle plants in desiccated potting soil. The door made an unsticking sound when Roberto opened it.

His father picked up after the first ring. "Yes—"

Casually: "It's me."

"Do you know what time it is?"

It was either a stupid question or a setup. Jason saw no reason to answer it.

"Did you hear me?"

"Yup." He looked around Roberto's kitchen. There were tin canisters in graduated sizes along the back of one counter, and a couple of dishes in the dish rack.

"Your mother has been worried sick. Another minute and you wouldn't have caught me here. I was just about to go looking for you."

He almost couldn't breathe. "Sorry." Casually.

"Sorry doesn't cut it. Where are you?"

"A friend's house."

"How long will it take you to get home?"

"Three days."

In the silence, Jason could see his father's jaw muscle working. Then he heard, directed away from the mouthpiece, "You talk to him," and the rattle of the phone.

His mother came on the line. "Your father is very angry."

"Right, and you're not."

"How dare you talk like that to me. Your father will come and get you. Where are you?"

"Uzbekistan," Jason said, still tense, and waited to see what would happen.

He could hear her breath, uneven, in the receiver. "Why?" she asked after a few moments, her voice on the edge of crumbling. "Why does it have to be like this?"

He wasn't the one to ask. He hung up.

It was kind of a gloomy house, he thought, and the furniture was ratty. When he went into the living room, Roberto gestured toward the phone. "Is everything okay?"

"Yeah. Do you want some help?"

Roberto studied him for a long time—nervously, Jason thought.

Despite his fear of being confronted by returning taggers, he crossed the dark street with a roll of paper towels and a bottle of lighter fluid from Zeb's office. It might be a decent solvent for spray paint.

The tag was still wet, and the metal wasn't porous, so it was easier than dried paint on stucco. Dry stuff, by the time you got it completely off, you ended up making big clean marks in the shape of whatever you were scrubbing.

He went through a lot of paper towels and emptied the bottle of solvent. Eventually, the rollup had a big clean spot, and he carried the paint-slickened wad of used towels back into the shop and jammed them into one of the gray trash barrels.

Roberto's room was a little smaller than Jason's, with a single bed and a blonde desk. The walls looked different from Jason's, too, cheaper somehow. A small bookcase sat near sliding closet doors. Some clothes on the floor, a black journal on the desk, an inkwell with a feather in it. Next to the inkwell was a figurine with an ovoid base about eight inches across, a beautiful Oriental man sitting crosslegged, a small blue stone in its lap. Past the open door was a small den and the living room. Next to the door was another, closed.

Roberto was in the adjoining half-bathroom, washing dirty suds and flecks of paint off his hands, scrubbing at spots of tar. Even with a long-handled scrub brush, they'd had to go onto the roof to reach the top third of the swastika. Jason bent sideways and looked at the bookcase. Dante, Poe, Plato, Marx, Shakespeare, Kafka. No real books, just classics.

"When my parents are home, we usually have dinner around seven," Roberto said nervously, wiping his hands dry on his pants. "But we can eat whenever."

"Have you read all these? Do you like them?"

"They're the greatest books ever written."

"Yeah, but . . . do you like them?"

"Of course." Roberto squinted at him as though confused. "They're the greatest books ever written."

"Oh."

"Let's go into the back yard and sit in the lawn chairs."

The back yard was small, with a thick lawn pierced by an oxidized metal clothesline pole. Jason took his shoes and socks off after Roberto did. The sun was behind the buildings, and would soon be below the horizon. Grass prickled, warm and cool between bare toes, the odors of unbloomed camellia and bottlebrush faint on the breeze.

Still wondering who in the family was Latin, Jason said, "Will your parents be here for dinner?"

"No. Mom's away and Dad's working. He's on a container ship. He's a merchant seaman."

The lawn cooled gradually in the small breezes. Jason wasn't sure what a merchant seaman was. Or a container ship. "Who paints all that stuff on your house?"

"We're not totally positive who, but it's probably some of the neighborhood kids."

"How come?"

"They get it from their parents."

"Yeah, duh, but I mean, like, why you?"

"They dislike me." Roberto shrugged uncomfortably. "I'm kind of geeky."

Jason paused. "I don't think you're geeky." But he'd paused too long.

They had Hamburger Helper for dinner, a nice change, both from the TV dinners Jason ate when his parents weren't home and the things his mother made when they were. He liked Hamburger Helper, but he never got to eat it. Maybe he'd start buying it on his way home. Some sugared breakfast cereals, too. His mother would disapprove, but he could hide them behind his desk drawers.

"Have you called the police?"

"We used to," Roberto said, serving himself again. "They came out the first few times and wrote down reports."

"So what happened?"

"Nothing."

"What do you mean, nothing?"

"I mean nothing. They said they can't do anything."

"That doesn't make any sense! They're the police!"

Roberto shrugged and put his napkin on the table. "I don't mean to be rude, but I need to take a nap."

"What do you mean, a nap?"

"I have to get up at ten for my night watch, so I only have two hours to sleep."

Jason felt it all trying to sink in, but instead it stayed merely a little odd. Anyone could see that this was probably a very serious thing, but the way Roberto was acting, it seemed like a passing inconvenience.

With only the slightest sense of import, he said, "Well, do you want some company?"

12

H E had never known anything so eerily normal.

It was just Roberto's dining room. They were just sitting in it. It was just the window and the dark porch and the street outside. Near the door, a wooden baseball bat stood against the wall. A clunky Polaroid camera sat behind them on the dining table, denting the folding green protective mat.

After the sunset had darkened to night, the darkness slowly gained density. Jason always paid attention during biology, so he knew the hunter-protector caveman notion was possibly bunk, but he felt a connection to something. Maybe not to a literal caveman ancestry, but certainly, part of what he felt was the fulfillment of something he was designed for. Young men had muscle and reflexes because they were the fists of the species.

Sitting in the darkened dining room, waiting for vandals, he understood for the first time, and thought that girls might not get it, any more than he got the baby thing.

The gap in the curtain was narrow. They'd be able to see movement directly outside and get the camera lens quickly up to the glass. The baseball bat was for something else. They weren't sure what. Pure symbolism, maybe. They sat and hoped the intruders would come.

13

AFTER some long minutes without vandals, they tried to talk about teachers, but they didn't have any in common. They didn't know any of the same students, either, and hadn't read the same books. Roberto seemed astounded when Jason not only asserted that Shakespeare was boring, but offered the author of *Sphereworld* as superior.

"William Shakespeare was the greatest writer in the history of the world, and you're equating him with some stupid sci-fi hack?"

"I don't get how you can call Lawrence R. Crabtree a hack."

Roberto eyed him uncertainly for a minute, and then recited, as though enraptured by the beauty of something he'd written himself, "'What light through yonder window breaks? 'Tis the east, and Juliet is the sun.'"

"Blah blah blah," Jason said. "Who cares? Nobody. Check this out, it's really cool. In *Sphereworld Protectors*, there's this ancient weapon so big it can destroy entire solar systems—"

Roberto shook his head.

"Wait," Jason said, "that's not the good part. There's these really ancient aliens, only nobody thinks they still exist—"

"You're equating this with *Hamlet* and *King Lear*?"

"No, it's better, because it's not boring. So, they find this probe orbiting the sun, *inside a Dyson sphere!*"

Enthused by the great story, he raised his eyebrows and nodded vigorously at Roberto to encourage interest that wasn't, for some reason, dawning. "But that's not even the good part. The good part is this whole book is just one part of the Sphereworld series, and the whole Sphereworld series is part of the Timespace series, which has whole other books and sets of characters and stuff, and some of them never even meet each other. Isn't that cool? You have to admit that's pretty cool."

"Yeah, you're right. It sounds a *lot* better than *Macbeth*."

Jason sighed. "Do you like *anything* that was written in, like, the last five hundred years?"

"Shakespeare wrote four hundred years ago."

"You know what I mean."

"I like Kafka."

"I mean, anybody who didn't write classics?"

"But once you've read the classics, why would you read crap?"

"*Sphereworld*," Jason said dangerously, "isn't crap."

There was a long pause. The silence of the room seemed to suspend. Then:

"I apologize for insulting your book. It was insensitive of me."

Jason looked over at him. Roberto's arms were folded tightly across his chest, and he was staring straight past his feet propped on the windowsill. Even in the dark, the bags under his eyes showed. Reciprocal apology was appropriate, but Jason's willingness to apologize had been hardening, of late, and though he struggled against his stubbornness, he lost.

"Okay," he said.

Nothing occurred in the stark black-and-white past the dining room window that Friday night. As fatigue increased, the air of the room became chill against skin, though the air was not cool. When dawn seeped in, the leaves and houses began to show pale color and exist in normal time.

14

ZEB took him to breakfast in the city. Very early mornings were wondrous, brassy things, and one or two of them a year was just right. The bustle and sincerity outside the diner window was heartening. Industry was what made America great. Jason was all for it.

"So." Zeb chased yolk with the torn edge of an English muffin. "You didn't die of boredom."

"Nope. Didn't get much reading done, though. I couldn't concentrate for some reason. I guess it was just the wrong book to be reading."

"It's really—I just want you to know how much of a help it is to know you're there watching the store. I can't thank you enough."

"Really, Zeb, it's . . . I'm just sitting up. It's no big inconvenience."

"Anything I can do."

"Dealer cost on a new synth would be just right, really. Speaking of which, do you have spec sheets I can look at? I couldn't find any."

"Most of them got thrown out with the mess. You know what, though: There's a second phone line over the back bench that we use for connecting to the Internet. You should be able to find specs online, no problem."

"You have a dedicated Internet line in the shop? Why, do you have a web site?"

"I need one, but I don't know how to do that stuff. I have the dedicated line because some of the new high-end digital mixers actually dial in and update their own software. I thought high-end customers would want to see it in action."

Jason gave him a look and shook his head.

Zeb did a don't-blame-me shrug. "It's a selling point. Three years from now, it'll be a standard."

"And the nice thing about standards—" Jason began.

"—is there's so many of them," they finished together. Outside the diner window, a young man walked by with two teeny miniature Dobermans on two woven red leashes.

"I tell you what I don't get," Zeb said, leaning forward to watch them depart, "is those fucking little dogs. What the hell good is a midget Doberman?"

Jason nodded. "I have actually given this some thought. I think they're for guarding individual valuable items. You get one dog for the VCR, one for the microwave, one for the TV . . ."

Zeb shook his head. "I hate those damn dogs. They're like—" he paused to divine the analogy "—they're like fucking little Fellini dogs for munchkin Nazis."

Jason squinted at him, something he'd picked up from Robert. "Considering all the truly stupid things in the world, why are you vehement about this one?"

Zeb shook his head sourly. "Gary wants one of the little fuckers."

"You're allergic or something?"

"Yes, to stereotypes."

Jason flipped quickly through his collection of stereotypes

and found no miniature Dobermans. He shook his head. "Sorry."

"Old queens with little dogs. You know."

A snapshot of Queen Elizabeth holding a Corgi flashed up briefly until some less instantaneous part of his brain understood and showed him a different slide: a plump, effeminate middle-aged man making kissy-face at a white poodle in a little sailor suit. It wasn't something he remembered having ever actually seen, but the image came readily.

"Oh. Yeah, but you love him, right? So what's a stupid little dog or two?"

Zeb glared at him disgustedly and didn't speak.

"Or three."

The disgust didn't break. "Perhaps," Jason said, "I will think of something else for us to talk about just now. So Zeb," he said cheerily. "You catch that awesome babe that just went by?"

"Yeah," Zeb said, trying to stay deadpan. "He was cute."

15

HE brought his laptop and Sarah's phone cord to the store that night.

After he had started the synthesizers arpeggiating—different notes this time, different sounds, different wash—he took the laptop to the back, stuck its phone cord into the wall jack, and logged on to check his e-mail. Several people thought he'd like to see other people naked, and had sent him links to their web sites. Some other people thought he might like to earn big money working at home. While it was true that he wouldn't mind earning big money at home, and did have a definite interest in half the naked people in the world, he deleted all the messages, and then there was nothing left in his box.

Zeb had mentioned wanting a web page, so Jason opened up a web browser and typed in *magicmusicshop.com* to see whether anyone already owned the name. After a moment, a page appeared, white with gray text.

"Damn." Someone else had beat Zeb to it.

There's a little shop in Brooklyn
In the middle of the street . . .
(come back soon for treats . . .)

That was all it said, and there was nothing to click on. Weird. If Zeb hadn't set up the domain name and the web page, who had? Gary Warren, maybe?

He went to a site where you could get information about who owned domain names, and ran a search. The contact info for magicmusicshop.com included a phone number and a Pennsylvania address. The contact name was listed as The Inscrutable Whom.

That didn't seem like Gary Warren's sense of humor. He went to a search engine and typed in The Inscrutable Whom. It got him a bunch of near-random results, none of which seemed relevant.

Come back soon for treats. Curiouser and curiouser.

As he pondered, a taxi slowed and stopped in front of the store and idled there. Snowflakes jittered, white in the beams of its headlights and red in the glow of its brake lights, and were swept in circles by cycling air from the engine heat and radiator fan. Jason hadn't realized it was snowing again; snow didn't make sound on the roof the way rain did. The cab bounced a little on its shocks as the person inside moved, and then the door opened and Robert stood on the sidewalk next to a battered white suitcase, looking up and blinking at the snowfall.

The cab pulled away as Jason slid off his stool and walked around the counter. Robert tilted his face up, squinted, and stuck out his tongue to catch snowflakes.

"It doesn't taste like anything," he observed as Jason came out. His voice, Jason's footsteps, and the doorbell sounded flat and nonreverberant.

"It's ice. What do you expect it to taste like?"

Robert frowned, but Jason had known him long enough

not to assume that this related to anything in their conversation. While he looked at his friend with affection and waited to hear whatever the thought was, he realized that he was hearing snowfall on the bare twigs and branches of the tree in front of the shop. It had the periodicity of soft rain, but it was softer (energy absorption by breakdown of crystalline lattice upon impact?) and more muted (sound absorption by snow layer?). There was no apparent sound when it hit the ground, only when it hit the branches, so the muted patter was all at ear level and higher.

"It's been—" Robert began seriously, and then looked surprised. "You can hear the snowflakes."

Jason took the suitcase. "I'll make us some coffee. It's nice to see you."

16

ROBERT was sitting on a stool on the other side of the destroyed counter, updating him. Their friend Martin and his brother Leon had come to live with them in Venice when Leon was twelve. Leon was now fourteen and, despite Robert's tutelage, not getting good grades in algebra.

Or, possibly, because of Robert's tutelage.

"What difference does it make how he gets the answers?" Robert complained. His mug was on a folded paper towel, balanced on the metal rail that no longer supported a glass countertop. Jason had turned off the arpeggiating keyboards, and snow rushed silently outside the door glass. "He gets right answers. Who cares if he gets some of them by doing arithmetic? The real problem is he's smarter than the teacher."

"And just for the alternative viewpoint, here, what's his class called, again?"

"I see where you're—"

"And the class is called?"

Robert paused stubbornly before answering. "The class is called 'Algebra,' but—"

"And does this class include the teaching of photon probability amplitudes?'

"No, but—"

"And are you teaching him photon probability amplitudes?"

"Yes, but he—"

"And the teacher is supposed to grade him on what subject, again?"

"Will you stop interrupting me? He's *able to learn* probability amplitudes. He *likes* them."

"Yeah, but—"

"He doesn't *deserve* a D on his report card. If he's capable of learning advanced concepts, why should he be forced to slog along with the rest of the class? He's learning. He's learning to learn. He's learning that his brain is more than just a passive receptacle to dump other people's facts into."

"Well, yeah, Robert, but . . . don't you think he also needs to learn algebra?"

Robert ceased speaking and looked dissatisfied. They both drank coffee and looked at the door, where snow swirled like they'd always heard it did.

"And is it possible," Jason said, "that you're distracting yourself from something else? I only see you get like this when there's something already bugging you."

Robert said nothing for a time. When he did, it was, "By the way, nickel and tungsten are elements. They're not alloys." But he didn't answer the question, and eventually, it was as though Jason hadn't asked it.

They saw the guy watch them as he stomped past in the snow. When he came back and peered in under his hand, they watched him back. In his forties, rough brown jacket, small gray ponytail sprouting from under a floppy knit hat. Big nose, scraggly beard, red scarf with yarn hanging off it. He waved at them in the snowy air and radiated hopefulness.

"Should I open it?"

"I don't know," Robert said. "Does he look dangerous?"

"Looks like a sax player."

"Maybe it's Kenny G. Don't open it."

Jason slid off his stool and went to the door and raised his eyebrows at the man, who responded by shouting through the glass, "You sell sneaves?"

Jason shook his head, frowned, and pointed at his ear.

The man cupped his mouth and shouted, "Do you sell gleegs?"

Jason turned to Robert. "I can't tell what this guy's saying. Toss me the key."

Frosty air hit his face as he yanked the door open. "Sorry, what was that?"

"Do you sell reeds?"

Jason shook his head. "Sorry, we're not open for business."

"Listen, man, if you could just sell me one, I'd really appreciate it. I was supposed to do a jam in SoHo tonight, but my last reed's dead. If I can buy a box from you, I can still make the gig. I only need one. Like I said, I'd really appreciate it. Hold on—" he held up one finger and dug in his pocket with the other hand. "Hold on. I'll pay extra for the trouble. I can give you . . . eighteen . . . nineteen . . . twenty-one dollars." He displayed the flattened bills.

Heck, Zeb would approve. Brotherhood of musicians, do unto others.

The guy specified alto sax and reiterated his gratefulness through the open door as Jason hunted through open boxes of unsorted spillage behind the counter. Feet resting on the counter, Robert did distracted "you're welcomes" and "no problems" back at him. When the reeds exchanged hands for the marked price, the man blessed Jason, tilted on one foot to bless Robert deeper in the shop—Robert thanked him—and hurried away as Jason locked the door.

Robert said, "You'd think New York would have a twenty-four-hour music store."

"Well, this is Brooklyn, not Manhattan," Jason said, putting the money in the cash register. "But even in Manhattan, it's not what you'd expect. There's a night life, but it's mostly nightclubs and restaurants. Contrary to the representation we get from New Yorkers in Los Angeles, you can't just stroll downstairs anywhere at three A.M. and find an open furniture store and an all-night driving range."

"Huh."

"So how'd Martin react to the D?"

Robert shrugged. "He's afraid that if Leon gets low grades, it could affect the custody situation."

"Do they still do parent-teacher conferences?"

"As far as I know."

"Maybe we should do one."

Robert eyed him for a few seconds, seriously at first, but then the idea seemed to renew his humor. "You at a parent-teacher conference might be interesting."

"Contrary to popular belief, I am able to refrain from telling people they're idiots."

"Jason, you can tell people they're idiots without even speaking."

Jason smiled.

Robert said, "That wasn't supposed to be a compliment."

They sat for a while.

"I thought you liked Kenny G," Jason said.

"But you don't, so the joke was still funny."

"Ah."

"This is awfully familiar." Robert sipped thoughtfully in the silence. "Isn't it."

17

Saturday morning at Roberto's house, Jason was tired, but he felt good even though there had been no vandals. Roberto made pancakes from a mix. As they washed the dishes, Jason said, "You seem sort of quiet."

"Hm," Roberto said.

"Hm what?"

"Hm."

"Hm what?"

"I just—hm."

"What!"

"You know how I asked that kid what it felt like to be a nigger?"

Jason cringed and put a plate on the rack. Washing dishes by hand seemed kind of classless. "Yeah."

"I was just thinking maybe you're right. Maybe it was wrong to do that even though I was just asking a question and didn't mean it badly."

"Duh, you think?"

Roberto didn't say anything further.

Jason said, "So what do you want to do today?"

"Take a nap," Roberto said. "Then maybe go to the library."

"The one by school? I want to see if they have *Sphere-world Rangers* yet."

"Don't you read anything but science fiction?"

"You still haven't told me what's so great about Shakespeare."

"How can you not see? He's just one of the greatest writers the world has ever known. Ask any teacher."

"Oh, please. Teachers think Henry James is great." Becoming a caricature of a pedant, index finger raised, Jason intoned, "'It was, as it were, in those days, such as it was.' Please. So you tell me what's so great about Henry James, because I don't get it. Or about Shakespeare, which you still haven't done."

"How can you not *see* it? 'Shall I compare thee to a summer's day? Thou art more lovely, and more temperate: Rough winds do shake the darling buds of May—'"

Jason listened attentively until it was over, and then shrugged, sincerely apologetic. "It just sounds like words to me."

On the bus, Roberto said, "How about this. I'll pick you a classic, and you can pick me some really good science fiction."

"Well . . . okay." Jason thought as Tujunga Boulevard trundled brightly by. "No, how about this. We'll pick out one book that isn't a kind either of us already reads. That way, we can start fresh. Deal?"

"Like what?"

On the recommendation of a librarian who listened and didn't patronize them, they left the library with two copies— a green hardcover and a battered paperback—of *The Night*

Men by Lester Kellogg. Then Roberto waited in the park as Jason ducked into school and scrounged almost eight dollars in change from his locker.

Going back toward Sunland on the 159, Roberto said, "Don't you have to call your parents or anything?"

"No," Jason said. "It's cool." He cracked open the creaking hardcover with interest and began to read. Roberto eventually stopped looking at him suspiciously and flipped open the paperback.

THE NIGHT MEN
Lester Kellogg

1

It was a dazzling August morning full of steam and traffic, and I looked like a civilized man and smelled of aftershave. Henry Clement's blonde secretary brushed me into his cream-colored office at Harkins, Clement, Radford and gave me coffee. Clement assured his dominance by not being there.

It was an expensive room made to impress its owner. My interest in ticking clocks and polished teak ran out before my coffee did. I put the cup and its pretty saucer on the desk, and stood to take my hat from the stand. A white-haired man with a beak like an egret ushered himself through the door and greeted me with a warm smile, as though he beat me regularly at cards and was happy to remember it.

"Ah, Mr. Carter." Our handshake would have been awkward had he been less adept with men who didn't know his last two fingers were paralyzed. They curled against my palm while the other three talons grasped my hand. "I must apologize for making you wait. I'm Tucker Radford. Please have a seat. I'm sorry Mr. Clement was not able to be here."

We sat on opposite sides of Clement's desk and looked at each other.

"I received a call yesterday that said you might have work for me, Mr. Radford."

"And you need work, Mr. Carter, is that right?"

"Generally, yes."

"And specifically?"

"Specifically, here I am in your office when I'd rather be eating breakfast and looking at the sports pages."

"Something of a live wire, are you?" The twinkle was built into his shockproof smile.

"Something like that."

He looked me over, as though I might be a forgery and he knew how to tell.

I said, "Do you want to tell me about the work, or shall I come back tomorrow when you've had a chance to write it down for me?"

Insults flitted right past him like ghosts past a carnival psychic. "Mr. Carter, we believe you are the man to handle—" his voice very low, he fixed me with a serious eye "—a matter of delicate and unusual nature."

"Sure," I said.

18

THIS worries me." Zeb pointed over Jason's shoulder at the computer monitor, which displayed the Inscrutable Whom's contact information. "This is weird."

Robert said, "There are a lot of things it could be, besides a reference to this store."

Jason turned around so Robert would see his skepticism. "Oh, like what?"

Robert shook his head impatiently and flicked one hand at the obvious obviousness. "Lots of things. It could be some other store."

"Some other Magic Music Shop in Brooklyn in the middle of a street."

Zeb studied the screen. "He's in Pennsylvania. You'd think that would be too far to go just to mess up somebody's music shop. Boy, I'd like to know what this is about."

Jason pointed. "Address."

"A visit?"

"Why not?"

"Today?"

"Maybe."

"Maybe."

They looked at each other.

Robert broke the silence of their consideration. "If I may interrupt these very terse and masculine sentence fragments, I'd like to iterate that if this is the person who vandalized the store, he or she is aware that Zeb can get his or her address. If he or she knows Zeb well enough to target the store and post something on the web, it's not unlikely that he or she would recognize Zeb if Zeb were to appear in Pennsylvania."

Zeb nodded. "That's a good point."

"Which," Jason asked. "The he or shes, or the butch sentence fragments?"

"But," Robert continued, "he or she doesn't know Jason, or me."

"Hm," Jason agreed. "At least, as far as we know. What do you think, Zeb?"

"I don't know. I feel like I should do it myself. But I think Robert is right about them recognizing me if it's some sort of setup."

"What about the police?"

Zeb shook his head. He gestured at the screen. "This is no actionable threat; it's just a bizarre riddle on a web page. I couldn't even get the police to take it seriously when I really have been threatened."

"You've been threatened?"

"No, not relating to this. I just mean generally. There was a wacko in Gary's past that we had to deal with. It was a long time ago, nothing to worry about now."

"Oh." In a murder mystery, that would be a clue, but in reality, Jason didn't know anyone—musicians, especially—who didn't have wackos in their pasts. "Well, what do you think? Shall we go to Pennsylvania?"

"Well." Zeb considered. "I need to stay here and keep working on getting the store back together. But if you don't mind doing it . . ."

"Not even slightly. I'm curious, and I've never been to Pennsylvania."

Robert nodded. "Sounds interesting."

"Okay," Zeb said, "but I pay for your travel and food."

To Robert, Jason said, "Say, I hear the lobster and filet mignon are good in Pennsylvania."

Zeb snorted. "Boy, do you hear wrong."

19

Trains weren't part of Jason's heritage. He remembered taking the *San Diegan* once when he was a kid, but in Los Angeles, unless you were one of the insane who commuted two hours each way from your affordable mortgage in Orange County, trains just weren't part of the contract. A couple of light rail lines had found a tenuous foothold in the arid climate, and a beautiful subway station had recently hatched in Hollywood, but in a car culture, use of public transportation is a social gaffe. If you're on the bus and you're not a student or domestic help, it's assumed that you still live with your mother and play Dungeons and Dragons every weekend with the other leprotic funguses from the Star Trek fan club.

The train went through New Jersey, which was kind of interesting to look at. A lot of New Yorkers expressed disdain for it, but, then, a lot of New Yorkers expressed disdain for any place that wasn't New York, by which they meant not New York, but Manhattan. The belief among the natives was that their tiny island was the axis of the universe, and that the rest of the world agreed and was jealous. He'd heard that about New Yorkers, of course, but he'd assumed it was a joke, along with cargo cults and people who ate live grubs without garnish and bathed in yak urine. As it turned out, all those things actually existed, and the advertising in New York subways exploited insular pride with separatist tag lines like "because you're a New Yorker!" and "capital of the world!"

When the monolithic parochialism made him tense, he tried to remember that Zeb wasn't at all like that, and neither was Sarah. But it was hard not to generalize when the stereotypes seemed so insistent.

Robert, apparently sincere, possibly just contrary, claimed to believe in New York exactly as advertised. He cited Broadway, the fashion industry, Wall Street, Madison Avenue, the Statue of Liberty, publishing, and the World Trade Center. When this list provoked only a halfhearted concession from Jason, he said with some impatience, "Well, what do you think is the center of the universe? Los Angeles?"

"I don't think there is one."

"You have to admit New York is at least the *artistic* center."

"What makes you think that?"

"Well, let me see—" In Robert's blank smile was the implication that Jason was slow today. "—All the art?"

"Such as?"

"*Such as?*" Shaking his head, Robert cast for an example, mounting an exasperated melodrama with eyes and hands because there were just so very many such-ases. "Okay, such as the painting of Van Gogh's shoes that's hanging at the Met?"

"Oh, was that painted in New York? I was misinformed."

Robert opened his mouth. Robert closed his mouth. Then he said, "Not only can you not do Bogey, but you're being obstinate because you know you're wrong."

"No, I'm being obstinate because it's fun, but I'm still right. Just because a lot of art ends up in one place after it's made, that doesn't make that place the 'center of art.' The center of art commerce, maybe, okay. Or *a* center, anyway.

But of art itself?" He shook his head. "Flagstaff is just as inherently artistic as the Upper West Side." Overriding Robert's response, he said, "The center of the artistic universe is wherever a good artist is working. In fact, I'll go one better and say it's wherever an artist is working and there's no *Cats*."

"*Cats* closed."

"What a shame."

"But don't you think it would be inspiring to be around a concentration of other artists?"

"Deadlines inspire me. Other artists are just fun to complain with."

Greenery and suburbs flowed by like sentences.

Robert said, "You're *such* a music snob. What's wrong with *Cats*?"

"The way I feel about *Cats* is the way you feel about Fabio—yeah it served a function, but so what? Does that make you an acting snob?"

Robert fell silent. The flow of scenery was measured now by the crumbling punctuation of old stone bridges. A few miles later, long after Jason had forgotten asking him anything, Robert said, "Probably. So let me ask you something. What do you like about New York?"

"Sarah's here. Pizza's good. TV commercials that try to sell four-wheel-drive sport trucks to subway yuppies are funny."

"Do the yuppies have that 'extreme' look here, too, with the tattoos and everything?"

"Yeah. I think they think it offsets the fluorescent lighting in their cubicles."

Robert lapsed into distraction. No shimmeringly obsequious waiters served prime rib from steaming silver platters in the dining car, but the snack counter guy sold them microwaved nachos with processed cheese, which made Jason just as happy. They spent the rest of the trip lounging in a small beige vinyl booth, eating nutritionally negligible mock-food products and reading.

20

THE Inscrutable Whom's address was on the second floor of a white building of small offices, on a street of red brick and white steeples too colonial to exist in Southern California, where the heritage was not Redcoats and rain, but conquistadors and sun, and the earth was prone to *grand mal* seizures. The sky was gray, the street and sidewalks recently wet. They trudged up an exterior staircase and stepped into a short, clean hallway of black flooring tile. Doors lined both white walls, and a dark-eyed woman glanced up from a desk in one of the open offices. A little sign next to the door said she was a notary, and a gold letter *I* was mounted next to the sign.

The door past her was *J*. On the other side were *F*—an accountancy—and then some storeroom-looking doors and then a few more with letters.

"Where's—" Jason said, and then saw Suite H as he turned. Next to where they'd come in was an enclosure of unpainted Sheetrock with a well-fitted but cheap interior door. Maybe eight by ten in square footage, much smaller than the offices. A gold *H* was screwed into the Sheetrock.

As they went toward it, the dark-eyed woman inside Suite I said, "May I help you?"

Jason stepped into the doorway. "We were looking for Suite H?"

The woman shook her head. "I haven't seen him around at all today. Was he expecting you?"

Jason opened his mouth to say no, but Robert spoke behind him. "Yes, but we didn't make specific plans. Would you happen to know whether he's been in already today?"

"If he came in today, I didn't see him."

"Let's just leave him a note," Jason said to Robert. "It was a long shot anyway, and I don't feel like waiting around."

The woman smiled. "If he wasn't expecting you, that's probably best. He only comes in late at night when no one's here."

"Oh, right." Robert nodded as though that jibed with what he already knew. "Okay, thanks." On the way down the stairs, he said, "Do you want to wait around for nighttime and see if he comes, or go back to Zeb's?"

"We need to be in the shop tonight. Let's call Zeb."

"Okay." Robert stepped onto the sidewalk and started toward the street, but Jason had stopped at the bottom of the stairs, looking up at the building against the beginnings of a speckling rain and the mottled gray sky.

Robert joined him. "What do you see?"

Jason pointed. On the second floor, about where the back of Suite H was, the butt end of an air conditioner hung out of a cutout in the wall. "And look." He pointed at a handful of black cabling that ran down from the roof and penetrated the wall next to the air conditioner. "I tell you what I think. I think that's an equipment cabinet, and someone's got a server up there."

"Whom?"

"Right."

"Whom?"

"Exactly."

"No, I mean whom do you think has a server up there? Who's the server owner?"

"No. Who's the person that vandalized the store. Whom has the server."

"Who has the server."

"Whom."

"I dunno."

They looked at each other, waiting to see who'd say "third base."

"I'm hungry," Robert said. "Let's go find a diner."

21

THE second night at Roberto's house, the weather suddenly turned October. The Kliban cat chimes moved in the tentative breeze without sounding, and under the streetlights, an empty potato chip bag scutted in lazy bursts, revolving and toppling as it meandered the length of the street.

Roberto whispered in the gloom of the living room, "What did you think of the bird symbolism?"

"What bird symbolism?" Jason whispered back. The Polaroid camera and baseball bat sat like totems in the same places as the night before.

"Tucker Radford in *The Night Men*."

"I didn't see any symbolism."

Roberto looked at him sideways. "His nose was like the beak of an *egret?* And his three working fingers were referred to as *talons?*"

"Yeah, but I don't think that's *symbolism*. It's just what the guy looked like and what Carter thought of when he saw him. It's not *symbolism*; it's just *description*."

"Hm."

"Okay, I guess it could be symbolism, but we'd have to see whether there's more of it. I wish we could read without turning the lights on."

"One of us could sit over on the couch with the flashlight and read aloud while the other keeps watch by the window."

While Roberto sat on the couch with the flashlight, Jason went into the cool night to see whether the glow was visible. It was, but only if he put his face right up to the window.

I escorted Radford's retainer check to Harkins, Clement's bank and had a girl convert it to legal tender.

I ate my breakfast at a diner and read the sports pages. The Dodgers were doing their usual. Then I drove to Ricky Tomato's little house near Beaudry and rang his bell. Ricky Tomato had a name like a Sicilian crime boss, but he was a Peruvian greengrocer.

I gave it a minute and went down the steps. When I was halfway to the gate, the doors opened on a black sedan across the street, and two men got out and strolled toward me. I knew big, blond Fred Baynes, but the mad-looking red-headed fellow hitching his belt was a stranger to me.

"Hello, Sergeant," I said.

"What are you doing here, Carter?"

The redhead broke in. "You know this man, Sergeant?"

"Yes, Sir, Lieutenant Corcoran." Baynes was polite, like the man hired to be friends with the king's rude son. "We know Mr. Carter, Sir."

"What's your business with El Señor Ricardo Tomatillo, Carter?"

I looked at Baynes. He was watching the

empty house, rapt, as though someone were about to appear in the window and do a puppet show.

"You nabbed me just in time, Lieutenant," I said. "I came by to kill him, but there was no answer, so I decided to kill someone at the next house over instead."

The redhead's smile was full of little teeth. "Sergeant Baynes, put this clever man in cuffs and charge him."

"With what, sir?"

"He's just confessed to intent to murder of a wetback in the witness of two officers of the law."

"Carter likes to bark when you come up the walk, Lieutenant, but he's harmless enough."

"Just an old bird-dog with no teeth," I said.

"Read that line again," Roberto broke in. "About the *bird* dog."

"I still don't buy that it's symbolism. What did you think of 'wetback'?"

"I think you have to judge books by the times in which they were written."

Jason's thought wouldn't form itself clearly. It was something about the immutability of humane behavior, and he knew he believed it, but he—

Bang!

Roberto jerked in his chair, and Jason froze on the couch with the book in his hand and held his breath, expanding the radius of his hearing. The nearly inaudible sounds outside the house magnified themselves through the walls and windows. Replaying the bang mentally, he could not identify it. It was neither the popbang of a car backfire nor the rattlebang of a market basket collision.

"What was that?" Roberto whispered, but Jason wasn't

seeing him. His pulse intense in his ears, he set his book noiselessly on the coffee table.

Breathing now, but shallowly, he moved to the baseball bat, taking it up, noting that if someone were in the kitchen, he should not swing it from the side, the way bats were generally swung, but should crash it down in a perfectly vertical arc or ram it end-first, so he would not damage Roberto's family's belongings.

Roberto watched him move to the door of the kitchen and whispered, "What are you doing?" There was a remote urge to answer, but that capacity had switched off. He acknowledged Roberto with a quick half-nod and prowled soundlessly back through the kitchen.

The window in the back door was covered by pleated fabric gathered in the middle. Wind rustled against the house and the fence, and a tiny draft, so small it may not have been there, moved over his face like a cold penciltip. He could hear no one outside, had no sense of anyone moving.

Roberto came into the kitchen behind him, carrying the camera. "Is anyone out there?" he whispered.

Jason shook his head tightly.

Outside, there was no motion. There was nothing there at all.

For an hour, they stayed at the door, frozen, hearing the hinged number tabs in the little digital clock on the kitchen windowsill flip at the end of each minute.

22

'M sure we'll be fine for one night without you," Zeb said over the pay phone. "Gary or I will sleep at the shop tonight. Thanks."

"Zeb . . ." Jason shook his head. "You gotta stop thanking me. Let me have dealer cost. Buy me breakfast. Give me your firstborn. Just stop saying 'thank you' all the time. It makes me feel like we're not friends."

"I can understand that. I just wish I could do more to show you how much I appreciate it."

"It's not necessary."

There was a pause. He could feel Zeb's next question, but it wasn't asked. He glanced around the diner. Robert was lounging in a red booth halfway down the aisle, grinning lopsidedly toward their petite waitress, who wasn't smiling back at him, busying herself at the coffee stand. "Um . . . I have some stuff to tell you when we get back there. We have selfish reasons for helping you. Something that didn't work out in the past."

"I had that feeling, but I wasn't going to ask."

"I'll tell you about it. For tonight, we just want to sit and watch for the Inscrutable Whom. It's a long shot, but we already bought thermoses."

"Well in that case, you have to. Is there someplace dry to watch from? Why don't you rent a car? I'm happy to pay for it."

"We don't have credit cards."

"You don't have *credit cards?*"

"We're the last two. We don't follow sports, either. We may not be Americans."

"Oh yeah?" Zeb paused. "Name the three branches of federal government."

"Animal, vegetable, and mineral."

"No."

"Larry, Curly, and Moe."

"That's close."

"Uh, executive . . . uh . . . ablative . . ."

"You're American. Call me back in a bit. I'll see if I can find you a car."

A thick, white, chipped diner mug full of diner coffee and a bowlette of individually sealed half-and-half mini-portions waited at his place. He'd always liked diner mugs. If he could find a place to buy them pre-chipped, he'd have ordered a full set for home.

He tore the paper from an individual mini-portion and decanted it, watching the dramatic billow in the black coffee. "Zeb's going to see if he can rent us a car to sit in."

"I was wondering where we were going to sit."

He opened and poured in a second portion. The second anything was always less dramatic. Who manned *Apollo* 12?

The adhesive of the third mini-portion was too strong, so the paper tore off in moist plies, leaving the portion sealed. He breached it with his fork—Blam! *Apollo* 13—before dumping it into his mug. Taking the last portion, he said, "Ever notice how convenient these things are?" He tore off the paper, added it to his coffee, selected three sugar packets from the ceramic holder, ripped open all three at once, and dumped them in.

One single cup of coffee—fifteen little pieces of trash.

He set his wet spoon on the empty sugar packets so the napkin wouldn't make sixteen. "They're good for the environment."

"Oh, I know," Robert enthused. "Especially the plastic ones."

They hung around and watched the diner not fill up. Into late afternoon, a man strolled in and sat at the counter, was greeted as "George" and given a pot of tea and no menu. Robert made friends with Cassie, the waitress, who was training to run in a marathon, and he and Jason eavesdropped in the direction of the kitchen as the bearded cook explained to someone that "beginner's mind" was a crucial ingredient of a quality Béarnaise sauce.

A little later, Ahmad Jamal played *Poinciana* in the little speakers around the ceiling, and it was so lovely with the warm diner, the legs stretched along the vinyl seat, the forearm on the table, the hand on the mug, the friend across the booth, and the bright leaden clouds outside the chilled windows that Jason reminded himself, as he did sometimes, to try to save a piece of it so he could have it again later. Which, as always, he couldn't.

In early evening, he rang Zeb, who said he'd rented them a car. Cassie went home and an actual gum-cracking waitress with a tag that said *Marlene* took their to-go dinner orders. Another named Judi took their money at the counter, called a cab for them, and filled their new thermoses with hot coffee.

"You don't see a lot of grown men with Hello Kitty thermoses," she mentioned to Robert.

✦

Since as far as they knew, the Inscrutable Whom didn't know them, they parked right across the street from his office building under an annoying spittle of halfhearted rain.

Robert struggled to adjust his seat, which he had reclined so that his head wouldn't press sideways against the headliner. The tiny red rental vehicle had the horsepower of a Malibu Barbie Corvette and the turn radius of a house trailer, and its designers had clearly expended a lot of thought and effort to place pointy things precisely where knees and elbows would be.

"What kind of car is this?"

Jason's shoulders were rounded uncomfortably by his own seat's ergonomic design. "I think it's a Dodge Blip. If you buy enough Happy Meals, you can collect the whole set."

"Oh. Speaking of Happy Meals. We took Waldo to the vet for his teeth cleaning. They tried to put him in a cat straitjacket so they could work on him."

Jason winced. "How's the vet?"

"She's fine, but both assistants needed mercurochrome. Aren't you going to ask me how I got from Happy Meals to Waldo?"

"I hadn't planned to, no."

In front of the office building, the single streetlight went on. During one of Jason's too-infrequent battles with his own ignorance, he'd had Martin explain light to him from an artist's point of view. Single-point sources made black shadows, with sharp edges. Multiple sources made converging shadows that were only dark where they overlapped. The shadows of the windowsills and ledges of the office building were sharp and black.

A car went by once in a while, and there were occasional pedestrians at first, bundled up in jackets, chatting with hands in pockets, but around ten, there hadn't been any for a while, and then there weren't any more for the rest of the night. The exciting part of the evening came around one, when a man in an electric wheelchair scooted down the side-walk and turned onto the side street, and then, a few minutes later, scooted back the other way. A while later, there was a stray dog, but it wasn't as thrilling as the guy in the wheel-chair. Just before it started to get light, a pickup truck stopped several times with its blinkers going, and a woman in a jacket got out and stocked the newspaper vending machines up and down the street. The rain never got its act together. Between the dog and the newspaper woman, nothing moved but the clouds, presumably, invisible in the dark.

A grainy, bleary dawn eventually showed up and lightened the shadows, and at some point, the streetlight switched off. Traffic started happening, a few cars at first. When the dark-eyed notary showed up at nine and went up the exterior stair-case with her keys out, Jason said, "Okay, let's get some breakfast and find out when we can catch the train back."

"Okay."

As they passed through the intersection, the side of the office building happened to line up in the little car's dirty side-view. He frowned as it flowed out of sight, almost kept going because he was tired, but sighed and made the U-turn.

Robert looked up and glanced around. "Where are we go-ing?"

Jason parked near the intersection and released his seat belt. "Check something out with me." Cold from staying awake all night, he shivered as they walked back toward the building through a pinpoint spattering of rain.

Robert said, "Is that another door?" A door-sized section was set into the wall facing them, painted white to match the building.

"That's how it looks."

As they crossed the street, Robert said, "Duh!"

"Just don't say it."

"Duh! We are idiots!"

"I just said not to say it."

It was a narrow metal double-door, knobless like the door

of an elevator, with a raised, shiny metal keyhole mounted on the inside of the jamb, about four feet up.

"It looks like an elevator," Robert observed.

Jason gave him a wide-eyed, shocked expression. Robert ignored it and looked thoughtful. "Did you see an elevator when we were up there?"

"No, did you?"

"No." After another moment, they went around the front and up the staircase.

All the office doors were closed. A pink flyer was taped to the door of Suite H.

???WHOM???
NORTH AMERICAN CAME-BACK TOUR!
**An assembly of alchemy & alternate angles of acoustical awareness
also coffee
Brought to you by inscrutable friends in
low places
Come to the show • Come to the show
$4 at the door • $5 at the window
Dishonest Abe's Coffeehouse
October 7 • 10:00 PM
handicapped access • muffins**

It was laser-printed. The font was fat and rounded like the old hippy-dippy split-fountain playbills from the Fillmore West. Shaky block capitals across the top said: BACK 10/7. LOOK IN ON ROCKY AND BULLWINKLE FOR ME. THANKS. —A.

Robert tapped him on the shoulder and pointed. One of the storeroom doors they'd noticed on their first visit was slightly open. Jason walked down the short hall and peered in. There was an elevator door behind it. No storeroom.

"Now you can say it," he said.

"We're idiots."

"Yes we are."

"Now what do we do?"

"Well, since he or she is not coming back until the seventh, first we say it again—"

"We're idiots."

"—and then we go back to New York."

On the drive back to the rental car place, Robert suddenly said, "Oh!"

"You just got it?"

"You already thought of him?"

"The guy in the wheelchair."

"We're idiots."

Jason nodded. "We certainly are."

He pulled to the curb instead of turning into the driveway at the car rental place.

"Want to?" Robert said, skipping an entire conversation and starting with the end. This happened with Robert sometimes. It happened with Martin, too, though to a less specific degree. It had never happened with Marisa, Jason's ex-wife.

"Yeah, I do."

"The address wasn't on the flyer."

"So we'll call information."

He put it in gear and pulled away from the curb.

23

and watched the sedan make a leisurely three-point turn from the kerb and prowl away toward Beaudry. I strolled around the block. It was a Spanish neighborhood, and I attracted no more attention than if I'd been a dancing rhinoceros. Two teams of kids playing street baseball called a time out and tailed me around the corner, but they stopped at Ricky Tomato's driveway when I went up it.

His one-car garage was as neat as a Navy deck. The garage doors were closed but not pad-locked. It had the empty sound of a neat, empty building.

THERE'D been no more bangs in the back yard, no motion, no vandals. Dogs, probably, they'd decided. Nothing dangerous. But Jason's thoughts were still jittery, and he kept rewinding the bang mentally, trying to identify it as he watched out the front window again.

He suddenly registered silence and glanced to his right. Roberto was sitting on the couch, looking at him, the open hardcover drooping silently from one hand.

"Why'd you stop reading?"

"Because you're not listening. It's been a full minute since I stopped. I bet you don't know the last thing I read."

Rewind, replay, recite: "'It had the empty sound of a small, empty building.'"

"*Neat* empty."

"Okay, neat empty." Jason shrugged. "I don't think that's even good writing. What else would an empty building sound like?"

Roberto tucked the dustjacket flap in as a placeholder and put the book on the coffee table.

Jason yawned and stretched. "What time is it?"

Roberto leaned over so he could see into the kitchen. "Um . . . three-thirty. We can stop watching if you want; everyone's probably asleep. Are you tired?"

"Yeah, but not sleepy." Another yawn. "I'm hungry, though."

"We don't have anything to eat. I have to go to the store tomorrow. Do you want to go to the Denny's near school and get breakfast?"

Riding in an empty, lighted bus at night was weird and exhilarating in a way that made him want not to show it, to contain it within him, in a compact three-dimensional shape that would never expand past the boundary of his skin.

24

BREAKFAST and coffee at Denny's at four-thirty in the morning was unconventional and adult, and Jason had a powerful, immediate taste for it. He sat lengthwise on the pliant bench seat, the window cold through the back of his jacket, ankles crossed, arm on the table, somehow across from this strange kid he didn't really know, calmly excited and oddly in control of this new nighttime world. School wasn't far; he sensed its existence off that way in the dark, but through a flawed connection, as though reality shifted at night, and all the neutrinos and cosmic rays that bombarded the school to make it material refracted somewhere else, leaving a hovering, school-shaped potential. His parents and their house were folded into the same shift, inessential in the solid darkness.

Roberto was reading the hardcover edition of *The Night Men*, his eyebrows beetled. The paperback was at Jason's elbow on the booth's table, but the night was too novel for him to give his attention to a mere story. Mist clung to the intersection, making colored nimbuses around the signal lights, and he imagined the nimbuses controlling ethereal traffic as the lights at their cores controlled the material. Occasionally, a lone vehicle of tangible metal and rubber would stop obediently, ceding right-of-way to the flow of invisible cross-traffic until the nimbuses switched colors again.

He saw the homeless and the nocturnal walking slowly along Burbank Boulevard, looked on as the night dissolved, watched floating, stationary vees of diffuse light lose their glows and coalesce into metal fixtures mounted on pale buildings.

The customers who came in early on a Sunday morning, when night was gone and the sun hadn't been up long enough to warm anything, were working people of a kind Jason had never associated with. He didn't know how he knew that. Their clothes held no clues, and at first, he thought it was in the faces and postures, but he came to notice how they talked to the wait staff. His family never did that. They ordered and expected to be served. But these people greeted them, had conversations, said goodbye.

The customers talked to each other, too. Nothing intriguing, nothing Jason would want to emulate. But sociable. He saw two men at the counter shake hands and introduce themselves after ten minutes of friendly chatting, and realized with surprise that they'd had no specific knowledge of each other previously, just some sort of conditioned recognition.

"It's interesting—" Roberto glanced up from the book, his face untroubled for the first time since Jason had known him, intent on the point he was about to make. But then he froze, index finger still marking his place, and looked past Jason in the direction of the entrance.

"What—"

"Don't look!"

"Why not?"

"Do you remember the kid I got in the fight with?"

"Not really."

"I think he just came in."

"Are you sure?"

Still looking past Jason, Roberto squinted. "I think so."

"How does someone 'think' they're sure?"

The squint widened into panic. "He's coming this way. Here's the plan—"

"It's a public place," Jason interrupted, irritated about not being allowed to look. "We don't need a plan."

A short, floppy-haired, dark-skinned kid carrying a dog-eared spiral notebook planted himself at the foot of their table and glared pugnaciously at each of them. Jason gave him a nod, but the kid had already turned his attention on Roberto, who radiated nervous waves of jumpy energy.

"I just wanna know something," the kid said. "I been trying, and I just don't get it." He jutted his jaw further out. "I just wanna know what the *hell* were you thinking?"

"I—I—" Roberto said.

"I don't know you from Adam. What gives you the right—" he paused to emphasize *right* "—to come up to me . . . in a public place . . . and use that kind of language?"

Roberto blinked rapidly. "I—I—I—"

The kid looked at Jason, expecting an answer.

"My friend is an idiot," Jason said. "You want a cup of coffee?" He slid his legs down off the seat to make room.

The kid narrowed his eyes, looking hard at him. "You're gonna buy me a cup of coffee."

"Yeah."

"Seriously."

"Yeah."

Roberto watched the dark-skinned kid with the focused alertness of a dog who's being very good so he can have a treat.

The kid paused, still looking at Jason. Then he shifted the notebook to the crook of his left arm so he could put out his right. "Martin Altamirano," he said warily.

They shook. "Jason Keltner. This is Roberto, uh . . . what's your last name?"

Roberto nearly fell over in his haste to stand. "Oh! Uh,

uh—" He shook his head briskly, as though dislodging earwigs. "Uh, Goldstein. I wasn't, uh—" He nodded emphatically and, attempting a broad, sheepish gesture of self-absolution, knocked over his coffee cup, drenching his pants, shirt, and the library book.

He looked down at his coffee-stained front with his hands spread, and then looked up at them in shock for a few seconds before thrusting his hand out cheerily. "Roberto Goldstein!" Martin took it, but he looked uneasy. Roberto grinned and pumped his hand vigorously, then pulled a wad of napkins from the dispenser and rubbed at the stains as one of the waitresses came by.

"Excuse me," Jason said. "Could we—"

Martin said, "Hi, Denise. You're looking fine this morning."

"Hi, Martin! Got some friends this time, huh?"

"Maybe so. Maybe so. So, uh, Cuteness, how's that man o' yours, and what can I do to convince you to dump him?"

She laughed. "Martin, you're a crazy kid."

"You know it, Denise, you know it. Listen, could I impose on your fine self to bring over some rags?"

"No problem, sweetie."

Jason said, "And two more cups of coffee, please?" He pointed at Martin. "One for him." When she left, he said, "Have a seat?"

"If you don't mind, I think I'm gonna sit over in my spot."

"No problem." Jason extended his hand again, and they shook again. "Nice to meet you."

Martin nodded and turned away, then turned back. "Thanks for the coffee."

Roberto looked up with a handful of coffee-stained napkins. "Want to come to my house for lunch?"

At the time, Jason couldn't read the expression that crossed Martin's face at that moment, the one that preceded the slow "Okay . . ." When he occasionally remembered it as an adult, though, it always made him smile.

25

THE stage at Dishonest Abe's was near the front door, about the same size as two of the mismatched little tabletops that had been jammed comfortably into the room by someone who suffered no compulsion to line things up in rows.

Jason surveyed the paintings on the two long walls, in their carved wooden frames. In ten years of coffeehouses, he'd seen no more than a handful of coffeehouse art showings that didn't include at least one female nude, usually in some weird color.

By the door. Greenish-white. The universe inches along its tracks.

Coffeehouse counter help generally comes in two mildly differentiated varieties. It's either hip, young, and resentful, or hip, young, and friendly. The girl at Dishonest Abe's had painted an alien face onto her own, and she had the bare-sliver-of-midriff, ring through the eyebrow, and dyed pigtails of a screw-you post-adolescent, but she looked in her mid-twenties and was apparently a happy person who didn't find it demeaning to provide a service and get paid.

She said, "Welcome to Dishonest Abe's" and gave Jason a beautiful smile. "What can I get you?" The music in the PA system was Ozomatli. This was a good coffeehouse.

Jason smiled back. "What's your favorite muffin?"

She looked serious as she considered. It made her look younger. "My favorite is pineapple apple bran, but we don't have any today."

"Um . . . why don't you just give me that big goopy chocolate-looking thing."

"And you, sir?"

Robert considered the muffins as seriously as the countergirl had, but instead of making him look younger, it just made him look very concerned about muffins. He pondered gravely. When Jason was about to repeat "And you, sir?" at him, he said, "What is your least favorite muffin?"

"My least favorite?" She deliberated. "I guess the peanut muffins, but I have a nut allergy, so if I ate one, I could go into anaphylactic shock and die."

Robert nodded thoughtfully. "I'll have one of those."

The leftmost part of the counter was a hinged leaf where the staff could get through, and to the left of that was a small bulletin board with a wooden frame. Jason had spotted the Inscrutable Whom's yellow flyer when they'd entered.

"I see you have entertainment here," he said, pointing back over his shoulder at the stage. "Anything tonight?"

"Just open mike."

"Is it ever any good?"

"Sometimes. The good ones usually get their own nights."

"Are there a lot of good ones?"

"Some. It depends on what you like. If you want to sign up, the sign-up sheet is on the bulletin board." She leaned over the counter to point at it. "The limit is eight minutes, but if you're good he lets you go longer."

"Thanks." He strolled over and looked at the dozen handwritten entries as she got their muffins. The Abe-ettes had already registered their intention, as had Amazing Steve and the Vertigo Puppies.

"Oo," Robert said behind him. "The Farts. I bet they're great."

"I bet you're wrong."

The countergirl said, "Will there be anything else?"

"Two mochas, please." Jason tapped the yellow flyer. "What about this 'Whom'? Are they good?"

"They're awesome, but they're a he. He started out playing at open mikes, but he just got his own night."

"What's he do?"

"Oh, you know. He just sings songs, but they're really good. *I* think they're really good. They're kind of folky, poppy, you know."

"Acoustic guitar?"

"Sort of, I guess. I don't know what it's called. That's eleven fifty."

"I got it." Robert dug in his pockets and came out with a wad of crumpled bills, ATM receipts, video rental coupons, and crumbs.

Sitting at one of the little tables, Jason said, "You keep crackers in your pockets?"

"Quiet, you." Robert sipped his mocha. "What have we learned?"

"I haven't learned anything. Have you?"

"Yes. You could be dangerous."

"Dangerous how?"

Robert looked past him for a moment, toward the counter, and then studied him. "I'm sorry. It's insensitive of me to point out a positive response you get from a woman when your girlfriend is out of town."

"Who, the little countergirl?"

"Yes."

"Huh." This information wasn't relevant to anything. "Have we learned anything besides that?"

"No."

"So now what . . . I guess we go back to New York."

Close behind him, the countergirl said, "This is him." He turned in his chair and she smiled and showed him a CD box. The cover said *Whom* in the same balloony font they'd seen before. "It's the guy you asked about, who's going to be here on the seventh."

He took the box. No photo or song list on the back; just vaguely psychedelic fractal designs in vaguely retro-sixties pinks and greens. "Thanks. Is it good?"

"I like his new stuff better, but it's pretty sweet. It's ten dollars."

"I'll take it." He put it down on the table, but she picked it up.

"That's the store copy. Somebody took the CD out of it anyway. I'll get you one that's still wrapped." She smiled at him again and departed. Robert smirked into his mug.

"Oh," Jason said. "Here's another reason to think it's a pair of servers up there on the second floor: People name computers after cartoon characters sometimes. Homer and Marge, Fred and Wilma, Ren and Stimpy."

"Rocky and Bullwinkle."

"One might be the backup for the other."

The countergirl came back with a sad face and the same empty box. "Sorry, they're all gone."

"Do you still need that box?"

"This? No, do you want it?"

"Sure, if you wouldn't mind."

She smiled. "It's okay with me."

He saw no evidence of attraction. Sometimes Robert interpreted things funny.

"Thanks."

"My pleasure." She went back to the counter.

He slid the booklet out. There was no text on the inside, just shiny white paper. A cheaply produced package. On the back of the booklet, though, was the same psychedelic pattern and the same balloony font, but with the addition of a title.

The Inscrutable Whom. Midnight at the Magic Music Shop.

26

As they came around the corner Martin stopped dead and stated, "Well, fuck me." Jason, who'd been looking at his feet and fearing his parents, looked up. In the afternoon light, a huge swastika gleamed pale yellow where they'd scrubbed it off. It hadn't been there right after they'd finished—the water must have disguised it until it dried—and they hadn't seen the house in the daylight until now.

Martin looked at both of them slowly. "Uh, I'm not taking another step until somebody tells me what *that*—" he jabbed a finger toward it, his sketchbook gripped in the same hand "—is all about."

As they looked at it, Roberto sat down crosslegged on the sidewalk and held his face in his hands.

Jason said, "Somebody spray-paints Roberto's house when he's not here. That's where we cleaned it off."

Martin turned and inspected it from a distance, then looked down at the back of Roberto's head. "Somebody did that to you?"

Roberto nodded, his face still hidden in his hands. Martin looked back up at the house. "Well," he said. "Fuck me." He stared at it some more, as though he thought it might do something surprising, and eventually said, "Is it safe?"

"Oh, sure," Jason said, not sure whether to look at Roberto or what to do. "We stay up nights to watch out." But they'd been watching through the arms of a swastika. This might be unsettling.

"Uh *huh*," Martin said slowly. ". . . Gotcha." He finally turned from it and bent to address Roberto. "Are you okay, man?"

Roberto nodded into his hands, wiped his eyes with his face still down, then scrambled to his feet. "Fine," he said brightly. "Yeah, I'm fine. Let's go."

They were sitting at the dining table, drinking sodas out of ice-filled glasses on gold foam placemats. The glasses had daisies on them. Either Roberto was playing host especially for Martin or it took two guests before his social graces kicked in. But he wasn't saying much, and there were long, strained silences that Jason felt helpless to fill. Roberto was slouched in his chair with his arms folded, staring past the tabletop, his expression dark.

"So, uh," Martin said. "What do you think of that school?"

Jason shrugged. "It's okay."

"I bet you're like a straight-A student."

"Me? No way."

"Oh yeah? Why not?"

"Most of my classes are stupid."

"What's your GPA?"

"Three point something. What's yours?"

"Two point nothing."

"How come? You seem smart."

"Right." Martin turned to Roberto. "How about you?"

Roberto sat and stared darkly through the table.

"Yo," Martin said. "Earth to Big Guy."

Roberto muttered something, and Jason and Martin both leaned forward and said, "What?"

Roberto shifted awkwardly in his seat. "I said I give up. It's too hard. I don't want to do it anymore."

"What?" Jason said. "Are you kidding me? You can't give up!"

"Why not?" Roberto looked up. The rims of his eyes were red. "They'll do it either way. Nothing I do makes any difference."

"You can't just let them win!"

Roberto's face showed nothing but exhaustion. "What do you mean *let* them win? I'm up all night, every night, looking out that stupid dining room window, trying to catch them. But I can't anymore. I can't do it alone." He shrugged. "I can't win."

"You're not *all* alone."

"Okay," Roberto conceded tiredly, "I apologize for my poor choice of words. But in a very real way, I am doing it alone. I'm glad to have you here, but I'm the man of the house, and there's nobody else who lives here. Are you going to come over every day to help me watch my house instead of going to school?" He studied Jason's hesitation. "Of course you're not. The weekend's almost over and you're going to go back to school. Sure, you could play hooky a couple of days, but my dad doesn't come back for two more *months*. Are you going to be here that long?"

Maybe, Jason thought. Maybe. "I don't know," he said, didn't know what to say next, and listened to the whirring hum of the clock in the kitchen and the gentle clucking when its numbers flipped.

"Now, this is none of my business," Martin ventured. "But do I understand that you're the only person living in this house? Or what? Or . . . how does that work?"

Roberto said, "My dad's on a container ship in the South Pacific."

"What's that? What's a container ship?"

Jason tried not to look as though he were suddenly paying attention.

"Oh," Roberto said. "I'm sorry. That just means a big ship that carries cargo in big containers. Like boxcars."

"Ah, gotcha." Martin nodded. "So, that makes him like what, like a sailor?"

"An engineer."

"Okay, that's Dad. What about your—"

"What's your dad do?" Roberto cocked his head and looked interested.

"Oh. Uh, well, when I was two, he was a machinist. I don't know what he is now."

Jason knew that families broke, but he didn't understand it, and he had only a vague idea of what a machinist was. Martin's life was completely incomprehensible. He nodded.

Roberto said, "Where does he live?"

"Your guess is as good as mine. So let's see. My dad ran off, your dad's off on a boat . . . What about you? I'm guessing your dad's still around, you got the two point five, the station wagon, the whole nine."

"I guess, except for the two-point-five," Jason said. "I'm an only child."

"Your mom stay home?"

"No, they both work."

"Latchkey kid, huh?"

"I guess. What about you, any brothers or sisters?"

"Nope, same same. It's just me and my mom." He turned to Roberto. "So you were saying—"

"What do you want for lunch?" Roberto stood and moved into the kitchen, "I thought I'd make tuna fish sandwiches."

Martin and Jason agreed, and they heard Roberto wrestle with a stuck wooden drawer and start rummaging.

Martin leaned in toward Jason and said softly, "What's the deal with his mom?"

Jason frowned at the non sequitur. "What do you mean?"

"Well, nothing, I guess." Martin looked confused. "I guess nothing."

27

As Jason unlocked Sarah's door later that evening, her phone started ringing, and he couldn't fight the key out of the lock, so he left the other keys dangling, dashed in, and snatched the phone from its cradle to say, "Hello?"

"You're there!"

"I am! I'm glad it's you. How's Peru?"

"Oh, it's so beautiful here. We should come together some time."

"How soon they forget."

"What do you mean?"

"Never mind."

"Oh ha ha," she said. Robert closed the door, the key ring in his hand.

Jason sat on her hanging wicker chair. "The shoot's going smoothly?"

"It's okay. You always know there's going to be *something* to go wrong, but it's going fine."

As she told him all about the plane trip, the local assistant, the models, and the day's obstacles, he gestured for

Robert to come in and get comfortable. When she seemed to be running down, he said, "So it sounds like it's going well."

"It is. It's going really well. I miss you, though. I wish you were here."

"I miss you too."

"So . . . how's it going there?"

He thought about it, tried to pin down an accurate answer. "Not bad."

"Do they know who trashed your friend's store yet?"

"No, not yet."

"That's too bad."

"Yes, it really is."

There was a pause, and then she asked, "Are you mad at me, Jason?"

Surprised, he said, "No, why would I be mad at you?"

Robert, who had been reading the spines of her books, looked over.

"You're being awfully uncommunicative."

"No I'm not."

"Well, you sure sound mad. I'm trying to talk to you, and all I get are one-word answers."

No I'm not was three words, but he intuited that this was not something to bring up.

"Well," he said, and got stuck.

Another pause. "I went out of my way to find a phone and call you, and you're acting like you don't care about me. Do you care how that makes me feel?"

"Well," he said, trying to find something that would address her concern without conceding wrongdoing inaccurately, "I would care if I made you feel bad, yes."

"*If* you made me feel bad?"

"Yes, I'd care very much about that."

"What's that supposed to mean?"

Another stumper.

"Hello?"

"I . . . you seem to have misinterpreted almost everything I've said, and I'm at a loss as to what to do."

"Oh, so now what you're saying is it's all *my* fault."

"What's all your fault?"

"I think you're still mad at me for going away and doing my job."

"I can't *still* be mad at you when I wasn't mad in the first place."

"You sound like you're mad."

"Well, yeah, *now* I'm mad."

"Look, I have to go."

"Would you still have to go if you didn't think I was mad?"

"Jason, I have a *job* to do here. People are waiting for me. Are you going to let me go or not?"

He wanted to say *not,* but that would be childish. "Okay, I'll talk to you later."

And there was the click and the dead line. He placed the phone in its cradle.

Robert pointed at the bookshelf. "She has Calvino and Wodehouse."

"Yes, Robert."

"Look: Steinbeck."

"Yes, Robert."

"Often have you had occasion to allude to her melodious voice. She abuseth not drugs, she cheateth not, and neither does she—"

"She thinks I'm uncommunicative."

"Well . . ."

"I didn't have anything to communicate, okay? All right, fine, what's the look for?"

"You and I just spent the night staking out a building in a part of the country we've never been to before, caught a glimpse of a mysterious wheelchaired figure called the Inscrutable Whom, and now have in our possession the box to his CD, which has the same name as Zeb's store. Are you sure you don't have anything to communicate?"

"I answered everything she asked me."

"Ee-*yeah*," Robert said. "I think that might be her point."

Jason looked at the phone and wished that someone had made this clear previously.

"Can you call her back?"

"I don't have the number there. Let's get some dinner and then head over to the shop?"

"I think I'd rather catch a quick nap."

"Can't quite stay up all night anymore, huh?"

"Unlike you," Robert said, "some of us are getting older."

28

T HEY came gingerly up the frozen steps from the subway to be attacked by the most vicious weather Jason had ever seen that close. The short distance to the store was a battle without armor; sneakers slipped on ice, eyes shut involuntarily against whirling splinters of snow, lungs stopped dead and refused to inhale from sheer shock of cold, and the body was needled and soaked where no muffler or glove blocked the onslaught.

When they piled into the store, Robert slammed the door and leaned against it melodramatically with hand to brow, the very model of a silent movie heroine.

"Aaaaaaaaaagghhh!" he emoted, gathered himself, and then said it again with exactly the same delivery. Unclear about what to do with the snow that was caked all over him—this not being a point of etiquette one learns in the City of Angels—Jason just stood there on the rubber floor mat somebody had put down and watched Zeb start to laugh.

The store was a little less of a chaotic nightmare. A new, inexpensive stereo tuner perched on the repaired back shelf. The old one was on the floor, at the bottom of a neat stack of other damaged things. Wet coats and shoes hung in the bathroom next to Zeb's office, and they were sitting on stools near the counter, absorbing uneven heat from a little space heater. Zeb sat on a road case with the empty CD case in his hand, listening intently to Jason's account.

"Did she say when they'd be getting more copies in?"

"I didn't ask."

Zeb's eyes widened. "You didn't *ask*? How could you not *ask*?"

His bare feet toasting on the rung of his stool, Jason spread his hands and tried to come up with something that wouldn't sound stupid.

"My friend is an idiot," Robert supplied, and smiled when Jason rolled his eyes.

Zeb clutched his head. "Aw, man! And the net's down over the entire Tri-State area, so we can't even go looking for info." Eyeing the increasingly violent storm outside the glass door, he let out a big breath. "I'm awfully tempted to see if I can get to Pennsylvania."

Robert did a big, sloppy double take that ended with his jaw dropped and his eyebrows way up. He pointed at the window. "In *that*?"

Battered by the wind, the glass clunked, the reflections on it wobbling.

"What," Zeb said. "You never seen a little snow before?"

But he went home to Gary Warren instead, vanishing into the white at a run.

Jason tuned in a news station, got some of the rack effects powered up, and ran the news through them, gently layering the sound into a newscast-flavored burble. He blended the burble with the arpeggiating wash of the synthesizers and the idiotic chuckling of the coffeemaker, and came back to the counter to be with Robert. When the coffeemaker gave a rattling sigh and subsided, he brought back two mugs.

Watching the icy maelstrom outside the window, Robert said, "I'm feeling an extraordinary sense of continuity. Even with the snow."

Jason nodded. "All it needs is *The Night Men*."

Robert cocked his head, started to move, hesitated, and then reached down to snag his backpack. Withdrawing the battered paperback, he said, "Should we start at the beginning again?" He held it in one hand, letting it fall open to its bookmark, an old Polaroid photo of indistinct darkness broken by a smudgy light flare. "Or should we pick it up where we left off? Except you read farther than I did."

When Jason finally spoke, his eyes were still on the bookmark. "Yeah, but I skipped around, and I was too upset to retain it. Why don't you back up a ways. Like after he finds the kid."

Robert opened the book.

Outside, the rain was banging down like God's mute resentment. I had no cocoa, so I scalded some milk in a skillet as the kid sat at my table in one of my clean shirts and watched me. My room didn't fit him any better than my shirt did.

"One of these days you'll have to talk," I told him. When I spoke, he put his cup down and showed me attention, but no flicker of understanding. When I reached for my glass, he drank again.

"Me llamo Carter," I said. He put his cup down respectfully. "Qué es su nombre?" I said. I pointed to my chest. "Carter," I said, and then pointed at him.

He picked up his cup as I walked to the telephone.

"Homicide. Baynes."

"Hello, Fred," I said. "I'm calling in a chit."

"Chit?" Baynes said, "Oh yes—I had one, but I gave it to you yesterday afternoon."

"I didn't need your help with that, but I need it with this."

"Look, Carter—"

"There's a minor in the picture," I said.

"Come down to juvenile hall and I'll introduce you to a few hundred more."

"This one's drinking hot milk at my table."

At first he didn't say anything, and I could hear his breathing. "You don't say."

"He's eight, maybe nine. He can't speak English, or won't."

"Where'd you get him?"

"A big stork dropped him here. I can't call about the mistake until open of business tomorrow."

"Carter—"

"All right, Baynes, I'll put too fine a point on it. You owe me one and this is payback." I put a lot of detail into my description of the child and left a lot out of the circumstances of my finding him.

"We're even after this, Carter," Baynes said. "And just so you know, I don't like you much."

I said that was fine and rang off. The kid was asleep with his head down on the table. I put him in my bed and left the dishes for the morning. I put the empty milk bottles out and left a note for the milkman to leave two more than usual, and two chocolate. My floor was more comfortable than some places I've spent the night. That's the rule: When you can't save yourself, save someone else.

29

THAT'S awesome," Martin said at the chapter break. "Show Roberto that," Jason said, pointing at Martin's sketchbook. From his post at the front window, he'd watched over Martin's shoulder, seen the evolution of imprecisely roughed geometric shapes into the silhouette of a hardboiled figure in fedora and overcoat, cigarette balanced between lips, smoking pistol down by its side, notched collar up.

Martin shrugged and rotated the sketchbook around to hand it to Roberto.

Roberto's eyebrows went up. "Wow. This is really great. I just thought you weren't listening."

Martin reached for it. "It's all right," he said. He didn't meet Roberto's gaze.

"It's much better than all right." Roberto handed it back. "You have a real talent." Outside, the wind was calm, and Jason could feel the October chill penetrating the window and robbing the first few inches of the dining room of warmth. There had been no sound or movement from the porch during his watch. Martin scribbled his initials and the date at Carter's foot and circled them, eyed the masculine figure critically, and closed the sketchbook.

"I didn't hear any more bird *metaphors*," Jason said.

Roberto sighed dramatically. "That doesn't necessarily *mean* anything. He could have just used them in that one scene."

"But then it wouldn't be a *metaphor*. It would just be a *description*."

"It could still be a metaphor. It doesn't have to be used all the *time* for it to be a metaphor. Do you even know what a metaphor *is*?"

"Yeah, I know what one is. Do you?"

"Of course I know, but I don't think you do."

"So what is one?"

"Right, like I'm falling for that."

"Well, I'm not falling for *that*."

"Well, I think you're weaseling."

"Well, like I care."

They glared at each other in the gloom. The growl of the little clock on the kitchen windowsill seemed to intensify, as though it had caught sight of a rival clock nosing around on the stove. A swell of aggression spread through Jason's body, strengthened his resolve, bolstered his distaste for conflict resolution.

Martin looked from one of them to the other, then shook his head. "*Jesus*, you guys get macho about weird stuff. Somebody got a dictionary somewhere around this place? 'Cause I don't have the slightest friggin' *clue* what one is."

Immediately outside the window, a shoe scraped on concrete.

Jason swept the Polaroid camera from the table, pulled the curtain open, aimed at the vague impression of a figure, and shot blind. The flash lit the room. He heard the receding slap of running footsteps and waited calmly for the motor to spit each photo out, shooting again, waiting, shooting. He set the camera and the photos on the table and took up the base-ball bat. Roberto was now standing; Martin's jaw was dropped. Both watched as Jason flicked the front door's dead-bolt, opened it, trotted onto the porch. They might have been saying something. The caressing breeze twined around him, and he went down the driveway with the bat at his side, watching himself precisely, a lone figure on a dark, empty street.

Roberto and Martin came out silently and walked out to join him. He turned and shook his head, which felt too dra-matic. It would be better next time to simply look at them.

They stood outside for a good twenty minutes, seeing nothing but the street and its listless leaves, hearing nothing but the distant communication of owls somewhere off toward the wash.

30

THERE'S a mood that happens at night with an old friend who remembers the same mistakes. In the still half-traumatized store, the arpeggios and the burbling newscasts washed and bubbled in the speakers, and the mood settled in comfortably. Raging snow suffocated the nearest streetlight to a dark gray blur and obliterated all others entirely. Jason tried logging on: nothing.

When the phone rang, the mood lifted momentarily. Like Waldo, Jason thought, when he'd open one eye and cock an ear before resuming a nap. He put his mug on the new counter glass, swung his feet down lazily, and reached behind for the phone.

"Magic Music Shop."

"Hey." Leon's new adult voice resided mostly in the neighborhood of high baritone, but it took spontaneous yodeling excursions into the soprano. Since the onset of the big change, he had affected a sort of faux-*pachuco* accent for maximum cool. Jason thought it was sort of cute, but it drove Martin nuts. "Is this Jason, yo?"

"What's up, Leon." The mood settled back in condition-ally, Jason's imaginary Waldo returning to his nap with the flat cant of ears that said he wasn't entirely trustful.

"Martin said I could call you? I found a washer fluid reservoir? From a junkyard, like you said?"

Jason's old Plymouth—no: Leon's new Plymouth—had parts that weren't exactly stock. After twenty years of engine heat, the original reservoir had cracked from sheer brittleness during a time when Jason didn't have fifteen dollars for a new one. The plastic bleach bottle still worked fine ten years later, but Leon wanted his washer fluid contained correctly. He wanted the translucent, trapezoidal reservoir with the snap cap, the embossed Plymouth logo, and the orderly search un-der a hot sun through rows of skeletal junkers in the Chrysler section of the graveyard, Philips-head jutting from back pocket, adult strut in the step.

"Did you test the new one for leaks?"

"I held it under the bathtub just like you said. What should I do next?"

"It's pretty easy, chief," Jason said. "You just pull all the black rubber tubes out and unscrew the pipe tape from the firewall. Screw the new one on, stick the tubes back in, fill it up, and let there be liquid."

"Martin said ask you if there's anything special I have to know."

Automotive sage and leader of boys into manhood. "Well, the main thing is not to drop the screws into the engine. If you always put them on top of the air cleaner, you won't lose them." After a few moments of uneasy silence, he added, "That's the big round thing on top of the carburetor."

"Oh yeah, with that *wingnut*."

"Right. Oh—and that black tubing is older than you are, so be careful not to bend it."

"Can you do it at night?"

"Well, it's certainly better in the daytime when you can see."

"But you could do it at night if you had a lantern, right?"

Jason smiled and said, "Hold on a sec." He punched the speaker button and hung up. "Can you hear me?"

"Loud and clear, *ese*," Leon's tinny voice said, and Jason smiled. A new adult-cool word from Leon. He'd have to be careful not to smile when it happened in person.

"I put you on the speaker so Robert could talk."

"*¿Qué tal, Leon?*"

"Yo, what up, Roberto."

"*Me llamo Miguel,*" Robert recited. "*Este es mí amigo, Ernesto. Y tú, como te llamas?*"

"Yeah, okay," Leon said.

"*Oye como va,*" Jason contributed.

"Hey." Robert gave him a big, cheesy thumbs-up. "Great."

"So anyway, Leon, you could theoretically replace the washing fluid reservoir at night, using my propane lantern for light, but it's probably better to do it in the morning."

Robert got the gist and grinned.

"Yeah, but . . . Martin said I could use the lantern and you could talk me through it on the cordless phone. If you say it's okay. I already put on my car-fixing clothes."

"Leon, what time is it there?"

"Like nine. It's still light a little."

"Leon, by what definition of 'light' is it light at nine o'clock P.M.?"

"*I* dunno."

No accent on that one.

From the front came the dull rap of gloved knuckles on glass. Jason turned in his seat. Outside the door, a small person encased in scarf and hat shoved its hands back in its coat pockets and did a shivery little dance as Robert got up. The neck of a soft black instrument case extended up behind it like a quiver. Jason said, "Hold on a sec, Leon."

Robert flipped the locks and opened the door, and fresh, icy air filtered in and brushed Jason's face and hands. He couldn't hear what the small figure said, but Robert turned and said, "Can we sell her some cello strings?"

When that was taken care of and the door re-locked, Jason returned to the phone. "Leon, you really want to do this?"

"Yeah, please?"

Jason looked at Robert, who indicated a shrug with his eyebrows, still smiling.

"Okay. But we only go 'til ten-thirty, okay? It's a school night. Whether it's finished or not. Deal?"

"Deal!"

"All right, then, chief. Go get the lantern." Jason put his feet up, getting comfortable again.

Snow pounded the boarded windows and rattled the glass door in the feeble light of the suffocating streetlamp. Robert looked out and shivered. "Remember the line from *The Night Men* about the weather in L.A.?"

"Yeah."

"I get it now." Robert watched the snow for a while, then stood and took their mugs to the coffeemaker for warmups. Across the continent, a boy in an old white v-neck and baggy jeans was about to cross Ocean Avenue under the warm, rustling palms, pop the hood on his first car, and smell old metal and coolant, dirty engine grease and mild Pacific breeze. Imaginary Waldo snugged his furry snout into the crook of his foreleg and sighed himself back to sleep.

31

JASON learned that his new unwillingness to back down didn't end at mere argumentativeness. When, on Monday morning, he spoke his intention to maintain his post at Roberto's house, his simple disregard of his parents became also disregard of the state. He was now truant. What he didn't mention was his fear: his life to that point had included arguing with authority, getting smart with it, and sulking at its unfairness, but he had never defied it outright, and this scared him cold. He understood himself to be forfeiting both the prejudices and the insulating properties of the middle class, and he knew the punishment for his defection would come not in words or silences, but in blows.

He had assumed all along that his adolescence would involve rites of passage, and that they would fall within certain proscribed areas of comfortable discomfort. To find himself free-falling beyond those boundaries without any memory of having crossed them—without having done anything but try to help someone—left him frightened and disoriented.

But: "Save someone else," he'd whispered, lying on Roberto's bed with his shoes off, trying to catch a nap during Roberto's watch. He repeated it more than once, testing it, feeling where it had already barbed his imagination. It was the first time he'd ever known in a concrete sense who he wanted to be.

As he left Roberto's bedroom, his curiosity was caught again by the closed door next to it.

Inside, a twin bed was made neatly with a thin, ribbed orange cover. A small, bare desk stood near a short wood-laminate bookcase with the rectangular footprints of half a dozen missing books blocked out of its gathered dust. The dust on the desk was similarly interrupted by an ovoid clean spot about eight inches across.

Roberto was at the dining room window, bleary and drooping in the unassertive morning light. Martin was asleep in the living room, on the couch. Jason picked up the fanned stack of Polaroid photos from the dining table and examined them closely.

"Did you find anything?" he said. All the pictures he'd snapped so calmly evidenced nothing but the reflections of flashbulbs on smudged, black windows. Nothing showed in the invisible darkness past the glass.

Roberto shook his head tiredly. "I was just going to wake you up. You only have twenty minutes to catch the bus."

"I'm not going to school."

"Jason—"

"I'm staying here until we catch the people."

"That's really nice of you," Roberto began, but he stopped when Jason shook his head.

"I'm staying here."

Roberto nodded jerkily. Jason aimed a thumb vaguely at

the outside world. "Do you have any money? I'll walk to the store and get us some more cereal."

Another jerky nod. "Sure." Roberto went through the living room and den and into the room next to his. When he emerged, he carried two wilted twenty-dollar bills. "This is all I have left, so you should get enough for three or four days. My dad's check will be here soon. Speaking of whom, shouldn't you be calling your parents?"

Dread leached up from where Jason thought he'd imprisoned it. "No."

"Are you sure? Don't you think they're worried?"

"I'm sure they are."

"Then call them!"

"I don't want to call them."

"Dude," Martin said from the couch, sitting up and squinting. "If you've got parents who give a shit where you are, you should call them."

"What the fuck difference does it make to you two? Just give me the goddamn money and I'll go get us supplies."

Roberto gave him a frustrated look and handed over the two limp bills.

Jason bought Boo-Berry cereal, Quisp cereal, milk, and a dozen little paper-wrapped cans of deviled ham. He bought Spam and Otter-Pops, hot dogs and buns, instant coffee, Fritos, and a tub of sour cream and some onion soup mix. He saved money on Kool-Aid by getting the smaller packets without sugar included. On a vague impulse, he picked up a lemon and a head of lettuce, then remembered the existence of sandwiches and got a loaf of Wonder bread, peanut butter, jelly, and canned tuna, and some macaroni and cheese and some margarine. Then he didn't have enough left for three large bottles of cheap cola and three Cup O' Noodles, so he put the lettuce back. But he kept the lemon.

That ought to hold them for three days.

The haul was greeted with approval, item by item, as Roberto put things away and made sandwiches. Jason felt bad about losing his temper earlier but didn't say anything about it. The routine resumed, day stretching into half-light.

32

Two rough men I knew came while I was shaving. One of them was Mattie Maloney, called Mutt, who didn't have a preference whether I lived or died, and the other was Jackie Boy Reilly, who did. I'd barely heard my door crash open when Maloney had crossed the floor in two strides. I dropped my shaving mirror as I turned and tried to lay the razor across his throat, but he reared back and took it on the chin as the mirror shattered in the basin; next my wrist was immobile in the grip of a fist the size of my head and he plucked the razor from it. Jackie Boy sauntered in from the doorway, glancing around. As I curled back my left arm and made the hand a fist, he pointed a Colt revolver at me. Mutt's chin dripped blood into the collar of his shirt.

"Hello, boys," I said. "How's it going to go?"

"Show him," Jackie Boy said behind his revolver, and as I threw my useless uppercut, there was a flash of silver and a flash of white at the end of Mutt's hand, and a searing pain and red blackness in the core of my left eye.

I was blinking through blood and shaving soap when I came back to myself, every flutter of my eyelids a dagger in the ruined flesh in its socket. I dangled from my right wrist, still clamped in Mutt's huge fist like a rope in a stanchion. My left arm hung limp. There was a horrible shivering endless moan in the room, and I knew it was me.

I heard Jackie Boy speak, wordlessly, through the terrible pain of my blinded eye and dislocated shoulder. I was hovering on the edge of a faint. I've been there enough to know you can fight through a faint, but only if you want to. I didn't.

I found myself awake, but I didn't know whether I was alive.

The pain was deep, its edges soft. My face and body were battered; I know the feeling through anaesthetic. I raised fingertips to my face in the darkness and met stiff cloth. The smells were of gauze and disinfectant. Distantly, voices murmured.

When I said, "hello," the sound was a whisper. No one answered. There was no doctor to ask about my sight, but I didn't need to. I was at least half blind and grateful for the bargain. For the miracle of waking alive, I'd have paid more.

I may have lain awake, or spoken with a nurse who might have entered, but if I did, it was of the moment only, and went uncaptured by memory before I fell back to unconsciousness.

I remember a thought of the boy, but I did not think of him again until later.

The pain was still there in the darkness, no worse. Fred Baynes' voice said, "About time. I was about finished with the *Herald*."

"Sorry I can't read you the captions," I said. My voice was dry and unused.

At first he didn't speak. I heard the rustle as he folded his paper. "The doctor bandaged both your eyes so the one won't move along with the other. That's why you can't see. Do you need anything?"

"Yes, help to the lavatory. I don't want to use the bedpan."

I heard him lay his paper nearby. Dragging my balky IV stand, we edged the poor invalid out of bed and started across the floor. It was slow going in the dark, but I managed without leaning on him too much.

"Speaking of captions," he said, "how about you tell me one for the picture in front of me?"

"I fell downstairs," I said. "How about that?"

"That must have been quite a fall. What would you say, about ten flights down?"

"Twelve, and then into a thresher. It's the damnedest thing; I'd never seen a thresher there before."

"By my lights, Carter, the evidence says otherwise."

"What evidence?"

We stopped. "Peek through the bandages with your good eye," he said. "You'll see it above the sink." I heard the door swing open.

"The eyes have it," I said.

I didn't peek. I already know what I look like whipped. I got a tongue-lashing from the duty nurse for getting up, and Baynes got one for aiding and abetting. He went out when the doctor came in to tell me in a resonant voice that medical science was advancing at an unprecedented rate. He was giddy with its rapid advancement. I told him I always give to the March of Dimes. He explained to me gravely that he'd done everything he could, and his voice trembled when he said that now it was in God's hands. It was a good show, but I didn't applaud and he left with his feelings hurt. Baynes came back in and paced in his squeaky shoes.

"What is it, Baynes?"

"The Lieutenant's not going to let me pass with a thresher story, Carter. You know that."

"Oh, did I say 'thresher'? I must have been delusional from the anaesthetic. I was ambushed. It was three little guys, maybe Albanians. I got a good look at them, these Albanians. They had long mustaches and one of them had a limp. They were dressed in white linen suits. Their ringleader wore a fez."

"All right, Carter."

"Tell your lieutenant to bring extra boys if he plans to corner these dangerous Albanians. They're desperate men."

Baynes' big sigh was freighted with disapproval. "You know the law casts a harsh eye on vigilantes, Carter."

"I don't know what you're talking about, Baynes, but I'm getting tired and I think I'll catch some shuteye. I'll have the butler show you out. Oh, James!"

"All right," he said, and then, "Is it bad?"

"Not so's you'd notice," I said, and I heard him leave.

I stared into the endless blackness of my bandages and felt the pain curl and magnify, the way it does. I don't know whether I fell asleep then or much later.

"Do you mind if we skip forward a little? I remember all this."

"Let's see . . . uh . . . okay, you remember his girlfriend loses the kid."

"Right."

"Okay . . . let me see . . ."

"But Tommy—oh, Tommy . . ." Fresh tears filled her eyes. "Why couldn't you save us?"

"Beth, I—"

"Tommy," she said softly, "please—please don't call anymore."

Then I looked at her, and on her face was misery, but also quietness. Outside her door, I sighed a shaky sigh, and then I sighed one that wasn't. It was for her and me and the whole sorry human joke. Then I thought of the boy whose name I didn't know, and I didn't sigh anymore.

When I came down the step in the moonlight, a cab was stopped on the corner, the cabbie eating his cold supper, but when he saw me he laid his meal carefully on its wax paper and leaned out his window.

"Need a cab, pal?"

He was a big, earthy man, and muscles stood out like knotted rope from the forearm he laid across his window. I squatted on my heels and showed him a fifty-dollar note. "I need a ride into a bad section and a cabbie who's not afraid to wait until I come back out."

He pointed at the note with one ruddy fore-finger. "A fellow who offers fifty up front is ex-pectin' a lot of waitin' or a lot of trouble."

"Trouble," I said.

A grin split his puffy face. "Good. I hate waitin'."

Jackie Boy Reilly did a lot of work for Borden Jarvis, an entrepreneur in the reaping of divi-dends from human frailty. His business had grown tenfold in recent years as it absorbed the local rings through superior organization and main force.

Rumors of Jarvis' ties to the Black Hand were in my thoughts when the cabbie said, "You ex-pectin' company, buddy?"

"How many?"

"One little blue coupé with two heads in it."

"Can you lose it without looking like that's what you're doing?"

He caught my eye in the rear-view. "You don't ask for much, do you?"

"No, I'm a model of self-sufficiency. I'd espe-cially like to get behind it, if that's not too much trouble for you."

He laughed and hung a sharp left onto a resi-dential street. As soon as we were around the corner, he opened the throttle on the Checker's big engine and the cab surged forward. He exe-cuted a neat, sharp left onto an unpaved, un-lighted road, where the upright beams of half-built houses loomed like gray finger bones until he switched off the headlamps. He rolled down his window and opened up the engine again, and we shot ahead in the dark, the cabbie

not braking until we had bumped well past the
edge of what terrain I could remember from the
headlamps.

I rolled down my window. As we listened, I
felt both my eyes see deep into the blackness.
The fantasy was short-lived, my vision's unbal-
ance returning when a sweep of passing light ac-
companied the growl of an engine on the road
we'd quit.

"One minute," I said, reaching for my door
handle as the cabbie reached for his ignition. "I
saw something on the ground that I want."

Jarvis owned a dozen warehouses, several apart-
ments, and one house that I knew of, but it was a
Thursday night, and this meant that for the first
time in a long while, I had something that could
turn into luck, if I were lucky. The Jarvis I'd
known was a man of reliable habits. Thursdays
were collection days, and he organized his weekly
rounds so that after he'd pressed the diseased
flesh of his assorted bookmakers, pimps, and
marihuana sellers, he would end up at Mickey's
Enchilada, a tiny three-stool lunch counter a
dark quarter mile from Olveira Street.

He was spooning Mexican sauce onto *huevos
rancheros* and watching Jackie Boy have a laugh
when I came in the open door. The proprietor, a
neat little ex-counterfeiter named Eliseo Rodriguez, came in from the back, wiping his hands.
He faded back again when he recognized my
face.

Reinforcing bar is common at construction
sites. It is nice, heavy iron, thick as a thumb and
ribbed for gripping concrete. It's meant to keep
buildings from collapsing in earthquakes. Jackie

Boy was still turning toward me when I smashed my recent acquisition across his temple. As he fell from the stool, I came back from my follow-through and broke his shin bone on the return. He cried out and hit the floor bloody and dazed.

"*Amigo,*" I heard from behind me. I knew my time had run out, and Rodriguez had returned with a gun.

Jarvis was salting his food. While Jackie Boy whimpered on the floor, he sliced off a bite with his fork, chewed it, took a drink of beer. When this demonstration was ended, he glanced down at Jackie Boy and spoke without looking at me. "You've done what you came here for. Now scram."

I said to Jackie Boy, "You'd better tell your bosom pal Mutt to look sharp."

Jarvis sliced off another bite. "I will tell Eliseo to kill you."

Jackie Boy tried to dodge as I dropped the re-bar on him and whimpered as the movement ground the fragments of his shin bone. Jarvis turned his pale eyes on me finally, showing me no more real interest than a hyena would show a bowl of plastic apricots.

I turned toward the door. Rodriguez was behind the counter, aiming a shotgun at my head. I aimed a forefinger at him and pantomimed pulling a trigger. When he smiled, a gold incisor glinted.

My cabbie was waiting around the corner. "That was quick," he said as he pulled away. "You do what you came for, pal?"

"No, I changed the plan. Didn't know I had one, did you?"

"I never doubted it for a second. How'd you change your plan?"

"I incapacitated the bodyguard and left."

"Just one bodyguard?"

"I took out the big one. There's still a little one."

"Armed?"

"Yes."

"Then he's another big one."

"That's right."

"What's your new plan?"

"I don't know yet, but there's another fifty in it for you to find a good place to keep an eye on that joint and twiddle your thumbs while I figure it out."

He found a spot a block away and we watched Mickey's Enchilada. I figured; he twiddled. I formulated dozens of plans. None was any good. Jarvis and Rodriguez came out with Jackie Boy and a tarp and put them both into the backseat of a two-tone Seville. "Follow that car," I said.

The cabbie straightened and cracked his knuckles. "You're a pro at this," he said. "I can tell."

We pulled into traffic. "It takes a hell of a plan to be better than no plan at all," I said.

"Ain't that the truth," he chuckled. "Ain't it just."

33

CRUMBLY snow lined the edges of the sidewalks. Down the centers, it was compressed unevenly and buffed into slippery ice by rubber, leather, and foot pressure. Whitened car windows were engraved to a half-inch depth by fingertips: peace signs; $E=MC^2$; a hasty and well-executed cubist nude. Yesterday's radical concepts, no longer potent enough to provoke anything but nostalgia.

On the counter was a note from Zeb:

> Alarm company coming out tomorrow——no more night watch! Gary and I want to take you both out for dinner. Where do you want to go? Will call.
> Z

Robert was measuring grounds into the coffeemaker, and Jason hadn't even started the arpeggiators going yet when the muffled knock came on the glass door. The blond man wanted a bass pick, so Jason had him come in and look at the selection. His companion browsed idly, twirling her hair around a forefinger. When the bassist had chosen half a dozen picks, a cable, two nine-volt batteries, and a shaker shaped like a plastic egg, he called her over, and she drifted to the counter and listlessly rotated a little velvet stand of cloisonné charms shaped like instruments.

Ten minutes of store time, Jason noted as they left. Total sale: $72 plus tax.

He tried to get online again. Still nothing.

When the arpeggiators and the newscast were going, he ran a microphone over to where Robert was starting coffee brewing, fed the percolation into the mix, pitch-shifted it down two octaves, delayed it a couple of seconds, and layered it back on itself. The door darkened and opened tentatively. A young man's voice said, "You open?"

"Not exactly," Jason said, adjusting a fader minutely and turning to greet the customer. "What do you need?"

"I saw that guy come out." The young man took a dance music magazine from the newly restocked rack near the counter and riffled through it in a flicker of brightly-colored pages. "Sweet chillout mix," he said. "Real ambient, down-tempo after-hours."

It sounded like English. Jason nodded vaguely.

The young man looked up from the magazine, saw incomprehension, gave Jason an I'll-use-small-words look. "Nice music?" He jerked his head toward the speakers.

"Thanks."

"Yeah." Now riffling through the magazine again. "Who is that?"

"DJ Coffeepot."

"Yeah," the young man said. "I heard of him. Real organic, right?"

"Right," Jason said. "He's known for that."

"Sweet."

"We're not exactly open. Did you need to buy something?"

"Uh . . . yeah, I'll take this."

As Jason rang up the magazine, Robert said, "So you're into South American DJs?"

"I like music from all over. DJ Coffeepot, he's from South America, right?"

Robert nodded. "He's black, from the mountains in Colombia. He's very rich."

"And aromatic," Jason said. "I need another fifty cents."

"Oh. Shit." An oversincere search through pockets.

"Bring it later."

"Thanks, man, I appreciate it. Hey, what CD is this?"

"*Two Sugars,*" Jason said. "It's a very hot import."

"Nice. I do a lot of parties. I'll check it out."

Robert locked the door after the young man left. As he turned to go to the coffeepot, he looked at Jason and said, "What."

"I was thinking on the way over here that some day, everything I thought was new would be old. It just happened sooner than I expected."

Robert prepared two cups (octave-shifted ceramic clinks amid the arpeggios, the clucking burble of pouring transformed into a cascade of quiet torrents) and brought them to the counter. "You are an old coot," he stipulated, hipping carefully onto his stool before handing over one of the cups. Doing it the other way around would have made more sense, but then it wouldn't have been Robert.

The coffee itself wasn't very good, but the milk ratio was flawless. They'd known each other a long time now. "I've been an old coot since my early twenties. I'm just finally getting good at it."

"You know, your early twenties weren't *that* long ago."

Jason inclined his head in concession, but Robert saw it as the silent disagreement it really was, and said, "Is that so? You feel that much different?"

"Yes."

Some music, some snow, some sipping. Jason warmed his hands on his half-full cup and eventually said, "Don't you?"

"Feel different?"

He nodded.

Robert shook his head somberly.

Some time later, he said, "I wonder if that's why—"

A rapping on the glass: the same young man. The biting chill invaded again as Jason opened the door and received the fifty cents he'd not expected to see.

"Thanks."

"Yeah," the young man said. He produced two playing cards from within his coat. "You into the rave scene at all? My man's spinning in the chillout room tomorrow night, but I got other plans. You guys seemed cool, so."

"Sure," Jason said, accepting the playing cards. "Thanks."

"A'ight, peaceout. Check out the chillout room."

Locking the door and wandering back toward Robert, he examined the cards. Someone skilled had done a lot of detail work to make the backs look like a Bicycle deck, but the bicycles were UFOs, and two naked spacewomen in bubble helmets—one right-side-up, one upside-down—floated in the line-art swirls at left and right. He turned the cards over. Above the date and location, there was the spacewoman again, scantily clad now, and larger, skillfully rendered in full color, brandishing a finned, bubble-barreled ray gun against a backdrop of huge, shadowy penis-shaped aliens, her lip gloss shining behind her helmet glass and the glossy plastic surface of the card.

"Is it advancement," he asked Robert, still looking at the illustration as he walked, "if a woman can now be depicted as protecting her own self from aliens instead of being rescued by a daring space captain—but the aliens are penises?"

Robert extended a hand. "Lemme see.

"Hmm," he concluded, handing it back. "I'm not sure she's not their leader."

Jason looked again. Could be. "Zeb doesn't need us anymore. Want to go?"

"Sure. I've never been to a rave."

"I played one, but I don't think they have bands anymore. It's all DJs doing mixes."

"What do you think of that?"

He shrugged. "It's no dumber than Kajagoogoo was when we were that age."

"You hated Kajagoogoo."

"Only as music. As adolescent crapulousness, it was pretty good."

The snowfall continued and the wash from the speakers gathered like a lengthening silence. Leon telephoned from under the hood again, desperate for the accomplishment of minor engine work, starved for the satisfaction of sitting one-leg-up on the cool steel fender of his own automobile, but unaware of how to do pretty much anything. This time, the second new battery he'd installed in as many days wouldn't charge. Jason explained the electrical system to the best of his ability, concluded with a recap of How to Not Blow Up a Car Battery, and suggested that taking a gamble and replacing the alternator would cost half as much as having the problem diagnosed. If it worked, Leon would save at least fifty dollars; if it didn't, he could return it and just be out a few hours' trouble and no money. Robert watched carefully.

34

—but after the electrical system lesson was over, Leon said, "Yo, Martin wants to talk to you," and the phone clunked as it passed from hand to hand.

"Hey, Jase."

"Martin—what's up? It's snowing here."

"Snowing?" Martin's voice said. "What's that?"

Jason turned to Robert, who was sipping from his mug. "Martin wants to know what snow is."

Robert swallowed and nodded. "Tell him it's like Styrofoam, only Waldo would get confused if he chewed it."

"Robert says it's like Styro—"

"Yeah, that's funny. Listen, can you put him on for a minute?"

"Sure."

Robert took the phone and Jason took their mugs for warm-ups. "Uh huh," he heard behind him. "Yeah." Then there was a pause, not so much a listening silence as a sudden stillness that made Jason look up. Robert's back was to him, very still, the phone up to his ear. Eventually, his shoulders shifted and he broke the silence: "Did he leave a number? Okay. Okay, thanks. Do you need Jason again? All right. Okay. Yeah. See you."

He hung up, took his coffee from Jason, and settled awkwardly onto his stool, sloshing a wavelet over the lip of the mug.

He said nothing. Jason drank coffee and watched the second hand move on the clock above the office door. After four minutes and thirty-three seconds, he said, "Well?"

Looking toward the countertop, Robert said, "As you've surmised, there's a development."

"Yeah, I've surmised."

"Leon was working on your Plymouth today after school and a man stopped and started talking to him."

"Is he okay?"

Robert waved this away. "He's fine. Nothing like that."

Jason waited like a patient friend until the pretense began to irk. "Big man? Little man? Sensitive man? Piltdown Man?"

Robert didn't look away from the countertop. "He was looking for me."

After another annoying silence, Jason said, "Modern man? Police man? Amazing Ham and Boiled Egg Man?"

Robert waved a shushing gesture in his general direction. "He said—" He stopped, but then sighed heavily, and the rest came out. "He said he hadn't seen me in fifteen years. Leon said he had dark hair and a mustache, and he was about as tall as I am."

Despite having intended to shut up and listen, Jason said, "No! How old?"

Without smiling, Robert chuckled. "Adult. Leon couldn't narrow it down any farther than that."

"Did he say what he wanted?"

"No. He told Leon he'd come back."

The pretty wash in the speakers was suddenly on Jason's nerves. He went to turn it down, and Robert sighed again and said, "What do I do?"

It wasn't really a question. Jason came back and sat, and eventually they both started drinking coffee again. After a while, he reached over and touched Robert briefly on the shoulder. It wasn't really an answer.

Outside, dense sheets of snow billowed and swayed. Every so often, Robert shook his head, and once he said, "Nothing ever lines up the way I want it to." After a while, Jason started up the wash again, powered up a CD recorder from one of the stacks of gear, adjusted all the sound levels minutely, and recorded about an hour of it to have when he went home.

35

As more days passed at Roberto's house, the more fluid became the hours, and the less regular the mealtimes. It was after ten o'clock when, to prove that he wasn't the jerk he'd been earlier, Jason made dinner.

Guided by the beam of Roberto's flashlight, they carried their plates into the dark living and dining rooms. The hot dogs had charred up nice and black in a cast iron skillet he'd found skulking behind the aluminum saucepans, so they were good and flavorful all sliced up into the macaroni and cheese. Nestled into a plate of Fritos was a gravy boat of onion dip, a concession to Martin's "Uh, how 'bout a bowl or something?" upon Jason's presentation of the repurposed sour cream tub and torn-open Fritos bag.

They settled in, Jason at the window and Martin and Roberto across from him in the living room. At first, it didn't sink in that there was anything weird about the left-side curtain making a popping noise and billowing into the room slightly. Jason's immediate reaction was to reach back and pull the curtain to him so he could look at it, which he did, and then he noticed another thing, which was that the left-most pane of the windowframe was cracked into three trapezoids converging at a common point, a pea-sized hole.

About to say something, he looked at Roberto and Martin; Roberto had half-stood, his plate in his hand, and Martin was saying, "Get—get— get—"

Roberto's flashlight hand was waving Jason toward the living room in mute agitation, and Martin came out with, "—get away from the window!"

Jason didn't understand what he meant by the recitation of this familiar line, which was—

(had there just been a quiet little popping sound?)

—what people on TV said when—

He almost went over backward in his chair, trying to lunge out of it, and although his trajectory had its point of origin at the dining room window, when he hit the floor, it was in the living room. His chair was on its back under the window. The curtain had settled. Most of this would fade with time, but that night gave him the first two of the very few snapshots he'd always carry. One was of the settling curtain, the dark bulk of his left hand reaching for it, the dim light catching on a short, oddly frayed thread that he saw later was at the periphery of the bullet hole. Although he hadn't seen the bullet hole yet, later memory made it a permanent part of the snapshot. The other snapshot was a frozen instant of the flashlight beam's frenzied bounce as Martin tried to urge him from the window, and in middle-shadow, Roberto's face, openmouthed in shock.

36

W HAT the shit?" Martin demanded. "Are you *nuts*?"
"If—" Roberto began again, patiently.
"Yeah, your old man'll get in trouble for leaving
you alone. I *got* that." They were sitting on the bed in the master bedroom, at the rear of the house, where their tactical retreat had taken them.

"Not just that," Roberto insisted. "They've already *been* here, Martin. They sat right on *that* couch with those walkietalkies and guns hanging off their Batman utility belts and said they're really, really sorry, but there's nothing they can do about the writing on the poor little Jew family's house. That's why the couch still smells like cigarettes."

"Well, what about your neighbors? Can't they—"

"The *neighbors*," Roberto said wearily, "are the people who are *doing* this."

Jason hadn't said anything since recovering from the window shot. He was looking off to his left at nothing, but he knew Roberto and Martin glanced at him uneasily as they argued.

Martin punched the bed. "Dude, your window was just *shot out* by frickin'—" he shook his head, searching for frickin' what. "Frickin' . . . white *supremacists,* Jack! And you just wanna sit here, doh-de-doh, like you *like* it? Please shoot me *again, sir*? You gotta be out of your ever-lovin' *mind.* You *gotta* do something."

"I—" Roberto started, and stopped, tightening his lips, stifled abruptly by his own frustration. He blinked rapidly, and his lips parted several times to begin utterances that never came to fruition, and then he became casual. "Jason, what do you think?"

Jason accepted the spotlight as it swung toward him, just as it had at last year's talent show, right before he'd pounded out "Buddy's Boogie" on the blindingly white keyboard of the school's carved-up grand. Buddy was the school mascot, some sort of dog, and in truth, Jason had just made up the title to increase his chances of being chosen for the show. There wasn't even a real piece; when the curtain rose, he'd launched into a thumping twelve-bar bassline, improvised over it until it seemed to have gone on long enough, milked a barroom walkout to near death, hammered the last chord into oblivion, and then sat unnerved by the roar of applause and whistling. Over the next week he ran into half a dozen girls who told him enthusiastically how great he'd been. He said thanks uncomfortably and parted with a sense of mild bafflement, wondering why girls he didn't know were suddenly talking to him. He went dateless for the rest of the semester and didn't add it all up until years later.

Now he took control of the moment and made his audience wait.

"Well," he said, drawing it out, enjoying the suspension of time and the isolation of the spotlight. He looked up, feeling on his face a smile he'd never smiled before.

At the moment when the suspense would evaporate if he didn't catch it perfectly, he said, "It takes a hell of a plan to be better than no plan at all."

✦

Thwack. Right in the pocket.

A beat.

   Roberto cocked his head and looked intrigued. "Hmm."

   Martin looked back and forth at both of them as understanding arced.

   "What the *fuck* is that supposed to mean?" he finally exploded.

   Jason nodded, still looking at Roberto, settling more firmly into the rightness of his decision.

   "I think what Jason is suggesting," Roberto said slowly, watching Jason's face, "is that we wing it."

   Jason nodded, quietly confident, riding the adult feeling, pretty sure he understood what "wing it" meant.

   Martin stared at both of them. "Jesus fuckin' H. Christ on a bun," he said, shaking his head. "You're crazier than he is, and I'm crazier than both of you."

   "Yeah," Jason said remotely, only half-hearing him. "I'm thinking maybe we ought to do something more than just sit here and wait."

37

THE convention center in Connecticut was roomy enough
for the boat show it would host when the rave was over.
Sheer sound pressure packed the concrete-floored
space, but it was neither the mindbending sonic exploration
Jason would have liked nor the pumping gonad stimulator
he'd been resigned to: if you weren't impressed by neato synth
sounds or the unfocused irony of samples from previous dec-
ades' hit songs, it was plain old four-on-the-floor dance music, meant for plain old booty shaking, played at levels so
utterly beyond "deafening" that there was no word for it, in-
ternal organs rippling like Jell-O at 140 beats per minute as
the drums and bass went off like bombs. Each of twenty-odd
slender columns that supported the roof bore three speakers
strapped just above head level, the speakers taller than
Robert and moving a hell of a lot of air. Whenever Jason
passed one, he felt his hair ruffle in 4/4 time. The columns
were sunk into concrete anchors that stood about two feet
high, and kids congregated on the narrow lips of the anchors,
directly under the speakers.

Robert wasn't there. He'd brooded for hours, at the shop, at the diner, and then at Sarah's apartment, still shaking his head. When the radio said the trains to JFK were running and flights were starting up again, he took it as divine intercession and left to catch the standby seat that God would certainly have arranged for him.

A hand-lettered sign near the entrance announced three breakdancing competitions, but there wasn't much dancing among the general population. Mostly it was socializing and glowstick twirling. The air was fresh and cold despite the hundreds of bodies, a mild acridity from the fog machines the only odor to survive the industrial-strength ventilation system. A soft drink vending machine restocked with fruit juice and bottled water stood against one of the long walls. Jason leaned against it and felt it pulse and resonate against his back. He glanced back to see if he could see it vibrating. He couldn't tell. Maybe if your eyeballs were vibrating at the same rate, it canceled out.

Along the adjoining wall were vendor tables: green or purple glowsticks in on-a-string and in-the-mouth varieties; puka-shell necklaces; sign-up sheets for Rock the Vote; cassettes of DJs Jason didn't mind never having heard of; incense; friendship bracelets; a Be All That You Can Be in the Army display; free posters of the naked spacewoman; free reprints of news articles about club drugs; free copies of techno magazines; big bowls of free foam earplugs.

The earplugs were still expanding in his ear canals as he reached another section of the vast floor, where a video game was running on three colossal projection screens. Sumo wrestlers, vampires, and Amazon goddesses twelve feet high battled in digital sound; ten feet back from the screens, half a dozen ravegoers sat the wrong way on conference chairs with their baseball caps on backward, clobbering each other by proxy.

The counterculture had taken far less time to go corporate this time around.

At the sudden understanding of what he was seeing, Jason relaxed and looked around a second time. This was just middle-class kids dancing to silly music and wearing stupid clothes, trying in vain to be at the forefront of irony, which no longer had a forefront. There was a fair chance that the most radical outlook in the place was his own.

The old guy.

It had a nice ring. He smiled affectionately at the kids as a group, nodded politely but without engagement at an answering twinkle from a very young woman half the size of a grownup, and strolled through the sea-floor crush of decibels in comfort, delighted that the sinister rave scene, with its evil music and demonic club drugs, was an invention of the press—and a little embarrassed that he'd believed it.

With some help from an awkward kid with three eyebrow rings and an arm so shrouded in tattoos that it looked moldy, he found the chillout room.

The room beyond the muscular, polo-shirted, ID-checking bouncer was a relative oasis in which sound levels were merely loud. Four beige sofas sat in a rough square, each bearing three or four socializing people. Small tables and chairs filled the rest of the space, which was a meeting room for trade shows.

A tablecloth-draped bar featured the same beverages it would offer when the kids returned in ten years to look at housewares. Against the opposite wall was a riser barely deep enough to accommodate a turntable; a silver stand that held two small synthesizers, a CD player, and a little mixing board; and miracle of miracles, standing proudly on four slender legs, one silver antenna sticking straight up out of its top and another forming a loop out of its side, frozen like a rectangular alien gazelle ready to bolt: a theremin.

Theremins turn up in electronic music circles sometimes, usually in the form of a black metal box perched on a microphone stand. But the sighting of an old wooden one is still cause for a specific happiness, along the lines of how a car enthusiast might feel walking around a corner in the mall parking lot and coming face-to-windshield with a '36 Duesenberg. Most of the people who happen to be around won't appreciate it properly, so the only thing to do is to find the owner and have a little mutual nostalgia. The best way to find the owner is to stand very close to the object and look as though you're admiring specific things about it.

Inordinately pleased, Jason stepped close to the riser, put his hands behind his back, and bent slightly to better admire specific things. The wood was nicked in a few places beneath its polish, and one of the legs had been broken and repaired—two slightly different grains of wood met in a careful zigzag join—but the instrument had obviously been taken care of. Its antennae were unbent and untarnished and it radiated a healthy glow, as though its master gave it lots of outdoor exercise and fed it a healthy diet including surge-protected wall current and Purina Theremin Chow.

Zeb had one of the old beasts, too, but it wasn't nearly as nice as this one. Jason had been there when man met machine; it was at a big music trade show in Los Angeles, and the theremin had been a geek-attractor in the booth of a small, innovative music software company that was, during the short span of the show, courted, acquired, reorganized to maximize effectiveness, and summarily executed, no survivors reported, for no apparent reason, by a large guitar manufacturer that was, despite having no business acquiring such companies in the first place, famous for leaving a scattered trail of their smoking carcasses strewn across the landscape. Zeb had been in the next booth over, where he'd been drafted at the last minute by an old bandmate to make an inexcusably flawed electronic mandolin look as though it worked and recite "that'll be fixed in the next rev" when anyone noticed that it didn't. To help the old bandmate, whose liquid assets weren't liquid, he'd driven a borrowed camper van three thousand miles from his home in Brooklyn and bunked down in the L.A. Convention Center lot. So while the shell-shocked software people were still reeling from their new masters' orders to sell everything in their booth so as not to incur the expense of shipping it back, Zeb—whose ear had cocked three days earlier at the nickname of the guitar manufacturer's CEO, a man whose nature he knew as intimately as Cratchit knew Scrooge's—stopped playing the perverted cyborg mandolin in mid-pluck, turned his back on the distributor's rep who'd requested the demonstration, and pounced.

Mary in her third trimester had glowed with less radiance than Zebedee Lindengreen with his new theremin, and as Jason helped load it into the camper van, he found himself caught up in the enthusiasm of future success. But like most musicians—including himself—Zeb started a lot of things that never got finished.

But this one. This one was beautiful.

The DJ who eventually stepped onto the riser in the chill-out room gave Jason an eye that stopped at the edge of blatant unfriendliness. In his twenties and spiky bleach-haired, with a dark little chin-beard and a tiny barbell through the septum, he stooped to place a napkin-wrapped bottle of water on the riser, well back from where it could spill on anything that was plugged in.

"Nice," Jason said, gesturing.

"The thurman? Yeah, thanks."

"Oh. Uh, *thair*-a-min, actually. It's named after its inventor."

"Oh yeah?" Interested despite the facade. "Who was the inventor?"

To be a wiseass?

As straight as he could, Jason said, "A Russian guy named Theremin. He made electronic instruments, some spy stuff, disappeared, reappeared, got kidnapped . . . weird life. Where'd you get this one?"

"It's my friend's. I just use it for effects, you know? Something a little different." He demonstrated briefly, wiggling his hands self-consciously near the antennae. From the speakers came a wobbling, uncertain tone.

"I'm not good yet." He dropped his hands, and the tone glissed down past the bass register and into the subsonic.

"Hey, even Clara had to practice."

"Yeah." Clearly, he had no idea who Clara Rockmore was. Usually, theremin players were oversteeped in its history, reveling in trivia nobody else cared about. ("Hey, remember Lothar and the Hand People? Lothar was the theremin!") But this person just saw it as a cute retro noisemaker.

So much for a little mutual nostalgia.

He knocked off a little after three A.M. Too tired to slog back to the train station, he got a room at one of two plastic hotels whose signs glowed high behind the industrial avenue.

For the first time since she'd left, he found himself lonely for Sarah. What would she be doing right now? Was she still upset? He thought about how she felt naked and looked at the hotel bed. It wasn't plush, but it was of decent acreage. Two mutually interested people could do all manner of things on it.

After he'd looked at the bed, he looked at the phone and thought about the long-distance fees from a hotel in Connecticut to a hotel in Peru. Even if he had the number, he was too bleary to hold up his side of a conversation. But it would be nice to hear her voice.

He picked up the phone and called her apartment so he could hear her say she wasn't in, please leave a message, and hung up and looked at the bed again.

He put his clothes on the chair and slid under the sheet. The convention center thundered a quarter mile away like a passing train, the powerful thump and boom bouncing against a million intervening surfaces to merge into a muddy rumble.

✦

Robert was huge and silver, but the KGB had him sur-rounded. Then Jason was awake, snatching after the edges of the dream as it slid away like a whisked tablecloth.

The desk clerk told him on the phone that it was seven in the morning. He couldn't hear the booming music anymore, but the rave was supposed to still be going. Maybe they turned the volume down in the morning. He dressed and checked out and, since he'd probably never see another one, walked to the convention center to look at the morning after an all-night rave, humming under his breath.

There were two cars left in the lot, parked at a distance in the spaces they'd been able to get the previous night. Litter blew around close to the ground. The building's doors were open, so he stepped in.

The capacious interior had been stripped down. There was litter, trash bags of leftover freebies, and a few people sweeping.

"Excuse me," he said to one of the sweepers. "I thought the rave was going through the morning?"

"It's still going." She pointed at the door he'd just come through, where a hand-lettered sign said AFTER-HOURS & BREAKFAST BUFFET!

Breakfast buffet sounded good. "Is that nearby? Like walking distance?"

"Sure, it's—Oh, walking distance? Well, it would be a long walk. You know how to get downtown?"

"I don't know how to get anywhere."

It was a forty-minute walk, and the sign in the bar window said CLOSED. Chairs were upside-down on the tables.

He turned to begin wandering and didn't quite notice himself humming again.

✦

He ate at a little joint where the waitress bellowed orders in the arcane jargon of diner kitchens. It was cheap and comfortable, and the coffee warmed spots in him that he hadn't known were cold. He finally noticed himself humming when he had to stop in order to swallow. A melody of five notes, the fourth with a trill. What was that? Usually if he couldn't remember what a melody was from, he could hum it through and the section that succeeded it would just follow on its own. He tried that. It didn't work.

The waitress appeared. "Anything else?"

"Yeah, what's this from?" He sang it.

"Oh, I know that." Her eyes narrowed and she sang it very softly to herself.

"It's stuck in my head," he said.

"Yeah, I know it. It's . . ."

They looked at each other as they both tried to pin it down. Then her face cleared and she pointed at him. "'Good Vibrations,'" she said.

"That's it! Thanks." Something tugged at a dangling thread of memory, but he couldn't quite see it. "You know what instrument it is?"

She frowned as though he were taking advantage of her. "It's somebody singing."

"Nope. It's a theremin."

Of course, then he had to explain what that was.

It got him thinking about the DJ last night as he walked toward the train station in a light morning mist. He knew it was a mark of incipient codgerdom to resent such things, but the guy should just have more of an idea where the instrument came from—at least know who Clara Rockmore was! It just wasn't natural.

He kept catching himself humming the "Good Vibrations" melody, and soon it was joined by the fear that he'd left something in his hotel room. He patted his pants pockets, felt cash, pen, ATM card, subway tokens. His jacket pockets were equally to spec: CD player and earbuds in the outside right, book in the inner left, the UFO-bedecked playing card stuck into it as a bookmark.

But the feeling wouldn't shake as he walked toward the train station.

He'd once found a lost keyring in a bag of kumquats by noticing that he was compulsively whistling "Strange Fruit," so he stopped on the sidewalk and concentrated on letting whatever it was struggle forward. What could he have left in the hotel room during the four hours he'd been there, besides the things he'd brought?

He stood absolutely still for a few minutes, trying to let it come. It approached tentatively a few times, but each time, it receded again.

When he got tired of trying to seduce it, he started walking again and thumbed open his book, catching the playing card as it flipped out from between the pages. It really was well done; both the spacewomen and the UFOs had that perfect old-fashioned pulp futurism to them, that *Forbidden Planet* aesthetic. Not quite *Forbidden Planet*. That was in color, with Robbie the Robot. The movie he was trying to think of was black and white, with a different robot, a big silver one.

The Day the Earth Stood Still. That was it. *Klaatu barata nicto,* and that great eerie—

!

—theremin music

The first use of the instrument in a movie score.

The curtains parted, and he saw what he'd forgotten in his hotel room.

✦

Klaatu barata nicto, Robert was saying. Robert was taller than usual, huge, dozens of feet high, fashioned of silvery metal. He came in peace.

"I bring you good vibrations," he intoned in his alien tongue, through the slot in his metal head. The KGB had him surrounded, their tanks like toys at his feet.

Jason rarely remembered his dreams, so when one managed to shove itself past the barrier and fang him in the cortex, he paid attention.

Okay, so I'm trying to tell myself *theremin.* What does that mean? Theremin what?

Look, he sent vaguely inward. *Drop the symbolism. Whaddaya want?*

Nothing. Crickets and tumbleweeds. You'd think the subconscious, having expended the considerable effort necessary to send a message through, would bother to phrase it clearly.

Screw this. He'd been thinking about theremins lately, so they were popping up when he was asleep. He shoveled the dream off onto the same compost heap where he discarded dreams about food, and decided to think about Sarah naked instead. He'd gotten as far as her collarbones when he stopped walking again, a new thought sparking and guttering.

Nah.

He started walking again, skipping a ways down Sarah to compensate for the interruption.

There was a working pay phone in front of Bobby's Place, morning moisture clinging to it in cold beads. "Hey," he said, grimacing at Gary Warren's sleepy hello. "It's Jason. I'm really sorry to wake you up, but I need to talk to Zeb."

Gary Warren said something inarticulate and the phone moved around. Then: "Yah," Zeb said in a loose rasp.

"I know this is going to sound really weird, but was your theremin one of the things that's missing from the store?"

"The theremin?"

"The one you got at NAMM that you were going to restore."

"The theremin's gone, Jason."

"Gone recently? Was it stolen from the store?"

"Um, yeah." His voice starting to come into focus now, Zeb said, "Why are you asking?"

"Just one more question, if you'll let me. Did it have a broken leg?"

"A broken leg? Yeah, it fell over in the van when I was bringing it back from NAMM, remember?"

"But you hadn't restored it yet, right? I just ran across an old theremin at the rave last night, and it's got a sawtooth join where one of the legs was repaired, but it's in really beautiful shape."

"Jason—" Zeb was awake now. "It wasn't fully restored, but all it really needed was stain and polish. Listen, can you still get close to it? I'll tell you how to tell for sure."

"I don't think so. The rave was supposed to still be going, but it's not."

"Oh. Well, if you do come across it again, mine's got some stains and a saucer ring near the antenna on the top."

"A saucer ring?"

"Yeah, when Rocket was still alive, we used to put his wet food up there so he'd make bio-stochastic music while he chowed down. It was pretty funny."

"Okay. Well, unfortunately, I have no clue where it might be. I'm walking to the train station now—why don't we try to find the rave organizers when I get back and see if we can hunt down this DJ?"

"Okay, see you then."

He hung up and turned to go and almost bumped into three guys.

"Sorry," he said, and then recognized them as three of the

huge-screen game players from the rave, now a little tired and shivery in the light mist.

"Hey," one of them said, recognizing him back.

Jason angled his head at the building. "Looks like it's closed."

A confused look. "Yeah?"

"Wasn't the rave supposed to still be going on here?"

"Nah," said the second of them. "They moved it. It's still going."

"Yeah," said the third. "A real rave, not like that shit last night."

"We just came from there."

"We just went out for smokes and breakfast, you know?"

"Pretty cold."

"Too bright."

"Way bright, man. Shit."

Unsure of which to address, Jason said, "Where's it at now?"

The second turned and pointed. "See that parking structure? Go past it and turn right. You can't miss it. What's the name of that club?"

The first and third shrugged.

"Cool," Jason said. "Thanks."

"You got any smokes, dude?"

"No, sorry. I don't do anything bad."

The first and second looked nonplussed, but the third laughed. "Yeah, us neither."

"I know where you can get some breakfast, though." He aimed them toward the diner and they said thanks and moved off, rubbing their arms briskly through their sleeves.

Bass and drums bubbled up faintly as he neared the corner of the parking structure, increased in volume as he turned. There were people on the street, some in jackets, hanging out, and some less covered, walking in the same direction as he was. The after-hours club was three blocks down, the only center of activity on a street of four- and five-story buildings, the crowd older and less happy. Just inside the door, a massive blond bouncer with the steroidal bulging and sharp WASP handsomeness of a GI Joe doll stood at ease in black T-shirt, camouflage pants, and unshined military boots, examining IDs, inclining his square, stubbled jaw at bags and waiting until the uncertain kids interpreted correctly that the bags were to be opened for searching.

When it was his turn, Jason said, "What ID do you require?" and waited for the man to break his impressive silence.

The bouncer's eyes were pale blue and unblinking. He turned them coldly on Jason and waited. Not being twenty, Jason smiled and waited back at him. Many seconds passed. Then the bouncer's jaw unhinged and he said in a voice he might not have used for another week, "Driver's license or state ID."

Jason flourished his California driver's license. The bouncer looked at him for another few years and then put out a palm. Jason placed the license in it and watched it travel away from him.

"Venice, California."

"Yes."

The bouncer looked at him for another epoch. The continents moved a few inches.

"Muscle Beach." The pale blue eyes without a flicker.

Not a place Jason expected to hear mentioned on the East Coast. "I'm closer to Abbott Kinney."

Philosophical movements rose and died. Generations of birds flew thousands of miles, south, north, south, north.

"I sometimes stay near Rose."

Jason nodded. "Egg white omelettes at the Firehouse," he guessed. The Firehouse's menu catered to bodybuilders.

The driver's license traveled back to Jason, and the thick neck swiveled toward the inner door. "Go on."

Jason pocketed the license. "Peace." That wasn't something he ever said, but for some reason it came out by itself.

The bouncer nodded and looked at the next person in line.

Inside, it wasn't as loud as the convention center. Humongous audio gear wouldn't fit here. Exotic anthropomorphic cat-women, UFOs, tequila bottles, and flaming dice fluoresced on the walls under black lights. The music was thick and pounding, and open boxes of Dunkin' Donuts were arrayed over every surface: counters, tables, sofas. On the sofas, people sat on top of each other. A chiseled, sneering man, anchor-tattooed and bare-chested, his shirt dangling from his back pocket to showcase his stunning upper body, strutted past Jason and slowed when hailed by a brightly curvaceous girl in a very small dress.

Drug dealer, Jason pegged him in a glance, with no evidence and no need for any.

He went up the dark stairs to the second floor, one blast of music fading into another. Here were swiveling red spotlights, the bouncing glitter of a disco ball, another DJ, more open donut boxes, and more tireless people dancing with serious, driven faces. Through a black curtain, he saw a few more sofas, some conversations between denim-and-chain-clad bodybuilders, a little club girl astride the knee of one of them, subtly grinding and eagerly making eye contact with whomever she could, looking proud and flushed.

Another flight up, another dance floor, more swiveling lights, more donut boxes, another DJ, more of the hardcore crowd. And another flight, tight and humid, the pulse of music reverberating inside it. To emerge unexpectedly into the brightness and crisp air of the roof was a minor shock, the same feeling as when it wasn't dark outside after a long movie.

The same donut boxes and sofas were here; the same dreds and goatees, waffle shirts and visors, eyebrow rings and nose studs, the awkward lumps of nipple barbells under fabric, messy morning hair, careful coifs, and fresh faces. The same overt types who populated the lightweight Bosch tableau inside now ate glazed donuts and cooled down in the open air. It was the chillout room transplanted, the same bleach-haired musician now dancing in small movements as allowed by the cord of his headphones, mixing up a formula of less frenetic dance music in the precise doses and ingredients required by the listeners, who weren't listening.

I have a jaundiced eye, Jason thought, this observation followed closely by *Good.*

The theremin was there next to the synthesizers and turntable.

The music didn't have beginnings and endings, but it did have periods of windup and wind-down. During a wind-down, he went over to say hello.

The DJ pulled one of the orange headphone cans away from one ear and laid it against the back of his head. "Whassup?"

"All right. Still going at it, huh?"

"Yeah, last set."

"Listen, I didn't think of this last night until after I left," Jason said. He withdrew the homemade CD from his jacket. "I dug what you were doing and I thought you might get into this."

Self-improvement thought: Don't say "dug."

The DJ took the CD and looked at it. "DJ Coffeepot, huh?"

"Yeah, he's, uh, South American."

"What is it, like real uptempo?"

"No, it's more of a, like a . . . sweet chillout mix. Real ambient, uh, downtempo after-hours."

"Sweet. Let's give it a spin."

"Now?"

Bleach-hair paused in mid-turn. "Why, 'zit got *copyright violations* or some shit?" He didn't wait for a response, inserted the disc, snapped the cans back onto both ears. One of Jason's nighttime cascades burbled up through other sounds.

It wasn't in the same key as any of the samples or loops, but it served well as one scrap of the collage.

"Yeah, okay," the DJ said loudly over the sounds in his headphones, moving around again to the music. "Yeah, that's all right."

Jason stepped forward, gesturing *may I?* toward the theremin with angled face and hands.

"Sure."

On the little stage, he eased around behind the instrument, hearing the tone rise up from its hiding place in the bass frequencies as his hands drew near the antennae. As he remembered, it was disorienting. There were no keys or strings, no buttons, nothing to touch. He'd once tried to describe it to Robert, who'd been prompted to say that making music by just moving around in space must be freeing. This sounded good from a certain artsy-cosmic perspective, but Jason's well-cemented belief was that the only thing "freeing" in any art was a hell of a lot of time spent practicing.

The theremin was so sensitive that minute changes of wrist angle or knuckle tension were enough to send the tone flat or sharp, and his hands sent wobbly swoops tumbling from the PA speakers. Luckily, the theremin wasn't prominent in the mix of sound layers, so all the *individuality* just added *flavor*.

He looked carefully, but the wood was newly polished. At first he thought there wasn't a saucer ring.

Shunting down through the claustrophobic, black-lighted staircases, Jason emerged not into the disco-lighted darkness of the ground floor but a wide, daylit commercial alley. He went the long way around instead of heading back in to find his wrong turn and waited behind half a dozen kids who, despite having adequate ID, were trying to get in good with the bouncer by calling him "man" and aping his stoicism. They exchanged private glances as they waited for each other behind him, the imitative nods now tinged with mockery and confined to where he couldn't see them.

The blue gaze was turned on Jason, who waited neutrally until the kids were gone and then opted for no preamble.

"I just found a piece of expensive equipment in there that was stolen from a friend of mine. How do you want me to handle it?"

It was impossible to tell whether the man was deciding how he wanted it handled, pondering the knowability of the Divine, or experiencing a paralytic seizure. His body was as casually inert as a desert rock, the contoured shadows of his face looking as though they wouldn't shift until the sun moved.

Finally, he stirred, slipping a walkie-talkie from his belt and bringing it to his face. "Front door."

The walkie-talkie said, "Yaboz."

"Relief."

"Roger dodger codger."

He and Jason looked at each other and waited. Comets inched along their elliptical orbits. The Amazon reforested.

"You talk too much," Jason said.

The bouncer didn't smile.

The door relief was outfitted identically in black T-shirt and camo pants, but he was young, bald, and energetic. Next to most people, he would have looked large. He took over and Jason followed his boss past the club entry and into a small office with two visitors' chairs, taking the one indicated. The big man sat behind a small wooden desk, and waited.

Jason took a moment to get concise, then said, "A friend of mine owns a music store. It was broken into. One of the things stolen was an old electronic instrument called a theremin. Right now, that instrument is on the roof of this building, being used by one of the DJs. It has a round mark near the top antenna where my friend used to put a saucer."

The bouncer absorbed or ignored this for a while, or possibly his battery had died.

"I'm Keltner."

"Barry."

Another glacial pause.

Barry said, "No police. No questions. No follow-up. No investigation. I get it for you; you leave with it."

Jason balanced the abstraction of justice against the return of Zeb's theremin.

"Fine."

"Your word."

"My word."

They shook hands. Barry left. Jason sat and looked at the office. There was nothing interesting in it.

When the door opened two minutes later, Barry was preceded by the bleach-haired DJ, who went from *puzzled but miffed* to *wary but innocent* when he saw Jason. Barry sat behind the desk and pointed at the other chair. The DJ sat slowly and said "What's this all about?"

Jason waited while Barry gave the DJ the long look.

"What," the DJ said.

The look drew out agonizingly. The universe expanded and contracted. Time itself got bored and looked for a magazine.

"Wha—" the DJ began again.

Barry said, "Possession."

The face went yellow-white under the yellow-white hair. "Dude, shit, you got to know Curtis is the main guy." He gave Jason a helpless glance before returning the full force of his appeal to Barry.

Jason watched him, trying to keep his attitude neutral.

"Fuckin' *what!?*" the DJ exploded at last. "Shit! It's not even addictive, Barry!"

Silence built up with nowhere to go, and Jason began to understand. The less Barry said, the more the DJ's imagination would do the job for him.

The DJ flicked one hand angrily. "It's Curtis, man! Fuck! You know it's Curtis. Fuck!"

Barry picked up the phone. The dial tone droned in the hard-walled room.

"Aw, man, this is *so* fuckin' bogus." The DJ shook his head, appending a disgusted *fsh!* to reemphasize the so bogusness of it. He stood. "I got a set to finish." But instead of exiting, he waited, as though for a cue.

Barry twiddled the phone handset meaningfully. The DJ dropped back into his chair and went for indifference.

Barry replaced the handset and laced his hands on the desk. He straightened one blunt forefinger to point at the phone. "No?"

"No, man!" Heartfelt, eyes closed, shaking his head with *feeling* so that his nose described a sideways figure-eight. "No! Fuck. Because this is bullshit, man. It's *so* bullshit and you *so* fuckin' know it. What the hell you want from me, anyway?"

"The *ther*—" Barry switched the pale gaze briefly to Jason. "*Thera*—?"

Jason said, "Theremin."

"Theremin, Matthew," Barry said, and they both turned to watch Matthew come up with a response.

Matthew did, a serious one. "Bull*shit*, man. It's not mine."

Barry lifted the handset again and let the dial tone speak to Matthew's future, put the handset to his ear and let his fingers hover over the keypad. Matthew shifted in his seat, watching uneasily. Eventually, Barry shrugged and punched 9-1-1, and Matthew shouted "Okay, shit!" and lunged across the desk to depress the switchhook, then barely got his fingers out of the way as Barry hung up.

Which is how on a Sunday morning, Jason came to be sitting in an alley in Connecticut with a theremin, waiting for a jubilant Zeb to get there in a rental van from New York.

It was turning into a good day for Zeb all around. His insurance company was paying up.

38

"S TEVE Keltner speaking."

"It's me, Dad."

Late morning, Jason sat alone in the master bedroom of Roberto's house with a knotted stomach, calling his father at work.

"Just a minute." It was the voice his father used in public when he wanted you to know you were going to be in trouble as soon as non-family was out of earshot. "I need to take this," the public voice said to someone. "Give me five minutes?" Jason pictured him in the office with the view, with his sleeves rolled halfway up the strong, sandy-haired forearms, the steel watchband and open collar, the dark blond head turned momentarily from the phone. "Are you all right?"

"Yeah, I'm fine."

"Where are you?"

"Do you promise not to make me come home?"

"I said where are you, Jason?"

"*I* said do you pr—"

"You think I'm bargaining with you, Jason? You're in deep,

deep trouble, and you're damn well going to tell me where you are."

"No I'm *not,* Dad." Wrong, wrong, embarrassingly wrong—too much of a little boy's whine.

"Jason . . ." The voice now quiet but the tone barely controlled, each word an individual extrusion between teeth. "Where—are—you?"

"I don't want to tell you." Still too much emphasis, not the way it should be. Better, though.

"Your mother is—"

"—worried sick," Jason said with him.

"I'm not arguing with you, Jason. You're going to tell me where you are—"

"Dad—"

"—and you're going to get your ass home—right—now."

"No," Jason said flatly. That was it. Carter would say "no" like that.

Except for the faint, angry sound of shallow breathing, the line was silent. His father was a man. Maybe he'd heard the new tone in his son's voice and understood.

"This is important," Jason said as loudly as he could, which was an uneven murmur, and his fingers jumped convulsively to the phone and broke the connection.

39

A CHEERY grayness spilled into the Magic Music Shop, diluting the colors of a glad clutter that hadn't been there long enough to start getting dusty. The OPEN sign hung jauntily on the door, and wind instruments and mouthpieces lay on soft folds of shiny fabric in the glass case. The sheet music had been sorted back into its black wire racks. Behind the counter, packets of guitar strings and boxes of reeds hung near a small flock of birdcalls on a stand, and on the back shelf, a jovial brace of obese little clay pots stood like tourists. Outside, a tall, bearded glazier with a white rag in his pocket was fitting the last of the picture window glass and glancing up at the light snowfall. The plywood he'd pried from the windows was out by the curb.

Gary Warren was putting green price stickers on heavy coils of guitar cable that hung in cardboard sleeves from floor stands. When Zeb and Jason carried the theremin in from the double-parked rental van, his sticker gun arrested itself in mid-stick.

"Oh my god," he said. "The Thing is back."

"You didn't—Careful . . ." Jason said as a wooden edge came close to the door jamb. "You didn't tell him?"

Gary Warren hurried over and leaned in to hold the edge back from the jamb. "*No*, he didn't tell me! He said he was going to look at paint and—" knocking snowflakes off Zeb's shoulder as he smacked it for emphasis "—carpeting." He sighed dramatically. "I guess I should have known something was up, since *I'm* the one with the taste."

Jason glanced at Zeb to see what he'd say, but Zeb had been married long enough not to say anything.

When the door was closed, they all stood around and beamed at the theremin as the glazier bent and tapped at the new window.

Gary Warren said, "Is this the same one? It looks so nice."

Then Zeb had to park the rental van, and Jason had to recount everything, and Gary Warren searched for furniture polish and told him about the insurance adjuster's phone call. Outside, a few fat, lightweight snowflakes buzzed in at shallow angles, caroming off a cushion of air before they could hit the ice and snow on the sidewalk and then being swept along helplessly, kamikaze crystals with serious intent and high velocity, but too little mass. Poor planning. It was a little frustrating to look at. And more kept arriving and doing exactly the same thing.

After Zeb was back and the glazier left, Jason said, "How'd you manage to get him to come out?"

"Oh, Joe? His workshop's just around the corner. I found his wife a hurdy-gurdy last month for a great price."

Gary Warren was standing back to eye the theremin's new polish critically. "Well, it's not a miniature pinscher, but I guess it'll do—" Interrupting this line of discussion before Zeb could, he said, "Oh!" and waved his furniture rag at Jason. "Oh! I knew I'd forget to tell you! Robert called. He said he'd call back."

"Did he say when?"

"No, he didn't."

"How's he sound?"

"Sad." Gary Warren looked sad too. "He sounds sad."

As Jason made coffee, Gary Warren started to clear a space in the back, where the theremin had belonged before its departure, but Zeb stopped him and moved the guitars out of the window to make room for it there.

"You're just asking for trouble," Gary Warren chided him as the theremin took its new place.

Zeb adjusted the beast's placement minutely, not speaking. "I know," he admitted finally, dusting his hands.

"Zebedee, we finally got this place halfway back together—"

Zeb took him gently by the shoulders. There was a long moment of communication and history between them before Gary Warren stated, "Okay," and got very busy doing very little, his mouth in a line, off in the back of the shop.

Zeb looked after him, then sighed and said without turning, "Do *you* understand?"

"Yeah, I understand totally," Jason said. "What are you going to name your little dog?"

Sarah's apartment had all the same things in it, but it felt desolate. Jason sat on her bed, tried to get online again, and then looked at the walls for a while. *The Night Men* was on the sofa. He plunked down next to it and opened it at random.

> thumbed back its safety, steering left-handed through the twisting cañon at forty miles per hour. There was a muzzle flash from the dark shape. I steadied the .44 on my left arm and

He tossed the book irritably into the air so it came down on the floor. Of all the scenes in all the chapters in all the book, he had to open it to that one. God had to exist; the world's disagreeable sense of humor didn't make sense otherwise.

He left it on the floor and pulled some paperback out of the bookcase, tossed it onto the bed, and went back into the living room and turned on the TV. When he noticed during a commercial that he didn't remember what show he was watching, he turned it off and went into the kitchen to stand with the refrigerator door open.

There was a beer in the door rack. He took it out and poured it into a glass. He'd never liked beer, so he left it on the counter and went back out into the living room. She'd been gone longer than the half-life of her vibes, the apartment now just a collection of inert matter. A shadowbox: Still Life with Taciturn Boyfriend.

The word *unimbued* came to him.

He noticed himself humming. Bill Withers, "Ain't No Sunshine When She's Gone."

Unimbued matter. Christ, I'm a geek.

The phone rang as Jason was staring, stonefaced, at a sitcom about a man who dressed well and wasn't funny.

"Hey," Robert's exhausted voice said in a din of airport blatter. "How are you doing?"

Jason turned off the TV. "This house just ain't no home."

Robert said, "I know, I know, I know, I know, I know, I know, I know, I know, I know, I know," but his comic delivery was fatigued and perfunctory, and he eventually realized he'd missed the exit to his punch line and stopped.

"How was the flight?"

"What's wrong with me?"

"Uh—which context are we—"

"I drop all my plans and fly home the moment Stuart shows up after fifteen years. What's wrong with me?"

"What plan, exactly, did you drop?"

A moment, during which someone was paged over the distant airport PA system. "The one where I don't drop all my plans and fly home the moment Stuart shows up after fifteen years."

"Right. That plan."

"Why am I going to him? *He* should come to *me*."

"He did come to you. You weren't home. Robert, which airport are you at?"

"Shouldn't he be the one making the effort?"

"I really don't know. Which—"

"It makes no sense for me to just jump up and run back home as though I'm some little child who's afraid he'll leave again if I don't do just the right thing."

"Are you still at JFK?"

"Jason, you're not listening to me."

"I am. I promise. What airport?"

Grudgingly. "JFK."

"You've been there all night? Did you even put yourself on the standby list?"

The airport noise jangled in the phone line. Robert would have the phone tucked on his shoulder. He'd have bags under his eyes from staying up worrying all night, and his expression would be a little baffled because of this uncharacteristic inability to decide what to do.

"All right," Jason said. Are you coming here, or am I going there? You're obviously not flying today."

No answer.

"Okay, we'll meet at the diner and eat lunch. How's that sound?"

"Why'd you ask *which* context when I asked 'What's wrong with me'?"

Jason rubbed his face tiredly. "I don't know, Robert. Bad phrasing, okay?" No response. "I said it wrong. I'm sorry. Let's just meet at the diner in an hour and I'll come up with some good-sounding explanation, and you can forgive me and then we'll talk about what's really bugging you, which isn't whether I think you have lots of things wrong with you."

"All right, fine. See you then."

He could have gotten to the phone in time if he'd been less distracted, but by the time the ringing broke through his thoughts and sent him running back down the hall to Sarah's apartment, he knew he was too late. He unlocked the door and hurried in anyway, but it had already gone to voice mail, the geniuses at Verizon having decided that three rings was enough.

Star-69 didn't have any information, as usual. He stood next to the phone for a few minutes. No one called back.

Robert was in a fouler, gloomier mood than Jason had ever seen him. His features bunched in an impatient, smoldering glower under his heavy brows. He was almost six and a half feet tall and dark-featured, and it was hard not to be intimidated.

"Just to get this out of the way," he said as Jason slid into the booth. "I don't appreciate being told I have a lot of problems."

Jason looked at the table as he wormed out of his jacket and riffled carefully through his response options. After he stuffed the jacket into the corner of the booth, he said, "Okay."

Robert nodded once, briskly, but the challenge didn't go out of his gaze.

"You want to talk about Stuart or not?" Jason said, opening a menu.

"Not," Robert said. He rotated himself abruptly and plunked his back against the wall to sit lengthwise with an arm along the seat back.

"Okay." Jason browsed the day's specials and then flipped to the desserts. *When you can't save yourself or someone else,* he thought, *order pie.* Robert's face was aimed into the diner, but he wasn't looking at anything but his own thoughts. Eventually, if left uninterrupted, he'd probably say whether those thoughts were of Stuart's offenses or Jason's.

Jason ordered coffee for both of them. Robert continued to glower at invisibles. There was no evidence that he noticed when their cups came, so Jason prepared both, and Robert grabbed his and slurped down most of it automatically without coming back from wherever he was.

This could have been the moment for Robert to sigh, turn to him, and start talking about what was bothering him, but as it turned out, it wasn't.

Jason decided that was long enough. "Are we okay or what."

Robert turned the glare on him. "The thing that really—yeah, we're okay—is why can't I ever—" He shook his head in frustration. "It never—" He blinked. "Oh." The glare softened somewhat. "Yeah, we're okay." One hand flapped dismissively. "Sorry."

Jason relaxed a little. "Okay."

"At first, after Martin told me Stuart had shown up"—apparently, they were talking about Stuart— "I wasn't sure how I felt. On the one hand, I wanted to be happy that he was back in my life—I was happy, actually—well, not happy, actually, but sort of . . . well, okay, happy—or, at least—or I would have been, but then on the other hand, it was all so unexpected that it was a little unreal. On the third hand, I also experienced some feelings of resentment and anger, which were hard to reconcile with being happy—or whatever—no, happy's right—I think—I *think* . . . anyway, da-da-da, I figure okay, fine, I'm going to have to deal with—yeah, I think happy's a good word—deal with these negative feelings, but the main thing is my brother showing up and wanting to see me after all this time is a happy occurrence. Or not happy, but—*anyway*—So naturally I want to focus on that. What do you think?"

Robert was staring at him intensely. "Uh—I'm not sure you get to decide entirely what to focus on, but I'm with you so far."

"Huh." Robert digested this only partially before rejoining the runaway flow of his narrative. "So I'm all . . . happy or whatever—whatever—anyway—not happy exactly, but—anyway, whatever—remember we heard the weather thing on the radio? so I decided to go home and see him—because—well, anyway—and it seemed like things were finally lining up for me, for a change. So I went out to JFK, and during the trip, I started to feel very angry."

He stopped and looked at Jason as though for consensus.

"That makes sense," Jason said.

"Does it? How?"

He'd only said it to say something. "Well—"

"I can see that it would be normal to feel anger at someone who'd abandoned you, but—it was really strong. Or not abandoned—well, yeah, abandoned—but that's not—" He shook his head a few times, then leaned halfway across the table to address Jason with greater intensity. "I was walking into the terminal, and there was a family there with their luggage. The mother—the *mother*—looked up and saw me, and gathered her child out of my *way*. What is *that*?"

His gaze bored right through Jason's head.

"Well, you're very big and kind of dark, so when you get angry—"

"That's such bullshit. Just because I'm—"

"Robert . . ."

"What?"

He let the silence grow a little just to break the rhythm. "We can certainly talk about how unfair it is for people to get scared because of your size, but then we'll still have to get to what's really bugging you."

"Which, in your opinion, is—?"

"I don't know. Maybe that your big brother, who was supposed to take care of you fifteen years ago, left you to fend for yourself."

Robert shook his head impatiently. "Even if he'd been there, he couldn't have done any—okay, what?"

"He left you on your own, and you've managed to go all these years without resenting him for it—"

"Resentment isn't productive."

"—and as long as it was Hypothetical Stuarts you were busy not resenting, it was pretty easy, and you even got a little cookie for it: you got to feel evolved and enlightened. But it's not Hypothetical Stuarts who're knocking on your door now. It's Actual Stuart, so your policy of Clemency for Big Brothers in the Abstract is about as useful as . . ." He gestured vaguely.

"A scuba tank at a baking convention," Robert supplied.

"Sure—"

"A diving board at a dance class."

"Fine—"

"Rubber legwarmers that reverse into oven mitts at a dance class for scuba-diving bakers."

"Right, so— Uh—" He stopped and added that one up. "No, less useful than that."

"Hmm." Robert shifted suddenly in his seat, one hand shooting up to squish his lower face thoughtfully. "Hmm. Hmm."

"'Resentment isn't productive' doesn't even sound like you. That's more like something I'd say."

A couple of minutes later, Robert said. "What, in your opinion, should I do?"

"I don't have an opinion of that."

"What would you do?"

"What, in my opinion, would I do? In my opinion, I have no idea. But we're talking about you."

"How unusual," Robert said dryly, flipping open his

menu. "Especially since I am an actor and all." He shook his head ruefully as he scanned the columns. "Forget it. I'm just being a goon. I'm fine. We're ordering.

"I'm buying," he added awkwardly.

Over the bang and clatter of the subway, he yelled, "Stuart took care of me for a long time when Dad was gone."

Jason nodded.

"When I was nine, he read me the Upanishads."

Jason nodded.

"I wouldn't have my spiritual interests as an adult if not for him."

Jason thought of the little Buddha with the ovoid base and nodded.

"None of that is the real problem," Robert said.

Jason nodded.

"Nothing's just been going right for a long time now. I go on an audition and I'm not *on*. Everything I line up falls through. I put on my clothes and they don't fit. I can't shave without cutting myself. Nothing just lines up. So I come out here, thinking at least I can help my friend out, and not only do I not do anything to help you, but while I'm here, not only does Stuart show up in L.A., three thousand miles from where I've gone, but when I try to go meet him, you go off on your own and find Zeb's theremin without me. Everything I do is the wrong place at the wrong time. You know?"

Jason nodded, which was once too often.

"You're nodding, but what do you *think* of that?"

"I think it felt truer than any of the other stuff we've been talking about tonight."

✦

In a little while, Robert blinked as though startled. "Oh. How are *you*?"

"Unimbued."

Robert studied him as the train wheels shrieked on curved track. "I know what that means," he shouted, "but I don't know what that means."

The train quieted on a straightaway.

"I might get a room at the YMCA for the next couple of nights until I go back home."

Robert looked concerned. "When did you decide this?"

A vacant, lighted station sped past, white tiles grimy.

"I didn't even know I was considering it until I just said it."

"You can *do* whatever you *feel*," Robert reminded him encouragingly.

"Oh. *Village* People. I get it. Greenwich Village."

"You West Coasters have no sense of culture."

"Cultcha. Say it right."

"Cultcha."

"Cultcha."

"Cultcha. Since I didn't fly back to L.A., I don't have a place to stay. How would you feel about a roommate?"

Jason glanced at him, then out the window, beyond which the dark wall of a tunnel sped by. The train clacked to itself on its rails. "Better," he admitted.

The Chelsea Y was full. Robert looked around the lobby while Jason checked them in at the one on 92nd Street.

It was a barren little room. He felt better already.

When they were settled, Robert held up *The Night Men*, raising his eyebrows. *Settled* meant they'd tossed their bags in the closet and assigned beds.

Sitting on his, Jason muttered, "I think I'm done with

that," and watched Robert stand the book prominently on top of the air conditioner. "You can read it yourself if you want."

Robert gave the book a look of sincere pleasure and patted it the way Sarah patted food she was preparing, as though assuring it, "Now you're *just* right."

It was cute when she did it.

40

Merchant sailors carried rucksacks up from the docks, passing under a single streetlamp in ones and twos before dispersing into the night. As I drove by, patches of rough conversation came through my open window on the dank wind, mixed with the smells of brine and crude oil.

A ragged line of cars stood at the kerb, engines idling. If I joined it, I could idle mine without drawing attention, and run the heater. But I knew a better place for watching. I turned away from the ocean onto a winding service road and followed it to its end, along the crest over the highway. I killed the engine and the lights.

The men were leaving a ship I hadn't seen from the street, hoisting their rucksacks and starting their leisurely ways home. A few women had left their cars and were shivering near the streetlight, waiting to be recognized and embraced.

The flow of men from the ship became a trickle. The last car claimed its waving sailor and drove away. A tow-haired man carrying a military duffel bag sauntered down the gangplank. He stopped at the bottom and dropped the bag at his feet, then cupped his hands over his face and I saw the spark of a lighter. He looked like a rough man trying to be a smooth operator, a nervous man trying to be casual.

He smoked and looked at nothing. I smoked and looked at him. The ship disgorged two eager men who slowed at the bottom of the plank to address him. He shook his head and gestured vaguely toward land, and they clapped him on the shoulder and hurried to where a taxi-cab had arrived to take them to their church meeting.

When they'd gone, the tow-haired man glanced at a pocket watch and made his way up to the street. I put out my cigarette and started the engine. Soon he stepped to a black sedan that pulled in from the highway. I couldn't see its driver. After the sailor got in, there was a pause, and then the man at the wheel bent down to release the hand brake. I saw the red hair and piggish eyes, a flash of small teeth, and knew if I hadn't been in for it already, I was now.

As I'd expected, there was no sign of the sedan by the time I made it back down the rutted service road. I turned to the South and picked it up again within minutes.

It was three in the morning, and the coastal highway was barren. I took my .44 from its shoulder rig, checked it, and put it back. We went through two beach towns and then I followed it at a distance onto an unlighted cañon road that twisted into the coastal hills.

Half a mile into the winding cañon, I stopped catching sight of it. I pushed the needle to fifty.

A cross-road came and went. If the road had curved the other way, I would have missed the moving silhouette of a car, dark against black, sliding through the side-view. The car was close behind me, but I couldn't tell whether it was the sedan I'd been following. I rolled my window down and breathed the cool burst of ocean air and night-blooming jasmine. I took my .44 from its rig and thumbed back its safety, steering left-handed through the twisting cañon at forty miles per hour. There was a muzzle flash from the dark shape. I steadied the .44 on my left arm and kept to the right, decelerating. When the dark car made its move and pressed in to my left, I ducked as far as I could and fired.

It was the same sedan I'd been tailing. Its driver braked to avoid my next shot at the same instant that I braked to avoid his. I fired again, then again, and dropped the gun onto the seat to shift into reverse. The sedan shuddered and accelerated sharply toward the right-hand cañon wall as I sped backward to put it into the beams of my headlamps. It smashed into the cañon wall, the small, high oval of its rear window facing me. I stopped, re-loaded, and re-armed.

I couldn't see them through the small rear window. They couldn't see me because they'd be blinded by my headlamps, and possibly because some of them were dead. But I'd fired three times, and I'd fired blind, and there were three of them. I hadn't any reason to believe I was that lucky.

Dirty though he was, the driver of the sedan was a police lieutenant, and he might already have put a call out. I left my car through the passenger's door and went in a crouch toward the sedan. I could hear now that its engine was silent. As I neared it, it rocked and the rear door flew open. It was a suicide door, and Mutt Maloney rolled out behind it and I saw a pistol. His shots went high, and I dropped onto the road, took aim, and shot his ankles from under him. When he fell, I shot him in the head and rolled to my feet. I went quickly over his crumpled body and through the open door into the backseat.

Fred Baynes' red-haired Lieutenant Corcoran was panting uncontrollably behind the wheel, his eyes rolling into his head. His skin was damp and pasty in the light from my headlamps, and blood gurgled from the hole in his neck. Next to him, the sailor gibbered, raising his hands and flinching to ward off my next bullet. The lieutenant scrabbled weakly at the two-way radio mounted under the dashboard. He would be dead soon if he didn't receive medical attention. I slapped the sailor's hands away and put my .44 to his head.

"I'm looking for a little boy," I said. "If you don't know where he is, I'll kill you."

"Manif—!" the sailor gibbered. "Manif— Manifests! Only!"

"You do the manifests," I said.

He nodded violently. Greasy sweat clotted on his face. The lieutenant had the handset of the radio now, but it was slithering out of his slippery hands. His mouth worked. Not a whisper passed his lips.

"You have ten seconds to tell me where the boy is," I said to the sailor. "And I'll shoot you if you don't answer in five."

"What boy?" he screamed.

"That's five," I said, and shot the seat-cushion. The sailor cried out. I put the barrel to his temple. "This is ten." Corcoran flailed weakly toward him as though in a panic, losing his grip on the handset.

"*Iohanna,*" the sailor gasped. The glass by his head shattered and his jaw blossomed. He slumped toward me. Behind him, Mutt Maloney couldn't bring his gun to bear on me in time, and I shot him dead.

Corcoran's eyelids flickered as his consciousness got flitty. I had one bullet left and we both knew it. I put the radio handset in his faltering grip and left him there with his ruined vocal cords. I put my last bullet into Mutt Maloney's corpse.

41

Dude, that's cold," Martin said without looking up from his sketchbook.

"There's no way Mutt Maloney could get up and fight like that if he was shot in the head," Roberto complained as he lay the book on the coffee table. "That's totally unrealistic."

Jason was at the window. "Yeah he could. I've read about people living with bullets lodged in their brains 'til they're like ninety."

"Maybe from like a twenty-two," Martin said. "No way from a forty-four."

These were just meaningless numbers, but Jason put on an expression intended to convey that Martin had a valid point.

"And besides," Roberto continued, "what kind of detective doesn't check a body to see if it's dead?"

"He was in a hurry to get into the car."

"He was in a hurry to get back to the plot. Doesn't the lapse of reality bother you?"

From the couch, Martin spoke up: "You mean the lapse of reality in the middle of this story about a guy driving around one-handed at night with an eyeball missing, and he kills three armed dudes with one shot, in their speeding car, from his speeding car, on a long, winding road, in the dark? That the realistic story we're talkin' about?"

His pencil scritched in his sketchbook.

"It wasn't one shot," Jason grumped.

"Oh," Martin said. "Yeah. Two shots."

"Three shots."

"Oh, three shots. Never mind, then. Everything's all *totally* believable." He bent pointedly over his labors as Roberto eyed him. Shortly he stopped and slapped the pencil down. "What!?"

"You're getting more comfortable with us," Roberto observed.

Martin stared at him blankly. "Huh," he concluded, picked up his pencil, and shook his head to himself. About to get back to work, he hesitated and said, "Sorry I punched you in the mouth."

Roberto shrugged self-consciously. "I'm really sorry I used that word."

"Cool," Martin said softly, almost to himself. "All right." He put down his pencil and extended a fist, which Roberto looked at blankly.

Rolling his eyes, Martin sighed. "First you make a fist . . ."

42

A CITY-owned shade tree towered darkly over the patch of city-owned ivy that ran along the curb in front of the house next to Roberto's. The tree's thick upper foliage was done up in a sort of split clown hairdo where the city had pruned it away from the power lines. Its shade fell for a significant portion of the early afternoon on four Caucasian male adolescents and a red-and-white El Camino with rotted wipers.

"See the bigger one in the fatigues and red baseball cap?" Roberto murmured as Jason put one eye to a hairline of light between the dining room curtains. "His name's Tiny."

Tiny was leaning against the bed of the El Camino, drinking from a crumpled paper bag and alternately holding forth and listening benevolently. When he moved, the car wobbled and an orange Union '76 ball jiggled where it was impaled at the top of the radio antenna.

The other three were sitting on the curb, looking skinny and tough with their elbows on their knees, butts against the ivy, rock concert T-shirts gapping in the rear, somewhere around Jason's age. A worn leather sheath and loop of chain jutted from one back pocket. Tiny extended his hand; a cigarette that was being passed was surrendered. He took a casual drag, then kept it to flick ash off of and gesture with as he spoke again. Thirty feet above him, two swallows rocketed straight out of the leafy gloom like escaping electrons and then plunged straight back in.

Jason jerked his face back from the curtain when two of the curb-sitters turned abruptly to look at Roberto's house.

"What is it?" Roberto was instantly worried. "What? What is it?"

Jason shook his head and returned to his watching position. Tiny was now drawing on the cigarette and gazing down the street as all three sitters looked at Roberto's house. The swallows careened and twittered. Jason said, "They looked this way, but I don't think they could see me."

Martin whispered, "Does Tiny live in that house?"

"The one they're in front of?" Roberto shook his head. "No, that's the Simonses'. Let me see out for a minute." He took Jason's place, saying "Pardon me," as he slid by, then looked out and said "Okay," as he moved aside for Martin. "From left to right, that's Jack Simons, Little Bert Simons, and Wayne Eckert. Wayne lives around the block. Little Bert Simons's father is Big Bert Simons. He works for the gas company."

"Okay." Martin kept watching through the curtains. "Gotcha. What's Tiny's last name?"

"That is his last name," Jason put in. "His first name is 'Big Fat Ugly.'"

"I don't know," Roberto said. "He doesn't live in our neighborhood. He just comes by sometimes."

"Is he in the army?"

"I don't know. He always dresses like that."

Martin nodded, then relinquished the watching post and shook his head. "You know many guys who aren't in the army but they dress like that?"

"Not well."

"Well, I do well, and I want you to listen to me when I tell you this. Guys like that are mean dumbass sonsabitches and you do not want to fuck with them."

Jason said, "It seems to me the fucking with is going the other way."

Martin looked at him and didn't speak at first. Then he went into the living room and sat on the couch. "Yeah, well, you just remember that nice distinction when he's stomping your face to mush." He picked up his sketchbook.

Back at the curtain, Jason eyed Tiny. "He's out of shape."

The one Roberto had identified as Wayne had removed the knife from its leather sheath and was idly pushing it into the dirt.

"So fuckin' what," Martin said as he drew. "Jesus."

By late afternoon, the bed of the El Camino was half in sun. Tiny and his disciples eventually strutted off down the street and turned in the direction of Sunland Avenue.

At the window, Martin said, "So who lives in that other bedroom?"

Jason was stirring a simmering pot of macaroni with a well-used wooden spoon in the kitchen.

"My brother," Roberto's voice said faintly from the living room. Jason slowed his stirring and turned down the heat to reduce the noise of the gas.

"Yeah? I didn't know you had a brother."

"He's not here right now."

"Yeah? Where is he?"

"He's at a Zen commune."

"What's that, like kung fu or something?"

"Well . . . almost. Zen is an Oriental philosophy of harmony through meditation." He stopped and added, "Stuart is a very spiritual person."

"So how long's he been there?"

"Not very long."

"So, what, like a month?" After a long silence, Martin said, "Just curious."

Jason stood at the stove, listening, the wooden spoon motionless over the pot.

Roberto's voice said, "A couple weeks."

"How do your folks feel about that?"

Another long silence. Roberto's voice said something very softly.

"Sorry, big guy," Martin said. "Couldn't hear ya."

A pause. Jason strained to hear.

"I said they don't know yet."

"Wow," Martin said eventually. "No shit."

Roberto was silent. Conscious of being a stranger to the house, Jason turned the gas back up as quietly as he could. As his weight shifted, the floor creaked that he'd been eavesdropping.

"Lemme ask you something else," Martin said as afternoon waned. "This check you're waiting for." He squinted. "How's that work?"

Roberto ate steadily. "What do you mean?"

"Well, your dad's out on this boat, right?"

"Ship."

"Sorry, ship. And here you are by yourself, right, so he sends you money."

Roberto's only response was a grunt as he shoveled macaroni and cheese.

"Except he thinks you're not by yourself, 'cause he doesn't know Stuart ran off. Right?"

No answer.

"So my question is, who are these checks made out to, you? or Stuart?"

Nothing.

"Do you even have a bank account?"

"Stuart. Has one."

Never having written or received a check, Jason was a step behind on the conversation. "What difference does it make? Can't family members cash checks?"

"Yeah, sure," Martin said. "If they're *married*."

Roberto chewed singlemindedly.

"So what does that mean?" Jason said when the conversation didn't progress.

With a one-handed sweep, Martin gave Roberto the floor.

Roberto said, "I'll think of something."

They ate without talking for a while.

"You know what you should do?" Martin said as he scraped his plate over the kitchen trash. "You should scrub the rest of that wall so it would be all one color."

"Keltner speaking."

Despite the strong feeling that he shouldn't, Jason had called his father again at work.

"Dad, I—"

"What do you want, Jason?"

He didn't know the answer, so he picked one he'd heard.

"I want to be treated like an adult."

"What makes you think you've earned that?"

"I don't know." His dad was being more reasonable than expected.

"Jason, when you get back—and you are coming back, whatever it is you're thinking—we're going to have a long talk, and some things are going to change."

"Like what?"

"We'll have to discuss the circumstances of your being allowed to continue living in that house. What do you think they should be?"

"Me?"

"Yes, you. What do you think you should have to do, to be allowed to live in my house?"

His father was talking to him like an adult. Not an adult he was pleased with, clearly, but this was two men discussing a problem.

"Well," Jason said, relaxing a little. "I think I should have to respect your rules."

"I agree."

"What do *you* have to do?"

"What do you think I should do?"

"I think you should trust me and let me make my own mistakes."

"Trust is earned, Jason. You haven't been earning it lately."

"So how do I earn it?"

"You tell me where you are, and be there when I come to get you."

"I can't, Dad."

"Then there's nothing we can talk about, Jason. Whatever you're doing, you've chosen it over your family. You need to think about that."

"What have you done to earn *my* trust lately?"

There was a long pause.

"Maybe we can talk about that when you come home. I'm not going to have that conversation now."

It was too odd, everything he said being taken seriously and his father not trying to get him off the phone.

"I drink coffee now," he started to say, and a mean adult male voice he didn't know said, "Is this Jason Keltner?"

"Hello?"

"The same Jason Keltner who ran away from home and refused to tell his parents where he was going? That selfish Jason Keltner?"

Fear rippled through all his limbs. "I didn't run away from home. Who is this?"

"This is Sergeant Frank of the police department, Jason. I'm on my way out there to give you a good beatin'."

Unable to speak, Jason stood with the phone.

"Did you hear me, Jason?"

Finally, he managed, "You what?"

"What did you expect, Jason? That's what happens to self-ish boys who run away from home and make their mommas worry. We trace their calls and they get beatin's. Now you're gonna sit your ass right there and wait for me, or you'll be in even worse trouble. Do you hear me? If you leave, I'll find you and things will go even worse for you."

Now catching up with the developing shape of things, Jason said, "Ah-yup." His fear was mellowing into a sort of a furious buzz.

"That a smart mouth you got on you, little boy? I like beatin' little boys with smart mouths."

"I'd like a medium pepperoni pizza, please," Jason said. "Dickweed."

The phone on the other end slammed, and the line clucked a few times and went to dial tone.

Roberto and Martin were staring at him as he strode into the living room. "What the hell is up with you?" Martin said, wide-eyed. "You look like you're ready to kill."

"I have to go," Jason said. The shakes were on him now as the buzz waned. "I'm endangering you by being here. Let's regroup at five at the Denny's near school."

"Dude, *what's going on?*"

As Jason headed into Roberto's bedroom to get his back-pack, he said, "Some policeman cut into my call with my dad. He said he was coming here to give me a beating. Oh, sorry—" he amended acidly on his way through the living room. "A *beatin'*."

"Fuck me!" Martin's jaw was actually dropping now. "Is that who you called a dickweed?"

Roberto said. "A *policeman* said that?"

Martin dropped his jaw even farther, turned to give Roberto a look of utter amazement, and said, "What planet are you *from?*"

"Five o'clock at Denny's," Jason said at the front door. "Okay? I gotta go."

Roberto was standing frozen. "What do we tell him when he gets here?"

On the front porch now, Jason said, "I don't care," and broke into a panicky run.

The 159 pulled away from the curb as he pounded toward it as fast as he could with an eight-ton backpack yanking his center of balance around.

"Shit!" he yelled, managing to brake before he overshot onto Sunland Boulevard. It would be at least twenty minutes until the next bus—and it was almost twenty minutes later when his father's Beemer flashed by, braked, and hung a U-turn to pull up into the red zone by the bus stop.

His panic had been joined by an odd combination of quiet coldness and simmering rage. He wasn't getting in without knowing how his father looked, and he couldn't see his father without bending down to the window. He shrugged his backpack higher on his shoulders and started walking grimly up Sunland Boulevard, toward the Bob's Big Boy. He heard the Beemer's door open behind him.

"I went sixty all the way here so I'd get here before that policeman did, Jason."

Jason turned and glared at him. His father wasn't happy, but he also didn't have the full-on "you're dead" look. "The least you can do is get in."

His tone of voice was hard to read. This was a different dad, a mom-independent dad he hadn't seen before. The dad he was used to mostly just enforced, but this guy seemed to be operating on his own recognizance.

Such initiative deserved a response. Despite his anger, Jason said, "How did you find me?"

"After you called me the first time, we had the police trace my incoming calls. We didn't know he was going to break in and threaten you like that."

"What do you want?"

"Now that I see you're okay, I want you to get in the car and come home."

"You tricked me."

"Look." His father spread his hands reasonably. "You want to deal with that asshole cop . . ."

The whole adult phone conversation had been a setup. His stomach churned and his chest clutched all the way home, and didn't stop when they got there. His mother bewailed and bemoaned. They finally left him alone, his mother cracking his bedroom door once to tell him she and his father were taking time off from work the next day so they could all go to family counseling. They'd decided that things had gotten that serious.

All privileges were suspended: television, telephone, visitors, freedom of travel. As evening fell, he closed the blinds, sat on his bed, and watched his clock-radio advance. A little after five o'clock, he punched a hole in his closet door, and then he had to go through the whole sullen "I don't know" routine.

Pushing past his parents and walking or bicycling the five miles to Denny's simply didn't occur to him. He was home. Home had him.

43

T'S as though Jason is a different person all of a sudden,"
his mother wept. His father sat stolidly between them on
the brown leather couch. A moment earlier, it had been
"Our marriage is just fine—that's not what we're here to talk
about."

Veronica nodded thoughtfully, at ease in her black leather
chair.

Tears: "Why can't I have my little boy?"

"He's not really a little boy any more, Lynne," Veronica reminded her.

A dotting of the eyes with a crumpled tissue. "It isn't supposed to *be* like this!"

Jason was sitting on the couch with his parents, feeling
surly about having to look at them sideways and hearing all
the same weepy crap he heard at home, and tense and upset
about missing his rendezvous with Roberto and Martin. His
stomach rolled. He stared determinedly at the gold carpet
and felt his face heat.

"What do you think, Jason?"

He risked a glance up. The look from the leather chair seemed genuinely interested. That alone was alien enough that Jason leaned toward it and asked, "About what?"

"About anything."

Anything? *Anything* anything? Which thing did that mean? "Well . . ."

Three pairs of adult eyes acquired him as a target: one stricken, one impatient, one interested.

"I don't know what to talk about."

Veronica did a little side-to-side tilt of the head, as though his answer to just about any question was important, and he had only to pick one. "How about what your mother just said? What do you think of that?"

"I think she's right. I am a different person than she thinks."

"In what sense do you think you're a different person?"

"Well—" Discussing Roberto and Martin would be outside the code. And they definitely wouldn't understand Carter. Carter was his. Denied the luxury of a truthful answer, he locked up again and stared at the carpet. His stomach rolled again, still upset from yesterday.

"Why won't you talk to us?" his mother blurted. "Why?"

Because you can't be trusted, he felt, but without the words that would have let him articulate it.

Instead, he muttered, "I don't know." He switched from staring at the carpet to staring at her wet face. If he was going to be a bad son, at least he owed her that much. She looked back at him searchingly and apparently saw something bad, because her face turned more hurt and teary.

Veronica said, "Jason, tell me—"

"What did I do that was so awful?" his mother cried.

Back to the carpet. "I don't know."

"Lynne, I'd like to—" Veronica began.

"Mom—" Jason started.

"Don't talk to your mother like that."

The enforcer speaks.

"All right," Veronica said slightly more forcefully, becoming everyone's new visual target. "I'd like to get a sense of how Jason feels. Can we do that?"

Uneasy assent.

"So. How do you feel, Jason?"

"Sort of pissed off," he admitted, and waited to see whether anyone would take issue with his choice of language.

"Jason—" his mother said, at the same time that Veronica said, "Lynne, please," and continued, "What are you pissed off about?"

This was confusing to consider, and he was additionally distracted by Veronica's use of his words back at him. He held her gaze as long as he could stand it and then stared at the carpet again and shook his head.

"It's not like we're really a family," he blurted, the thought striking him as incongruous as he heard it spoken. The impulse to say it had seemed germane, but the words hung jaggedly. He didn't look at his parents, but his mother would be stricken and his father would be glaring at the opposite wall.

Or not. He sneaked a glance on the off chance that he was wrong.

Nope, stricken and glaring.

"And how do you feel about that?"

"I think it's stupid to pretend we're a real family when we're not. I don't see how we're supposed to fix things that are wrong if we're pretending they're not wrong in the first place."

As she replied, Veronica glanced at his mother. "We've talked about what your parents want. Now what do *you* want?"

I want things. . . .

I want to be told what to do. I want to be punished if I don't do it. I want to be listened to. I want to be appreciated. I want to be Carter. I want to save Roberto. I want to understand Martin. I want to be accepted by the rich kids I don't like. I want a driver's license and a car. I want a job. I want that policeman not to have threatened me. I want to have been at Denny's at five o'clock yesterday. I want all my teachers to give a shit. I want my beard to come in. I want a driver's license. I want to give you a true answer. I want to sit in coffeeshops at midnight. I want to be accorded respect. I want to be a solid friend. I want to be stoic. I want to save someone. I want to be an object of adoration. I want to eat what I want. I want to bestow my great, powerful heart and stride the earth like a king.

"I don't know. I guess I just want to be left alone. Mostly."

He glanced at his mother. She hadn't melted down yet, but the color in her face and the enraged set of her mouth meant klaxons were going off and workmen were abandoning their posts. It was coming.

"What do you mean by left alone?"

Another stumper. Family counseling was interesting. A glance at his mother: only a few seconds before catastrophic core breach. "I don't know," he said helplessly, watching his mother's face change as her containment failures began to cascade.

"I'd like to clarify this. Do you mean you want to move out of your parents' house?"

He didn't think that was what he meant. He said "Um—" and everything blew up, his mother lunging to her feet and shouting, "This is *not* why we came here!"

"Lynne, it would help if you would please sit down."

Emboldened by the presence of an ally—or at least an enemy who listened—Jason said, "See? She doesn't—" and then felt stupid complaining in the third person when the object of his complaint was in the same room. He swiveled. "Mom, can I please *finish*?"

Veronica eyed him appraisingly as his father said, "Don't talk to your mother like that."

"This is *not* why we came here, and we are leaving *this instant*!"

"Lynne—"

"Mom—"

"I can see this was a mistake. We're not paying you a *dime*!"

He and his father stood awkwardly and followed the white-hot mass of seething plutonium into the waiting room. Jason turned back to see Veronica watching him from her leather chair.

"Thank you," he said politely.

She nodded.

"Can I come back by myself?"

He saw her pause thoughtfully before opening her mouth to speak.

"Jason! Let's go! *Right now!*"

"Do you feel you got something out of this session?"

"Yeah. Well. I *think* so."

The appraising look. "Why don't you call me and we'll talk about it," she said, and got up and found a business card in her rolltop desk.

"He doesn't need that," his mother snapped close behind him. His father loomed next to her in a display of protective solidarity. If Veronica turned into a vicious werewolf and went for someone's jugular, he'd be ready.

Go, Dad.

The vicious werewolf stood in the middle of its office, holding its business card.

"Bye," Jason said.

"Goodbye, Jason," the werewolf said viciously.

He and his father went through the waiting room and out to the elevator, where a molten, blinding mass was vaporizing the walls and floor. He glanced back through the two open doors. The vicious werewolf was scratching its head and sighing.

"Just in case you didn't know?" he offered on the way home, after stifling the comment about a hundred times. "Regular bullets won't kill her."

Death was instantaneous for everything within six hundred miles.

His father dropped him off in front of school the next morning and watched him walk, shaking, up the lawn and into the Admin building. It was arranged that he would check in with his grade counselor, which he did, donning an attentive expression as she spoke at him. Then there were still twenty minutes before homeroom. He went out to the pay phone across the street at the Taco Bell and got Veronica's phone number. When she answered, he muttered, "This is Jason Keltner. My family was there yesterday."

"Yes, hello, Jason. What can I do for you?"

"How much does it cost to come see you?" He fingered the change in his pocket, hoping to hang on to at least three-fifty for lunch.

"I charge sixty-five dollars an hour."

"Oh. Okay, I was just asking. Thanks very much."

"I do put a few slots aside for people who can't afford to pay my standard rate."

"How much do those cost?"

"It varies. Sometimes I'll take it out in trade."

"You mean like work?"

"Yes. Why don't we make an appointment and talk about it."

"Could I—when could I come in?"

"I have a cancellation today at three . . . but you're in school then, right?"

"Right."

"Could you get here Friday at four?"

"Okay."

"We'll talk then about what you could do in trade for sessions. So I'll see you at four on Friday."

"Okay—Um . . . did you—I know you only saw me for a little bit, but . . . did you—do you think I'm wrong?"

"We can talk about that on Friday."

His heart fell. Not all the way; just a few floors.

"Are you there, Jason?"

"Yeah."

"We'll talk Friday."

"Okay."

"All right." She seemed to hesitate. "Without getting into right or wrong, why don't I just say that I think you have a pretty good BS detector."

He wasn't sure quite what that meant, but it was apparently good. "Really?"

A smile in her voice. "I'll see you Friday, Jason."

With only a few minutes left before homeroom, he rushed to his locker to swap books from his backpack. From locker to backpack went his fifteen bucks, *Health for Morons*, *A Sanitized History of White People*, and *Imbecilic Spanish Conversations Between Brain-Damaged Shop Customers*. From backpack to locker went Geometry and Biology—

—and *The Night Men*.

Paperback library copy, frayed, lying facedown on his textbooks, back cover staring up at him, lurid:

WHEN YOU CAN'T SAVE YOURSELF, SAVE SOMEONE ELSE!

That's Thomas Carter's rule, the law he lives by in this two-fisted action tale of corruption, salvation, and the warrior's code of hot lead.

When gangsters kidnap his ward, a foreign child who can't talk—or won't—Carter is forced to take on his toughest case, the case no detective should have to take!

Bullets can't stop him.

Torture can't stop him.

The devil himself can't stop Tom Carter
as he hunts down . . .

THE NIGHT MEN!

His white hand, still extended, trembled.

On the bus, too upset to read, he fretted fearfully over parental anger and the disembodied phone voices of sadistic police sergeants. It was too late to change his mind and return to school; he would already have been marked absent from homeroom. He wondered how long he'd be able to help at Roberto's before they came for him.

A shock: They might be there already.

"That was really dumb, Jason." (His father, holding a briar pipe and standing in a book-lined study.) "Dumb move."

"Why?" (His mother, decked in streaming lace and a tiara, hovering over a verdant meadow.) "Why are you so bad to us?"

"I'm sorry," he said guiltily, loudly enough to count as tangible evidence of his conscience, but low enough to be subsumed by engine noise. "I'm sorry," he said with a little more force so there could be no argument later that he hadn't really said it. *I'm sorry.*

College, family, and a decent life lay dead behind him. He would never have a nice place to live. He might already have a police record, which he understood would interfere if he ever wanted to hold a sensitive job for the government. Statistically, he was probably now at risk for drug abuse or alcoholism. All because he was being stupid. Everything was stupid. The code he was trying desperately to follow was stupid. His journey on the bus was stupid, and the world outside its window was bright and menacing. He was intimidated by the only other passengers, two dredlocked men trading loud, incomprehensible jokes and chewing on little sticks. The older wore a jersey on which the word *Uprising* was worked into a cartoon of a black man rising with fist aloft. The younger man's shirt said Free Nelson Mandela! Jason didn't know what any of this meant, but he felt himself accelerating exponentially into its lawless outer territories.

He barely saw the sidewalk as he stepped off the bus.

Consumed by terrible worry, walking automatically, he didn't notice that his stomach had stopped churning.

The pale yellow ghost of the big swastika loomed over Roberto's front yard, but the house looked okay otherwise. No one answered when Jason knocked. He bent to peer through the gap in the curtains where Martin or Roberto should be watching, but the gap wasn't there.

He went and looked over the wooden gate into the back yard.

Past the low, open fence that delineated the adjacent properties, the front door of Big and Little Bert Simons' house opened and Tiny in his fatigue pants and T-shirt emerged from the dark rectangle of the doorway, holding the screen door. The girl who followed him onto the porch wore a halter top and faded flares over sandals with plastic flowers. They were both smoking. Tiny noticed Jason, took a long drag, then pulled the girl to him and French-kissed her, squeezing her butt with both hands. She wasn't that pretty, but her sexuality was blatant. She locked her hands around Tiny's neck, her cigarette sticking out behind his head, his burning by her hip.

Jason stood by Roberto's gate in the shade, feeling cornered in the open air.

They walked slowly to a yellow VW Bug with peeling flower decals all over it, kissed and kneaded some more, and she got into the Bug and rolled down her window to talk and kiss, until finally its little engine blatted in the stillness and she drove away.

Tiny strolled up the Simonses' driveway with his cigarette. Jason went casually back to Roberto's porch, opened *The Night Men,* and stared into it as Tiny put one foot up on the low fence and watched him. Sparrows squabbled in the trees.

"You like that pussy?"

Jason stared harder at the text. Tiny laughed and stepped

up on the fence's cross-member, balancing on it before dropping onto the wide strip of grass the posts were sunk into.

He strolled to the porch. "Mind if I sit," he said, sitting. He smelled like stale cigarettes and Jason didn't know what else. An act of bravery: Jason looked at him and held his gaze.

Tiny pointed with the cigarette. "That like a really good book or something?"

Jason couldn't concentrate on glaring and think of a response at the same time, and he'd already committed to the glare. Something like bubbling started somewhere in his body.

"What'sa matter, cat got your tongue?"

The bubbling grew. Hoping to become uninteresting, he turned slowly back to the open pages and dragged his gaze across the typeset lines. In a moment, he turned a page. He saw his hand tremble.

Tiny laughed and took a drag. "Hey, you like Jews, right?"

The words were lines of black wire, scattered with dots and serifs.

"Yeah, you're a Jew-lover, right? Well you should like me, then, 'cause I'm Jewish."

Another turn of a page, spiky black lines traversing paper.

"I'm adopted, right? So my old man tells me like a month ago to make sure I'm home for supper, and right after supper, the doorbell rings and it's this old Jew rabbi with this long beard, wearing the beanie cap and all that shit, and he tells me my real mother and father were Jews, so I'm one. So I'm like, no way, you old Jew fuck, go fuck yourself, and he takes out this book and showed me my birth certificate. Well, shit. That's totally official. Can't argue with that, right?"

The sparrows chattered and rocketed. The black wire pricked and blurred. Tiny's clothes stank of cigarettes. He sucked in another drag, twisted his mouth to aim the exhalation away from Jason. "So next Sunday, I go to temple and everything, and did the whole thing, you know, and the rabbi hears my confession and gives me communion and all that shit. So I'm like, one of you now, right?"

The silence grew in volume. Jason grunted meaninglessly.

Tiny flicked ash onto Jason's shoe, smashed the end of his cigarette into the porch and stood. "Bye, kid."

He went into the Simonses' house, then came out again, locked the door, and drove away in his El Camino. Jason sat rigid on the porch, not looking at the cigarette stub, but smelling it.

44

We rounded the next corner smoothly and the cabbie doused the lights. The Seville had stopped in front of a cheap stucco house in Lankershim, the residence of one Donny the Doc, formerly Dr. Donald L. Hancock, M.D., formerly of Sing Sing, and, if men are born innocent, formerly innocent.

The cabbie got comfortable in his seat. I nodded at him in the rear-view. We settled in for a long wait that amounted to five minutes before Jarvis and Rodriguez got into the Seville and its headlamps went on.

"Follow that car, Mac?"

"Not this time." We watched the Seville make a U-turn and go back the way we'd all come. I handed the cabbie the other fifty-dollar note. "I'll be back in ten minutes, but just in case."

"Watch your tail, Bub. Say, what do they call you?"

Shaking his hand was like being engulfed to the wrist in dry canvas.

"I'm Carter," I said.

"O'Connor."

"You're a handy man to have around, O'Connor. What was your outfit?"

The ruddy face split in a cocksure grin. "First O'Connor Division, *Sir.*"

"Stand down, soldier," I said. "I think I know your boss."

In other cities, the seasons occur one after the other. In the City of Angels, they blend constantly in layers, the year a fluid change of their combinations. This Autumn night, April's leaves still fluttered in a cool breeze edged with Summer warmth. The temperate coastal Winter would soon commingle, dotting the calendar with rain.

I went down the dark suburban driveway between two houses. From the other house floated the soft strains of a music show. I thought of the young Negro girl who'd parted with her hard-earned dollars to die here, and the slower death of the ideals of a rookie cop whose arrival only terrified her further. Donny the Doc taught two dumb kids a lot in a hurry. I still owed him for both lessons.

The last notes of the music were washed by a low tide of applause. The announcer came on. I could hear the modulated trustworthiness of his speech, but I couldn't hear what he was saying. I looked into Donny the Doc's window. Past a sink of dirty dishes and a gas stove, a bright line glowed yellow at the bottom of a closed door. A woman's happy voice performed a commercial announcement. A few houses away, a dog barked a brief statement. The moon was a blue smudge behind woolen clouds, my vision whole again in the trick of darkness.

The rotted window screen crumbled to powder under my hand. Dark shapes moved within the yellow line and I heard murmurs of speech. One voice had the affect of bedside manner and insincerity. The other was Jackie Boy, responding in clenched whimpers. On the faint music show next door, the announcer came on and a band started playing something fast and excited.

The glass shattered under the butt of my pistol.

Half an hour after Tiny's departure, Jason was still on Roberto's front porch, staring very hard at his book, leafing almost at random, sometimes reading passages, sometimes turning pages automatically. He'd casually kicked the ash off his shoe, but some still clung. Don't show weakness when they might be watching.

Finally he stood and stretched, looked up at a clear blue sky inked with black telephone lines. The angular silhouette of a crow fluttered on one of the lines, cawed, and flew over the Simonses' house. Further down the street, black dots of sparrows adjusted themselves on the wires.

He picked up the cold, crushed cigarette butt and walked around the fence and up the Simonses' drive to put it through their squeaking mail slot.

As he turned to leave, the bubbling got so bad that he started shaking.

The glass shattered under the butt of my pistol.

Loose ornamental bricks lined the walkway.

45

ZEB's broken windows are all fixed and he's getting his stuff replaced," Robert said in the dark as a smattering of frozen raindrops went *tick-spink!* on the air conditioner housing. The beds were set in an L. Robert's head was across the room diagonally from Jason's.

"Yup."

"You got the theremin back for him."

"Yup."

"The police are on the case."

"Far as we know."

"Okay. Just—forgive me; I'm slow. Why did we take a room in Manhattan tonight, again, instead of flying home, again?"

"I don't know."

"That's what you said a minute and a half ago."

"I'll say it in another minute and a half if you ask me the same question again."

"I'm not asking questions. I'm making a rhetorical—"

"—failing to make—"

"—point."

"And I'm ignoring the rhetorical point you're failing to make."

Robert's bedclothes shifted. "Are you going to do the thing where you stir up stuff everybody else is content not to stir?"

"I haven't decided."

"You know, the thing where you piss people off for no good reason—"

"—I don't—"

"—and get into unnecessary trouble you could have avoided?"

"I don't—"

"Where you irri—"

"Look! Robert! I don't know why I'm still here. Okay?"

"Okay."

"Okay."

Rain pattered. Unable to sleep, he counted breaths backward from a thousand. Around the mid-700s, the numbers turned into men's names, and then into people and scenes.

I go motionless through liquid air toward the sedan.

Sergeant Frank is panting behind the wheel. Blood gurgles from the hole in his neck. I'm looking for a little boy, I say.

("Manif—!" the sailor gibbered. "Manif—")

Manifest destiny, I say.

You—

The glass by his head shatters and his jaw blossoms. Behind him, I see myself, and I kill it in the heart. I carry it to the roof—the bucket clatters on the ground below—

—the bedclothes jerked against his skin as he startled from half-sleep, shocked by the jarring sensation of not falling.

The overpowering comfort of the dark room, the tap of rain—the dream disintegrated, but he was fast enough to snatch up a handful as the rest ebbed to nothing.

His dream analyst snored in the next bed.

Allegedly a diner: half a dozen tables and two booths, the sky-blue cushions mended with fibrous strapping tape; olive-hued coffee, whitish liquid in the cream pitcher; swarthy men behind the counter, dollar-fifty for egg on a roll. Past the window, the street of dirty snow and the few bundled-up people were stark in ugly yellows and blacks: New York sleeping fitfully in the freezing cold.

Robert yawned. "So you were basically Carter."

"Among others."

"You usually don't remember your dreams."

"I wasn't really asleep. It was all mixed up with counting backward."

Staring at a point somewhere between their booth and the cash register, Robert dismissed this amateur viewpoint with a desultory flick of the hand. "Well, okay, what does Carter mean to you?"

"I dunno. Tough guy, I guess. Ideal man in a bygone-era way. Detects stuff. Saves a kid. 'Warrior code of hot lead.' Do you remember yours?"

"My heroes? Oh, my dreams?" Robert snorted. "Unfortunately. For instance, last night while you were committing violence upon the oneiric underworld, I was flying over a gigantic mountain range that turned out to be Jennifer Lopez."

"Subtle."

"Yeah, my dreams are real hard to interpret. What does Carter mean to you?"

"Uh . . . I dunno. Archetypal protector figure."

Robert mulled. "While that's true . . . it's probably too informed to be of much use. Jung said stories in which the author includes interpretation are of the least interest to the analyst."

"You're the analyst?"

"Am I analyzing?"

Robert got more Talmudic with each argument. "Okay."

"Without interpreting what he might mean in this particular context, what does Carter do when he's not showing up in your dreams?"

"Shoots people. Drives cars. Looks for a lost kid. Breaks up with his girlfriend. Gets blinded. Gets played by Whatsisname, the guy who shouldn't have played him, in nineteen-whatever." He paused, then continued straightfaced, "Has a thing for *bird metaphors*."

"Ha!" Robert bellowed, bonking the table with his nearly empty mug for emphasis. People in other booths turned to look. "You admit it!"

"No, actually, you're still wrong. I'll go as far as *motif*, but no way are they metaphors. Metaphors for *what*? You never have an answer for that. You can't have metaphors unless they're *for* something. What, in your opinion, are the birds in *The Night Men* metaphors for?"

"They're birds! Birds stand for flight, freedom, escape—"

"It's not a dream, Robert. It's a novel."

"So?"

"So you can't just make a nice-sounding case for what you want it to mean and suddenly it means that."

"Sure I can. Haven't you ever heard of postmodern criticism?"

"Oh, Jesus Christ, Robert; postmodernism's head is so far up its own butt that it's popped out the other side and looks normal."

About to respond, Robert stopped, closing one eye. Then he narrowed the other. Then he cocked his head and shook it a few times, blinking. "What?"

Jason took a deadpan sip from his mug, but unwisely glanced up in mid-swallow.

Robert, watching him mop coffee spew from his face, said, "So let's get this straight."

"No, no, let's not."

"No, no. Really. I want to understand." Robert nodded enthusiastically. "So according to you, an entire artistic and philosophical intellectual movement is wrong. Is that right?"

"Hey, it happens."

"You realize—"

"Anyway, they're not metaphors—"

"—they *are* metaphors." Then Robert expounded upon this thesis, but Jason was looking into space and chewing the inside of his mouth.

After a few moments of silence, Robert said, "What is it?"

"Um. You're right."

"Really?"

"No, not about that. You're still wrong about that. About me going off and bothering people. I don't actually think there's any chance we can find out who trashed Zeb's place, but I want to know I gave it my best shot before I give up. I'm going to start after breakfast. Do you want to help, or do you want to go home?"

"Start where?"

"That's the problem. Now I wish I hadn't given my word that I wouldn't pry into how Matthew the DJ ended up with the theremin."

"You got it back, though."

"Yeah, I know. I wish we could get online and do some research on the—" he blinked. "Hey. What's today's date? Is today the seventh?"

"As of two hours ago. Why?"

On his feet and digging for money, Jason said, "You coming?"

✦

"It's not just that I'm not in the right place at the right time," Robert explained as they went cautiously down the ice-slickened staircase into the freezing subway station. In front of them, a somewhat attractive woman in a long white coat, dangling earrings, and four-inch heels picked her way awkwardly. "It's bigger than that. It's like I have no effect on the world. I audition, it goes okayish, then they don't call. I go to the store and the shelves are full of things that I don't buy. It's not just that I don't buy them," he clarified as Jason opened his mouth, "it's that the same thing happens whether I buy them or not. I come here to help you, and you do all the same things you'd do if I weren't here. And then Stuart shows up in Los Angeles—where I just left! It's like—"

The woman tripped and went forward, flinging her arms out for balance. As though they'd practiced it, Robert hooked her elbow with his and held her steady while she recovered her footing.

She looked at him only briefly, as though embarrassed. Flushed, she murmured, "Sorry—thanks."

"No problem," Robert said as he released her. Jason listened to him gripe as they waited for the subway train, but he couldn't stop seeing the woman, her arms out as though in flight, the sleeves of her coat spread and angelic in the air, her earring pointing toward her chin, horizontal like a skydiver over the diagonal descent of stairs.

It was a long time before the next Amtrak train to Pennsylvania. "Just ignore me," Robert said about his mood, which had deepened again, so Jason left him to brood on a couch and killed time reading old newspapers, drinking old coffee, and chatting about e-mail withdrawal and network infrastructure with the woman who ran the Amtrak lounge.

"Do you live around here?" she asked when their departure time neared.

"No, just visiting."

"That's too bad," she said, and gave him a heartstopper of a sizing-up from under black lashes.

The tiny stage at Dishonest Abe's Coffeehouse wasn't big enough for the three-piece band that was setting up on it. The stand-up bass was off the stage on the floor, and people bumped into the bassist when they came in. The drummer was sitting at the back of the stage with the nonchalance of a pro, his instrument an empty five-gallon plastic water bottle, which he was holding between his knees and playing distractedly with brushes. In front of him, a short woman stood with a scarred acoustic guitar. According to a laser-printed paper banner pinned above the drummer's head, this was The Gregs. Handwritten after that was "With Special Guests Lavonne and Kim." The s in "Gregs" was crossed out.

The paintings on the walls now were luminous rainbow-colored fantasies with naked women and unicorns, in thick, carven wooden frames. The tables were still in a fashionable scatter, and most of the few dozen seats were filled by people who didn't yet know where their wrinkles were going to be. Dark boys wore khakis, sideburns, and black leather jackets; light boys wore buzz cuts, T-shirts, and baggy pants; girls wore black gothic gear or coveralls over a short white shirt, the bare skin of the stomach flashing at the sides, the occasional glint of a navel ring in baby flesh.

"When did adults get so young?" Jason asked Robert after they stepped in. "No one consulted me."

"Careful," Robert warned. "You're getting crotchety ahead of schedule."

The same counterperson was flinging herself around behind the counter, filling orders from a line of a dozen people, and she sent them a warm smile after a pleased double take. Her hair was now blue, her alien makeup less severe. Her face, as it turned out, was pretty, her dark eyes bright and lips sweetly full.

The singer said, "Hi, we're The Greg," and launched straight into a surprisingly professional-sounding song about junior high school gym class. The crowd could relate; it applauded and yelled "yeah!" at all the right moments.

"They're actually good," Jason said as they inched toward the counter.

Robert turned to shoot him a look of surprise and interest. "You like them?"

"Not even a little."

The song wrapped up and the audience clapped and whistled. The drummer pretended to drink from his water bottle as the others retuned.

"Hi, guys!" The countergirl smiled as they stepped up.

"Hi," Jason said. "Wasn't the Inscrutable Whom supposed to be playing tonight?"

"Oh." Her face went sad. "Yeah. He canceled, sorry."

"How come?"

She shook her head sympathetically. "I don't know, sorry."

The front Greg said, "This is a sensitive ballad called 'My Girlfriend is Pretty.' One, two . . ." The space was assaulted by a mass of loud, untuned strums and random bashing.

"Do you know when he'll be playing again?"

"No, I'm sorry."

"Want to stay or go?" he asked Robert, who turned to consider the band.

"George Dubya is shitty!" the Greg screamed. "But that's tough titty!"

"Go," Jason answered for Robert.

"Sorry," the countergirl sympathized.

On the way to the door, Jason glanced back. The countergirl smiled at him. He smiled back and said to Robert, "Feel like walking a couple miles?"

Outside in the cold, he said, "Oh, wait," and went back in.

✦

There was no line at the counter, and she smiled especially warmly at him, so he smiled back.

"Have you gotten a new shipment of *Midnight at the Magic Music Shop?*"

Her eyes sparkled. "Sure," she said, and wiped her hands before leaning across the counter to pick one out of a little cardboard stand he hadn't noticed. She placed it matter-of-factly on the counter. "Is that what you came back for?"

"Uh . . . yeah?"

She smiled indulgently, plucked a napkin from a stack near the cash register, and wrote on it: *Courtney*, and a phone number.

He came back out and showed the CD and the napkin to Robert.

"Is that hers?"

"Am I broadcasting alerts on the emergency bachelor channel? That's the second pass in a day."

"She thought you were coming back in to talk to her."

"Apparently."

"What did you say?"

"I didn't know what to say. I said thanks."

"What are you going to do with it?"

She looked pleased when he came back in again, plunking her elbows down on the counter to meet him squarely.

"I, uh," he said.

She cocked her head attractively. Pretty eyes, and he hadn't noticed her figure previously. It was awfully cute inside the coveralls.

"I . . ." he said. "I . . . have somebody." He placed the napkin gently on the counter but kept his fingertips on it.

"Ohh." She blinked and bit her lip. "I'm sorry."

"No—really, you made my week."

She studied him long enough that it became uncomfortable, finally saying, "You're a good guy, huh."

He took his fingertips from the napkin. "No, not really. I'm . . . Well. Anyway."

She did a detached little smile. "Yeah you are. Well, have a nice night."

"You too."

"So?" Robert said.

"I hurt her feelings. Let's go."

"You still know her number, don't you?"

"Can we go?"

It was another mile to the Inscrutable Whom's office on its quiet street of brick buildings. A wedge of weak light spilled down the side stairs from the open door.

No one answered the tentative knock and greeting. Inside, the office doors were closed and silent. Narrow tire tracks, light-colored where they'd dried on the dark tile, snaked down the hallway under yellow light, their path truncated by the elevator door. The elevator had up and down arrows in a little brass plate instead of numeric floor indicators above its door. The arrows were dark.

Jason turned silently to Robert and spread his hands.

Robert shrugged uncomfortably. "Maybe we should leave," he whispered, then followed Jason to Suite H and watched him put an ear to the door.

"What do you hear?"

"Sh." Listening intently, he put up a hand. "Cooling fans," he whispered. Half a minute later, he said, "I think two."

"For the servers?"

"That's my guess. Uhp!—I think a little generator just kicked in. Maybe a cooling unit."

They went back to the silent elevator doors and looked at them. The arrows were still dark.

"Wow," Robert muttered, and Jason looked up in time to see wonder flickering through the cloud of angst.

Robert looked at him as though in awe. "Wow. That woman on the subway stairs—"

A *clank* triggered the childhood impulse not to get caught and the up arrow lighted green. Exchanging a meaningless look as the clank was followed by a hydraulic whine and the tick of coiling chain, they stepped back a few feet.

The green arrow went dark and the whine ceased.

"Do—" Robert said after a few moments, and the doors lurched apart.

They were staring at a man who was staring back at them. Waves of silver hair fell loose to his shoulders, and a pair of zippered alligator boots were parked on the step of his electric wheelchair, draped by clean, new-looking blue jeans with stars-and-stripes flares. The jeans were matched by a denim jacket, out of fashion, the collar up. Inside was a pale green polo shirt, open to reveal a wiry tangle of chest hair and a gold sun medallion.

It was an ungodly awful ensemble, but it worked because of the man's outstanding face, which shone first with surprise and then with friendly curiosity. The face was missing wrinkles, as though the aging process had stepped out for a cigarette break and been hit by a bus. It was the face, Jason thought, of a man who's given away everything ten times over but somehow never missed a meal. Or who's nuts.

"You seek the Spinning Wankel Stick," the man said. His eyes twinkled and he nudged a toggle on the arm of his wheelchair. His silver hair glimmered in the dirty light of the elevator as the chair rolled forward.

Stepping aside, Jason said, "The Spinning Wankel Stick?"

"Rotation Nation Station." He looked at Robert. "Altitudinous dudinous. How high are you?"

"I never touch the stuff," Robert said. "I'm six-foot-five, soaking wet."

The man cocked a sly glance at him and pointed as though awarding a high grade. He rolled past them toward the Sheetrock enclosure of Suite H and unlocked its door.

Jason said, after some rewinding and puzzling, "I see. No, we're not looking for the Rotary Club. I'm assuming you're the Inscrutable Whom?"

"Whom you seek," the man said, "and whom you find." He whirred into a three-point turn to face them, then raised a loose fist as though raising a forefinger, but the fingers didn't open. "The one is meek, the other blind. But what is weak, and what is kind, when love's your only reason?"

"We came out to Dishonest Abe's to hear you tonight."

"The Universe gives," said the Inscrutable Whom, "and the Universe makes a way. What can I do for you?"

The sudden lack of cosmic encryption was jarring. "Uh, there's a little shop in Brooklyn," Jason said, "in the middle of the street."

"And all the children know that this is where they find their treats. Down below the boulevard the battered beater beats; the player plays, the dreamer dreams, the creeper slowly creeps." He leaned forward, gesturing again with an unraised forefinger. "And here, my child, will you stay, until the day you go away, returning not 'til you are young and wise and tattered gray."

"We're from the little shop," Jason said.

There was a transformation in the remarkable face, as though a joyful sun had ignited behind it. "The wheel turns," said the Inscrutable Whom, "and thereby turns back."

46

BEFORE the Inscrutable Whom started crying, he told them about the Magic Music Shop. Robert and Jason were sitting on folding chairs, and he was in his wheelchair in the wide part of the hallway, outside Suite H.

"In nineteen seventy, nobody did that. Nobody. But Diz loved music, so there was the music store at street level, and down below he had an eight-track recorder and a couple of couches, which he called a recording studio. Now, any kid with a Soundblaster can do the same thing, but then! Then! Magical implements from the gods, my friend! Diz didn't know how to use it, and nobody else did either, but you could record a few love songs for a few shekels."

"No acoustic treatment or anything?" Jason said. "How'd it sound?"

"It sounded like what it was, but who cares? We were making music. There was a place nearby where you could go make a record—on *vinyl*—if you wanted to sing a song to your girlfriend or send a voice letter back to the farm. I had a few dollars, so after I recorded a few songs at Diz's, I took my master tape there and had three hundred records made. When I went to pick them up, the owner wanted to sell me sleeves, but I didn't have the money for them, so I put the records in paper bags and tied ribbons around them.

"So I go down to the local record establishment with these bags with ribbons, and they take them on consignment. That's pretty cool, so I go around to a few other record stores, and they take a few here, a few there."

He nodded at Jason and Robert as though that made sense. They nodded back because yes, it did.

"A few weeks later, I notice that one of the records is gone from one of the stores, so being a little short of shekels, I go up to the counter and I say, 'Hey, I noticed you sold one of my records, so can I have my money?' He says, 'What do you mean?' 'I brought so-and-so many records in here on consignment, and I notice one's gone, so I want my money.' 'I don't know what you're talking about.' Well! This bloodsucker's got me mad now! So I take back all my records. Then I march around to all the other record stores and I take all those back, too.

"Now I've got two hundred and ninety-nine records. What can I do with two hundred and ninety-nine records?"

The open face was earnest. He was actually asking.

Jason shook his head, "I don't know. What did you do?"

"What could I do? I went out and stood on the street corner, and when a car pulled up, I knocked on the window—" He pantomimed it and made the sound with his tongue. "—*clock clock clock*, 'Hi, want a record?' I gave all of them away but five. I washed my hands; I walked away. That was thirty years ago. End of story, right?"

Obviously not, but: "Right."

"Fast-forward thirty years. I get e-mail from this guy in Switzerland who's desperate for another copy because the *grooves wore out* on his! Then I get another e-mail from a collector in Finland, and then another one in California. Pretty soon, I'm getting e-mail every few weeks from people looking for this record that I just—" hands fluttered suddenly upward like startled birds, fingers swaying loosely beneath them "—gave away."

Robert said, "Wow."

"Wait!" Leaning in like a conspirator, he said in a low voice, "There's more . . ." He let the suspense build, then sat back and winked. "One day my wife's dropping the kids off at school, and one of the teachers comes up to her and asks if she's related to Allan Stegner." Adopting a puzzled expression, he said, " 'He's my husband . . .' 'Oh, I love his record!' Naturally, there must be a mistake, right? so Peggy asks, 'What record?' 'Oh, isn't he the same Allan Stegner who did *Midnight at the Magic Music Shop?*" He paused for dramatic emphasis. " '*I just heard it on the radio!*' "

He looked at them in amazement. "On the *radio!* And *then!*— I get e-mail from this guy in Florida who tells me they're bootlegging it in *Japan!* so do I want to do an authorized reissue on CD? He'll put up the money and do all the work. So obviously, that's a big problem."

Jason was still frowning in confusion when Robert said, "Why's that a big problem?"

The eyebrows rose in surprise, as though this were obvious. "This is a record I *gave away* thirty years ago. I *washed my hands* of it." He demonstrated by brushing his hands together, one-two-three. "We *parted ways.* That's its *karma*, right? So this becomes a serious spiritual question: Should I accept money for it thirty years later."

Leaning forward intently, Robert said, "What did you do?"

"Wrestled with it. Like Jacob. With his angel."

"And?"

He seemed embarrassed. "I let him go ahead and do the pressing."

"Why?"

"Peggy said if I didn't, she'd kill me."

All three of them nodded.

Robert said, "So what happened to the studio?"

"When Diz died, a few of us snuck in at night and bricked it up." One lax hand demonstrated, tapping a brick into an imaginary vertical barrier. "It was a holy place."

"So how come you canceled the gig tonight?"

"That's an epic of epic proportions, man."

"We don't mind."

"I'll give you the Weeder's Digest version. I had to stop playing the guitar when bugs ate my brain. Peggy paid a nice lady to stick knitting needles in me, but I still couldn't play. A couple months ago, she finally got tired of my complaining and said an intelligent gentleman such as myself should be able to find a way. My first reaction was, well! How dare she? You know? But one thing about Allan Stegner: If you kick his ass hard enough, the scales do fall from his eyes. Guess what I did."

They shook their heads.

"Jimi's nightmare. The schoolboy's musical friend."

Blank looks. More headshaking.

As though confessing a beloved naughtiness, he leaned in again. "I ordered an autoharp!" The beautiful face registered surprise at its own statement. "An autoharp? Yeah, a *nice* auto-harp! Did you know they even *made* nice autoharps? But hey, it worked. I could make the chords and sing the words to all my old songs, and that's where it's at anyway, right? The song's the thing. So once my chops were up a little, I did a couple open mikes and people seemed to like it. Abe gave me my own night. But—" He lifted his left hand. His eyes filled, and when he blinked, tears rolled. One silver lock fell; he pushed it back with the ball of a thumb. "Never have a good time where the gods can see you. I woke up this morning and I couldn't even play the autoharp." He brightened. "Hey, that's a blues song. 'I woke up this morning/couldn't play the autoharp.'"

"Men's room?" Jason asked, went to it down the hall, and brought back tissue.

"Woke up this morning/couldn't play the autoharp," came the thoughtful murmur as the tissue was accepted clumsily. "Thank you, Jason."

"Is there anything we can do?" Robert said.

Dryer-eyed, his face blurred but still beautiful, the Inscrutable Whom lifted his hands slightly. "Can you fidget with my digits?"

Robert said, "If you don't mind my asking . . . what happened?"

The beautiful eyes widened in terror—or mock terror. "Bugs ate my brain, man! Oh, shit!" He shot his cuff and consulted a digital watch. "Time to shoot up."

Wheeling around in the open space, he pushed into his office. Racks of computer gear and a mini-refrigerator showed briefly until the door swung almost shut behind him.

Jason and Robert looked at each other. From within the small office came:

"May I offer you some green tea? The tea is free, but the cost is to steep."

The door opened ten minutes later, and their host sat in the doorway, offering two steaming ceramic teacups that lay on a red lacquer tray on his lap. Jason and Robert rose to accept them and breathed opulent floral vapors, as though the cups held hot perfume. A few tablespoons of dry tea leaves lay scattered across the office floor.

"Is this jasmine?" Robert asked, inhaling deeply over his cup as he sat again.

"Dragon Pearl," the Inscrutable Whom verified, rolling back into his office. "A gift from a girl who drives a wagon and scripts in PERL." He came back out with an empty cup and a red-and-black teapot ornamented with willowy branches and kingfishers. "She leaves tea leaves—and so it unfurls." He beamed. "I usually drink Lipton's."

Jason wasn't a green tea drinker, so as always, it tasted like slightly tinted hot water. Smelled amazing, though.

"I need to ask about your web page," he said. "What's it for?"

"For music. I was going to put up some songs. I just haven't gotten to it."

"So it's just a teaser."

"For the songs, the gigs, the CD—" He gestured ornately. "Whatever transpires."

Jason nodded.

"So," Robert said conversationally. "Bugs eating your brain. What's the Latin name for that?"

The Inscrutable Whom raised the pot clumsily to his own cup, the handle resting across one palm, the heel of the other hand tilting the spout. One did not pour one's own green tea, and Jason's impulse was to offer an inviting hand, but he didn't want to appear to condescend. As their host poured his own and set the pot on the tray, he decided it fell into the same category as opening doors for women: He would do what was gentlemanly, and if someone took offense, screw 'em.

The screw 'em part wasn't gentlemanly, but life is paradox.

"From *scler,*" said the Inscrutable Whom, "meaning *scar.* Many scars: multiple sclerosis."

Robert eyes expressed horror over his teacup. "Wow," he said. "I'm really sorry."

"Tragic magic. But . . . When bugs eat your brain, you may go insane, but at least you know you're not to blame."

Where, yet again, was Martin's empathy when you needed it? "Well." Pausing to breathe the intoxicating floral steam, Jason said, "I don't have any friends who could get your dexterity back for you, but I can push chord buttons and strum in time if there's a chart."

"Wow." The Inscrutable Whom looked surprised and very

pleased. "Wow. You have a heart." He looked at his watch and shook his head. "And I do have a chart. But it's too late."

Robert's eyes narrowed. "You mean for tonight, right? Or generally?"

An eloquent spreading of unopening hands. "Man plans, God laughs, and even the moon is an evanescent crescent."

Robert shook his head in admiration. "How do you *do* that?"

The beatific face shone. Jasmine steamed from the cups and pot. "LSD," said Allan Stegner, "set me free."

Jason refilled their host's cup.

Robert held his on a crossed knee and said cautiously, "You seem like a man who's . . . in tune with the universe. What do you do when nothing's lining up right?"

"Mm—" A swallow, a shake of the silvered head. "I just happen to be having a good day when you're having a bad one, my friend. Tomorrow you could find the key to all your dreams and I could roll into an open sewer."

Robert nodded in acknowledgment, but pressed on. "But—if you don't mind the question—this day started with the discovery that your hands no longer work. How can you find the prepossession to call it good?"

After serious thought: "I don't know, man. All I can tell you is listen to the Universe."

"What if the universe isn't saying anything?"

"Oh—" The Inscrutable Whom frowned and shook his head emphatically. "That *never* happens. But sometimes you can't hear it because your own crap is in the way."

"What do you do then?"

"You screw up a lot." Humor lit the beautiful face. As though hearing the punchline of an eternal joke for the first time, he laughed and repeated it, nodding to himself with pleasure. "That's it. You screw up a lot."

Robert said, "Okay," discontentedly and put his cup on the floor.

His face now suffused with compassion, the Inscrutable Whom said, "The thing is, Robert, you can't fight the universe."

"I'm not fighting it. I think it's fighting me."

A delighted laugh. "Then you're *really* not going to win!"

"Did you always have this point of view," Jason ventured, "or did you develop it after you got sick?"

"As I said." The Inscrutable Whom raised his cooling cup between the heels of both hands, fingers curved over the top like a white lotus, and sipped. "It's a good day."

At the door, Robert seemed to be thinking. Then he said, "Thank you," and extended a hand.

"You're welcome," said their host, and extended his own. When they shook, it didn't look awkward.

"I have something to tell you," Zeb said on the phone, "but I'll tell you over dinner."

"Great," Jason said. "See you then," and hung up without letting on that they had a few somethings, too.

47

I T was to his credit, he thought, that he hadn't run from the scene of the crime.

He'd steeled himself against the consequences, but so far, anyway, there had been none. He sat on Roberto's front porch and waited for Tiny to come back and find what he'd done to the window, or Roberto or Martin, or his parents, or the police, or anybody. No one did.

He watched someone come out of a house halfway down the block and get into a car, the slam sounding an instant after the door shutting. The cough of the starter introduced the sudden blare of the radio, and the drone of the engine threaded weakly through the birdcalls and breezes, layering with the baritone hum of washing machines.

He didn't know what time it was, but suspected he'd been sitting there for a long while, and he guessed from the light that it was midafternoon. He was skipping around randomly in *The Night Men* because he couldn't concentrate on the story, and his butt was cold and sore from the concrete.

He stood and brushed the seat of his jeans, turned to look at the house, and stared at the pale yellow swastika.

He'd already walked around the house a few times, looking for unlocked doors or windows. Leaving *The Night Men* on the porch so if Roberto and Martin came back, they'd know he was around, he walked out to Sunland Boulevard.

A few hundred yards of empty parking lot past the Bob's Big Boy was a Thrifty drugstore. He spent all but a few cents on a rectangular wooden scrub brush, a three-foot wooden handle that screwed into it, a plastic bucket, and dish soap, and then the cashier let him spend the few cents on a granola bar, even though he didn't have enough for the tax. The gravity of the morning's deeds was settling on him, forcing up fear that, in turn, displaced his resolve. But he'd done it, and it was just. There would be punishment.

But there hadn't been punishment.

He was pretty sure it was just.

Back at Roberto's, he ate the granola bar while he made suds in the bucket and screwed the handle onto the brush. At first he was afraid the various shades of clean and dirty yellow would all brighten by a set amount, leaving a newly pale wall with a double-pale swastika, but as he scrubbed, everything got evenly brighter. In a couple of hours, the bottom two-thirds of the front of the house was clean. He knew from last time how to get onto the roof.

Roberto wasn't there this time to hand the bucket up to. The roof route started with a step onto a cinder block planter box and another onto a tall sprinkler valve with a sprinkler key hanging from it. A quick push of a sneaker against the top of the gate put you nearly waist level with the roof. Then it was upper body and getting a knee over.

Sort of scary even without a bucket. He got partway several times before giving up and standing on the soaked concrete, staring at the roof.

Duh. The sprinkler pipe had a spigot. He connected the garden hose, carried the bucket up to the roof, sat up there and filled it, and hooked it over a ten-inch tin vent stack near the peak.

There was maybe half a foot of overhang, and the slope was toward the sides of the house, so he could lie along the roofline and reach the top of the swastika with the long-handled brush. It was slow, dirty going, but the breeze, the focused work, and the slow cooling of the afternoon made the minutes blend. There had still been no consequences, and Roberto and Martin had still not returned. As he looked down at the empty driveway, he realized that Tiny had walked straight across it. Roberto's family's station wagon wasn't there.

Why would that be?

Few cars passed, and the only people he saw for an hour were kids playing down the block. It was such a shock to glance up and see Little Bert Simons' head fifteen feet away, silhouetted over the line of the roof peak, that he said, "Hi," involuntarily.

Little Bert's face wrinkled in disgust. Wayne Eckert's appeared at the roof line beside him.

"This the fucker that broke your window, Little Bert?" he said. "Looks like the fucker to me."

They clambered up and sat on the roof peak with their elbows on their knees. Lying along the overhang, Jason had to look up to see them.

"You the fucker that broke my window, fucker?" Little Bert asked.

Jason said nothing, looking back and forth between the two.

"Just askin'," Little Bert said, "fucker." Wayne Eckert hawked and spat, the glob landing a foot from Jason's head, darkening the shingle.

"Hello, boys," Jason said. "How's it going to go?"

They stared at him.

"Fuckers," he added.

"You are so dead," Wayne said.

Wayne hawked another one, and as Jason ducked his face, he felt the soft impact on the top of his head. Neither Wayne nor Little Bert commented. They just got comfortable. There was nowhere for him to go. Besides jumping off the roof, all the escape paths were toward Wayne and Little Bert or toward the back of the house, where he'd have the same problem when they moved to block him again.

He craned back to see the roof edge behind him. He could jump off there, but if he landed wrong on the hard dirt next door, he wouldn't be able to run.

"You gonna jump, fucker?"

"Bitchen. Go for it." Wayne hawked and spat. Bubbly spittle dribbled from another shingle edge, an inch from Jason's eyes.

His right hand ached—it was still clenched around the brush handle. A lightweight club, at best, and he could lose his balance swinging it. Still looking up at Little Bert and Wayne, he set it down and flexed his fingers.

"Your hand hurt, fucker?"

"Make your body hurt, soon enough," Wayne said, aside, to Little Bert, and they both laughed falsely.

"Not so's you'd notice," Jason said flatly.

Wayne frowned and shook his head as though trying to understand gibberish. He half-stood, hands out to balance his shaky stance, said, "I'ma go get my Bowie knife," and clomped down the other side of the roof where Jason couldn't see him. The sounds of the gate rattling and feet landing on concrete preceded Wayne's appearance in the front yard. "Now, you make sure that fucker don't move while I go get my knife," he called up.

"Okay, Wayne," Little Bert promised.

Before Wayne had doubled the hunting party, Little Bert

by himself had looked like too much to handle. Now he looked like a godsent reprieve. Without his older brother's friends, he looked suddenly younger than Jason, and a little scared to be left alone.

Jason lunged left, toward the back yard, and Little Bert, startled, rose to a low crouch and almost lost his balance, one hand shooting back to grab the peak.

From then, it was like music.

48

"I CAN'T tell you how much of a load you two took off my mind," Zeb said, holding up his wineglass. "And Robert, I'm glad to have gotten to know you better. So—to knowing who your friends are."

"We would have taken you someplace nicer, you know," Gary Warren said after the toast. "We didn't have to eat in the store." He and Zeb sat on the two tall stools; Jason and Robert were across the counter, seated on stacked road cases. Between them, foil take-out containers of Italian food and two open bottles of wine sat on the glass counter.

"We had a reason for eating here," Jason said. "But first, you said you had something to tell us?"

"Yes. More like ask your opinion, since you gave me the idea in the first place. Tell me—do you think there's enough business to keep the store open twenty-four hours?"

"Boy, I don't know. We had only three customers in three days. But that's without—"

"Yeah," Robert cut in.

"— any kind of advertising or enough time to really establish word of mouth."

"Right," Robert said, nodding.

"You know, though, I think it's possible. You're thinking about it seriously?"

"Well, if I can offer something unique that there's a demand for, it's another way to compete with the chain stores. Well, thanks. If you hear of anyone looking for a casual night job, let me know."

Jason reviewed the list of people he knew in New York: Zeb, Gary Warren, Sarah. "Nope," he said. "Sorry."

"No . . ." Robert said slowly. "Me neither . . ."

"Well," Zeb said, "if you think of anyone. So what was this reason you said you had for eating here?"

"Well," Jason said, looking at Robert. "First we want to ask you some questions."

Zeb, chewing, glanced at both of them and shrugged. "Sure."

"What did you know about this place's history before you bought it?"

"Well . . . I know it went disused for a number of years until the neighborhood started to turn around. We bought right before the prices went through the roof. It was the Magic Music Shop in its past, since the sign was already here. I've been too busy to really track down the history, and most of our neighbors have only been here a few years. So we don't know as much as we should. Why?"

"Just a couple more questions. Was there any kind of structural analysis or building inspection before you bought it?"

"Yeah. The way it works is the buyer hires an engineer. It's not required, but we did. Why do you ask?"

Robert said, "Is there a basement to this building?"

"You mean a cellar?" Zeb said. "Not enough to mention. Only that little storeroom—you've seen it, Jason. Barely enough to put anything in. The engineer said there must be a rock shelf here that got in the way of making a full cellar. That's part of how we got the price down a little. I keep Ultimate Support tubes down there, that's about it." He pointed with his fork. "All these buildings have cellars. What's going on?"

Jason said, "So we were in Pennsylvania last night."

"You were?"

"We had tea with the Inscrutable Whom."

Zeb and Gary Warren both said, "You *did*?" Zeb leaned forward. "Who is he? Or she?"

"He." Jason slid off the road cases and pulled *Midnight at the Magic Music Shop* from his hanging jacket.

A moment of confusion on Zeb's face turned to surprise and he stood abruptly. "You found a copy!"

"You haven't done any research on this yet, I take it," Jason said.

"No, the Internet's still down and I haven't had a chance to make any calls."

Flipping open the case, Jason withdrew the disc and indicated the CD player.

"Of course! Go ahead!"

The music was of another time, suffused with psychedelia, acoustic guitars and plucked sitars, twinkling wind chimes, incense, and wooden recorders, and—thirty years younger and walking upright—the Inscrutable Whom:

> *There's a little shop in Brooklyn,*
> *in the middle of the street.*
> *And all the children know that this is where they*
> *   find their treats.*
> *Down below the boulevard the battered beater*
> *   beats,*
> *the player plays, the dreamer dreams, the creeper*
> *   slowly creeps.*

The beat suspended momentarily as the guitars strummed and the sitar swelled and buzzed in loose time behind the spoken refrain:

> *And here, my child, will you stay,*
> *until the day you go away,*
> *returning not 'til you are young and wise and*
> *   tattered gray.*

And then it returned for the second verse:

> *The reel turns, the teacher learns,*
> *the student growing older*
> *sees seasons change and rearrange,*
> *the summer blowing colder.*
> *On his courtly carousel, the ragged reaper reaps.*
> *But down below the boulevard, our secret ever*
> *   keeps.*

> *And there, my child, will it stay,*
> *until the day we go away,*
> *returning not 'til we are young and wise and*
> *   tattered gray,*
> *returning to unseal the past and watch the*
> *   children play,*
> *returning there with you, my love, to sing another*
> *   day.*

Zeb was smiling after the fade-out. "That's nice. Nobody does that anymore."

Jason hit the stop button before the next track started. Gary Warren flared his eyelids dramatically and snapped his fingers to make beatnik applause. "It's far out, man. It's totally groovy."

Jason and Robert joined in the finger-snapping. It sounded like rain.

232 ◆ KEITH SNYDER

Zeb said, "So what, then? The big mystery web page is just a song lyric?"

Taking the CD from the tray, Jason said, "He was quoting it as a sort of a teaser. 'Come back soon for treats' just meant there'd be more up at the site soon, so come back and see it."

"Well, that doesn't sound very ominous," Gary Warren said.

"There's nothing ominous about this guy, believe me." He boxed the CD and handed it to Zeb.

"So why's the store in the song?"

"What's that little storeroom wall made of?" Jason asked.

Puzzled, Zeb said, "It's brick."

"What's behind the brick?"

"I don't know. Dirt? Sewer lines?"

"Dead bodies?" Gary Warren contributed.

Jason looked at Robert again. They were both smiling broadly now.

"Look," Zeb said, finally losing his patience. "What's the joke?"

"You're not going to believe this," Robert said.

49

UNEQUIPPED with sledgehammers, picks, or pry bars, there was nothing they could do but crowd through the trapdoor in Zeb's office and down the tiny staircase to the little storage area, pull out all the modular black aluminum tubing that Zeb kept down there, and rap on the bricks with the butt ends of gong beaters. It was impossible to tell anything. It all just sounded like hitting bricks with the butt ends of gong beaters.

"Well," Jason said, examining his. "Here's your battered beater."

"Maybe we should leave it," Zeb said. "He did say it was holy ground."

Gary Warren's eyebrows about leaped off his head. "Are you *nuts!?* You *own* this place! You can't not at least *look!*"

"I know, but . . ." Zeb grimaced. "I feel weird breaking in."

"Zebedee—it's *your place!*"

"We don't even have any tools."

"Any all-night hardware stores here in the city that never sleeps?" Jason asked from his seat halfway up the staircase, and then had to stand and scramble into the store when Zeb declared, "I have a five-pound sledge and a cold chisel at home," and charged up the stairs.

"Can you *believe* him?" Jason heard Gary Warren say downstairs, and Robert say, "Huh? Oh, sure. Everyone I know is nuts. So—you guys are really thinking of keeping the store open all night?"

"Well," Gary Warren began, and since Jason had never known those two to have their own conversation, he said, "Wait up, I'll go with you—" and caught up with Zeb.

The snow that had whipped and raged during previous days now slumped, gray and grubby, the few patches of untrammeled white persisting only around trees and inside the black iron fences that caged apartment building trash cans.

"Feel like telling me?" Zeb asked as they strode toward the subway station.

"Now? With the basement thing?"

"Sure."

"Well . . . sure, if you want, okay."

"That is, if you feel like it. You did make me awfully curious."

"Well. Uh. Okay. When Robert and I were teenagers— and Martin; I think you met him at your party—"

"He's the one who didn't like the Chinese bluegrass."

"Right. Wow, you remember. Anyway, we had sort of a similar situation to what happened to your store. We stayed up watching at night, and the short version is somebody got hurt."

They had music in common, so Jason rarely felt their substantial age difference. But when Zeb said, "I see," it was a more experienced man talking. "Want to tell me about it?"

He never discussed it. Almost never. When he did, he got it out and over with, leaving out any details that might paint him in a sympathetic light, skipping right to his culpability.

"It's a pretty long story."

Zeb looked both ways, shrugged. "We do have a train to wait for."

"Well . . ." He struggled to get a grip on where to start. Not only was he unused to talking about it, but no matter where he started, it would sound weird. It wasn't a story where one thing came after the next—it was more like layers.

So he just picked one.

50

H E was fascinated by the flow of it.

It was all just like music, the lovely friction of the shingles as he gripped with the ball of a foot, the over-balancing thrust of weight that he knew he could compensate for before it was too late. Above him, Little Bert had no flow; he was shuffling back and forth, one awkward hand behind him on the peak line, keeping him from falling, but also keeping him clumsy.

Another second, and it could all have been different. Another two seconds, and Little Bert might not have panicked in Wayne's absence and gone for the bucket, which didn't want to unhook from the little conical roof of the little vent stack until Jason had nearly reached him. By the time it was disentangled, soapy water was rushing down the shingles toward the side of the house, and the only thing Little Bert had time to do was swing the wet, empty bucket desperately, without balance, with way too much follow-through.

His body torqued around by the momentum of his swing, his soles slid enough to break their friction with the shingles.

The bucket bounced against Jason's forehead and clattered off the roof. Little Bert landed on his ass and went sliding as the bucket hit the ground.

Jason's balances were lined up perfectly and he saw Little Bert's trajectory and momentum; he could have stopped him with a well-planted leg. It was a split-second decision, but he felt himself make it: He leaned left as Little Bert slid by on his right, down the soapy roof, and over the edge after the bucket.

He listened, heard nothing, and crept up to the peak to look out for Wayne Eckert and his Bowie knife. He didn't know what a Bowie knife was, but it had to be bigger and more murderous than a regular knife, or Wayne wouldn't have named it specifically. Maybe it was the one Wayne had in his pocket when he'd been sitting by the ivy the day Roberto had first pointed him out.

The wave of fearlessness, having swelled, was breaking into a flat, receding tide that left him afraid to poke his head over the peak line. But Carter had gone toward the crashed sedan even when someone might have been in there with a gun, so Jason tightened his mouth, gathered himself, and did it.

Nothing—dry roof. Trembling now, he scrabbled down to where he could step onto the gate and made his way to the ground. He was by the porch, shoving *The Night Men* into his back pocket, when the Simonses' screen door opened and Wayne came out, holding the dirty leather sheath with the loop of chain dangling from it and grinning as though the whole thing were funny.

Wayne was bigger and probably faster than he was; running away would work for about ten seconds. Jason ducked back through the gate to dodge line-of-sight.

Wayne called cheerfully. "You pussy, you let him get away."

Jason cast about wildly for a weapon, grabbed the two-foot sprinkler key from where it hung from the valve handle, and backed a ways down the side of the house. The key was long and rigid but insubstantial. When Wayne appeared at the open gate, he hurled it.

Wayne jerked back and the key clanked dully as it hit the grass along the drive. "Hey, Simons!" he yelled as he stepped into the open gateway. "Where'd you go?" He grinned at Jason. "Hi there, fucker." Unsnapping the sheath, he pulled a hunting knife only half an inch out and nodded encouragingly as he advanced. "Want some of this, kid?"

Scrambling backward, Jason emerged from the side-of-the-house walkway and stood in Roberto's little back yard with nowhere left to go. There were kids who could scale seven-foot block walls, but he'd never learned. He tried the kitchen door. Locked. He could wait like a willing victim, or he could try to get past Wayne Eckert's Bowie knife and end up half blind. He backed warily to the middle of the yard.

"You're not afraid, are you, fucker?" Wayne asked as he came into the yard. "You know we're just messin' with you, right?" He pulled the knife out now and held it in one hand, the sheath in the other.

"C'mere, kid," he said. He waved the knife mesmerizingly, then tilted it suddenly to reflect the sun into Jason's eyes. The white flash was blinding.

"Simons! Where the hell are ya?"

"He fell off the roof," Jason whispered, backing toward the cinder-block wall and watching Wayne's shape obliquely as he tried to blink away the blind spot. His left heel encountered the rise of dirt that meant he had maybe two feet left. To his right, the house met the wall.

"Bullshit, fucker," Wayne said, as though bored with being lied to. "Simons!"

"He fell off the roof," Jason said again, breathing hard, his vision fogging at the edges, the blind spot persisting.

"Jesus, little man, give it—"

Jason closed his eyes and screamed, *"He fell off the roof!"*

He stood panting on the grass with his eyes nearly closed, the yard closing in.

Uncertainty halted Wayne's progress. "Where?" he challenged.

The blind spot was clearing. Jason thrust a finger toward the edge of the roof where Little Bert had gone off.

"If you're shittin' me—" Wayne went cautiously past him and did a little jump to see over the block wall into the next yard. "Shit!" he said. He sheathed the knife and stuck it in his back pocket, backed up, and leaped to catch the top of the wall with his hands, running up it with his feet and pushing with his arms so the top of the wall was at his waist, and Jason darted in and grabbed the chain that dangled from the sheath and nearly yanked him off the wall. The sheath flipped out of the pocket and lay in Jason's hand.

"Hey, whoa," Wayne said, his full weight on one forearm, trying to kick Jason or get him with the other arm, and Jason, his entire body rattling with fear, unsheathed the knife. It was cold and heavy, and it had a hand-fitting grip that he must have been holding wrong, because it felt clumsy. He wrapped both hands around it.

Wayne dropped from the wall but didn't turn around, protecting his front, and said, "You fucker, I'm gonna kill you," his left arm raised to fend off knife attack, but wavering, because he wouldn't turn far enough to really see, and in his blind flailing, he pasted one on the side of Jason's head, which Jason thought was the beginning of the end, so he sobbed in terror, braced the pommel against his chest so it wouldn't shake so badly, and rammed it into Wayne as hard as he could, at his chest level, which was even with Wayne's butt, his face pressing into Wayne's jacket, which was warm.

The denim resisted. The pommel bruised his chest, and he waited for Wayne to finish him off, but then the tip broke through the fabric and sank in, and Wayne spun away, sliding off the blade. Jason stumbled back a step, holding a six-inch knife with a three-inch smear on it, and felt himself fill with a different music than before, a shocking cold one that made all the hair on his arms and body—hair that hadn't even been there until recently—stand at attack.

This fucker was dead.

"Shit!" Wayne's voice was fearful; he reached back to touch the wound and brought his fingers away bloody. He twisted around to try to see it, and Jason saw his jacket and T-shirt lift away from the side of his torso and expose his flank.

51

'M listening," Zeb said as he unlocked his apartment door. "I'm just thinking."

As they came back out with the sledge and chisel, he said, "Maybe we should invite this Whom to the unsealing,"

52

HE was running and vomiting without the knife, running toward Sunland Boulevard and vomiting into a smelly trash can he barely made it to, empty at the curb. Coming out onto the bright boulevard, he pelted after the 159 already leaving the bus stop, and the driver stopped and let him on.

"Kids after me," he managed through his gasping as the bus pulled into traffic. "No money."

"Uh huh," the bus driver sighed. "All right, young man, sit down." She shook her head and muttered "Mm, mm, mm" as he staggered toward the back. He sat for about a second and then lurched up to the front, gasped, "Thank you," and stumbled back again.

He wasn't a tough guy. He was a gentle guy, and once that returned to him, he was horrified. *The Night Men* was a lump in his pocket under him, riding with him like an unwelcome familiar.

Riding with him where? He couldn't go home, he couldn't go to school, and of course he couldn't go to Roberto's. Those were his only three places. Okay, the library—but he couldn't stand the thought. Denny's—

That's where he'd go. His parents didn't know the place had any meaning for him.

Maybe it would go like a story, and Roberto or Martin would be there, and maybe even tell him it was okay that he'd missed their 5:00 meeting two days ago.

Or maybe he'd be alone again.

53

I buckled in the chair as I felt bone crack.

"Give us a minute," I heard a voice say, and Fred Baynes stepped into the light.

"That time's over," said the stocky cop. He rolled his thick neck and steadied himself for best leverage.

Baynes repeated in a low voice, "I said give us a minute." The stocky one turned to him as though to crack wise, but saw something that made him stop. "I'll just be outside," he said. He went out looking hard at Baynes.

Baynes lit two cigarettes and put one in my mouth. Sitting in the other wooden chair, he said, "You know a man with a cosh uses it."

"So does a man with a badge," I said. "I know the drill, Fred, so nix the routine. You might be all right, but even if you are, you're in over your head."

"Enlighten me," he said.

I shook my head slowly.

"You're a hard man, Carter. Harder than most. But you can't win this. You don't have the cards."

I laughed bitterly. "You want to know if I know you're in it. And if not you, then someone. Corcoran wasn't dirty alone."

His eyes went hard. "Corcoran was rotten, but he was a cop, and you left him to die."

"It's true I left him," I said, "but the dying was up to him."

Behind his cigarette smoke, Baynes' face was a mask carved from cold stone. "You've made your bed, Carter." He rose and knocked twice on the door. "Sweet dreams."

They got a few more good licks, and then the door opened and Tucker Radford breezed in and said, "Another application of that cudgel, officer, and you'll spend the rest of your career wishing I'd simply turned you into a toad. My dearest client, Mr. Carter! I expect you've been duly apprised of your inalienable rights under the law, which include your right not to be handcuffed to a chair and tenderized?"

"I don't recall," I said.

"Who's this bird?" the taller cave-dweller said.

"Radford," said the bird, flourishing his card. "Esquire. That's the important part, son. It's a French word meaning 'you get those handcuffs off my client before I count three, or your next uniform will have a picture of an ice cream cone on it.' One."

"I didn't know you were a linguist, Sir," I said, wincing as I brought my freed arms forward to shooting pains.

"Oh, yes. One must diversify if one is to stay in business in this increasingly specialized age. I see you're confounded, son," he addressed the stocky one as we left. "My advice to you is to stay that way. It's the healthiest state for a limited intelligence."

Baynes watched impassively from across the squad room, saying nothing as we left. That was two I owed him.

54

ALLAN and Peggy Stegner were to arrive at Penn Station on the 6:30 P.M. Amtrak and then take the F subway line out to Brooklyn. By seven, the sledgehammer and cold chisel had been leaning lazily against the brick like city workmen for almost twenty-four hours. The sturdy pick with the clean white price tag had been there for eight. The Coleman lantern had been there for five. The four impatient people upstairs had been there for, it seemed, most of their adult lives.

"Seven-fifteen," Gary Warren stated with slit-eyed finality. "Then I start sledging."

The clock in Zeb's office said seven-thirteen when the Stegners rolled up, a guitar case sticking up out of Allan Stegner's lap. When Jason opened the door, they were gazing up at the old sign as though it were the Mona Lisa.

Peggy was a small, slim brunette with large brown eyes, a girlish voice, and long hair. As the wheelchair bumped through the doorframe, she said, "Allan! Watch the—" but the exasperation held no malice and more than a hint of affection.

Jason made the introductions.

"You look familiar," the Inscrutable Whom said to Zeb.

"Yeah, I was just thinking the same thing about you. Did you play at ——" This was followed by a list of extinct venues.

"I don't think so. Did you ever play at the ——?"

"I played everywhere," Zeb said. "Were you . . ."

This went on for a good two minutes before Gary Warren finally lost it, blurting, "Can we *please* knock some bricks down?"

"Yeah!" Peggy Stegner concurred good-naturedly. "Do this later!"

"I'm glad you two said it," Jason said. "I was paralyzed by conflicting codes of machismo."

"I can walk," the Incrutable Whom said to a roomful of amazed stares and the affectionate smile of his wife. "Just not every day."

"It's coming loose." Zeb tried another good thwack and the sound of sledgehammer against brick changed from resonant to flat. He stopped and looked at the brick that had just rotated a few degrees within its rectangular space.

"Zebedee?" Gary Warren demanded after a few seconds. "What *aren't* you doing?"

"We should turn the lights out," Zeb said.

In the dimness, Zeb knocked the one brick through and sent a few dozen more after it. The dark hole was big enough to stick an upper body through, the unsealed air that wafted from it damp and fungusy. In the darkness, a faint blue, localized glow persisted through corrective blinks, back a ways from the hole.

"Buddy Blue," the Inscrutable Whom intoned. "I see

you." The glow had a fixed shape to it, but Jason couldn't resolve what it was.

No one moved.

"Get my guitar, honey."

Peggy kissed her husband on the cheek and went up, and Jason pointed at Zeb, who said, "Yeah, if you wouldn't mind."

"And there, my child, will you stay," the Inscrutable Whom recited in the gloom. Sitting next to him on the step, his wife slid her right arm around his back and rested her head on his shoulder. Her left hand waited on the guitar neck.

"Until the time you go away . . ." He nodded, and Peggy fingered the first chord as he strummed softly with his knuckles. Standing by the opened wall, Zeb followed by ear with muted strums on his banjo, keeping it soft until he learned the progression of chords.

Jason was highest on the stairs; he went softly up into the quiet store and got a clay pot, a couple of egg shakers, and one of the exotic birdcalls. Down by Zeb, Gary Warren caught the birdcall, and Jason handed the shakers past the Inscrutable Whom to Robert and then sat on a high stair with the vase-like clay pot, starting a soft, simple pattern on its rounded shoulder and flared mouth.

Robert held the shakers awkwardly and looked lost until Jason played a bar of two-beats-against-three at him. Robert had wasted significant time learning how to do that, and his face lit in recognition. He nodded and frowned, and soon he began a soft, more or less regular shaker pulse with one hand. When he looked up for approval, Jason flicked a quick thumbs-up at him in the near-dark. Gary Warren, it turned out, wasn't musical at all, but the birdcall was, so his clumsy choices of placement didn't threaten the fabric.

The Inscrutable Whom began to sing his song against this newly woven accompaniment, giving it new words and rhymes that later, no one could remember. Up the stairs and outside, kids yelled faintly and sirens passed. Down below the boulevard, time seemed without end, and Jason's heart, so easily closed, opened.

Then came the refrain again and a long pause, and Jason did a sort of soft, birdwing riffle on the clay pot and then rapped a little pickup statement, and everyone—even Robert and Gary Warren—came back in together. And when Robert came back in, he was even using both hands and doing the cross-pattern—and then, from nowhere, it became one of *those* moments. Everything changed, and everyone knew, and Jason started humming a descant to float over the Inscrutable Whom's sung melody. Zeb smiled dreamily, his fingers picking a gentle pattern and later, he wouldn't quite be able to recall what the hell *was* that pattern? Gary Warren laid off the bird call. Jason felt his eyelids half-close—

and Robert had drum face, which drummers get when they're in the groove, and they can't think or they'll blow it. He'd never expected to see it on Robert.

The music flowed from all of them and returned to them. He looked at Robert and thought this would be the last he'd see him for a while, and he looked at Zeb and Gary Warren and thought they looked just fine, and the store was fine, and Gary Warren would get his little dog, and Zeb wouldn't actually mind. Allan Stegner was his wife's hero, and not just since the wheelchair, and Peggy made the chords as though she'd just been waiting for him to ask all these years.

Himself?

Well, himself . . .

55

I T was a little industrial cell of an interrogation room, the walls clumped and clotted with a thick application of bile-yellow paint, the same color as the windowsills and rain gutters at school. There was a table and two chairs, like on TV, and they sat him in there without his book. He stared at the ruler-straight crack where the metal edge of the tabletop came all the way around and met itself. He didn't know how long. Maybe as long as he'd sat on Roberto's porch.

When the two officers finally came in, they gave their names again, but he didn't retain them. When they walked, they sounded like loose change. One sat; the other stood.

"Jason Keltner," said the sitting one, opening a manila folder.

It wasn't a question, so he observed the metal crack and didn't answer.

"You speak English?" the sitting cop asked.

"Yes."

"Just checking, since you didn't answer me."

"You didn't ask me anything."

The manila folder closed halfway. "Are you a wise guy, Jason?"

"I don't think so."

"You don't *think* you're a wise guy?"

"That's right."

"That's right, *sir*." The sitting cop gave him a long look, then repeated: "That's right, *sir*."

"Right," Jason said dully. "That's right. Sir. That's right sir."

"Look at me when I talk to you, Jason."

He looked until the sitting cop opened the folder again, and then he stopped looking. "Now you're going to tell me what happened, Jason, and you're not going to leave anything out. We already know most of it, so if you lie to us, we'll know."

He didn't know where to begin. There were too many beginnings. The answer was too complicated for the question. Why would they tell him not to lie? That was offensive.

"Jason."

He looked again.

"What happened up on the roof?"

Everything happened up on the roof, he thought. The question is too big. I'd help you if you'd just ask a reasonable question.

The standing cop shifted from his position at the wall. "Let me ask you this, Jason. Do you understand that Little Bert Simons is probably paralyzed for life?"

He nodded.

"And that he could have died?"

Nod.

"Okay. And you knew at the time all this happened that when people fall off roofs, they can be very seriously injured or killed, right?"

"Yes."

"All right." Standing cop glanced at sitting cop. "So you

can see that your own actions might not look too good right now?"

"What do you mean?" His gaze flickered over the two policemen. The manila folder seemed to have too much paper in it. There couldn't be that much paper about him—

They were lying.

The police were lying.

"What do you mean, *sir*," said the sitting cop, closing the folder.

Jason picked at the edge of the metal gap with a fingernail and rocked a little in his seat.

The standing cop raised one hand toward his partner and said, "Stay with me, Jason, all right?"

Still rocking, he nodded.

"Okay, Jason, you just said you know falling off a roof can cause serious injury or death. But after Little Bert fell off the roof, first you attacked the friend who was trying to help him, and then you ran away without notifying any authorities. Is that right?"

He nodded and rocked.

"So you left him to die."

He looked up.

Behind his cigarette smoke, Baynes' face was a mask carved from cold stone.

He laughed bitterly.

Finally. A question he knew how to answer.

56

THEY pressed him longer, but he had nothing important to say. He told them what happened, several times over, understanding that they were looking for inconsistencies or rote recitations. He told them about how he hadn't stopped Little Bert's fall and how he'd stabbed Wayne Eckert in the butt, how he'd intended to stab Wayne again in the side but was overcome by a shaking fit. He told them how he'd run away and vomited in the trash can—he described the can so they'd be able to find it when they checked his story—and caught the bus to Denny's. He described the bus driver. He concluded each recounting by stating that he expected to go to prison.

"You know your friend Robert told us where to find you," the standing cop said.

"Robert?"

"Roberto," said the sitting cop.

It was an odd thing to say like that. Wasn't it supposed to be *good* when you cooperated with the police?

Then they released him without pressing charges, into

the custody of his parents, and the standing cop returned his book, standing and tapping it thoughtfully first.

His father was quiet and furious. His mother was drawn and silent, which was behavior he'd never seen from her. It suited his own mood, so they rode home in a state that had the ease of a companionable silence, but none of the companionability.

They stopped at the supermarket, and his father went in and bought cold prepared food for dinner. At home, the closing of the car doors and the rattle of the paper bags were the only sounds. His parents went into the house, but he stopped at the front door as the bags of food were laid on the dining room table.

"Come in the house, Jason," his mother said levelly, without looking at him.

"Why?"

The way she turned communicated both the admirability of the effort she was making in not yelling at him and, by implication, the enormity of his transgressions. "We have a lot to talk about, but this is not the time, so why don't you just come in the house and go to your room, and we'll talk about it when your father and I have cooled down a little."

"What's in it for me?"

His mother's eyes widened. "*What?*"

"I don't see any sort of benefit here for me at all. I get in the house, you ground me, and we have another long, pointless conversation—

"Don't you talk to your mother like that."

He turned to appraise his father, who was giving him the dangerous look. After a few moments, he said, "Dad, do you ever have any opinions of your own?"

"Steven—" His mother, the voice of reason as his father took a step toward him. "Okay, Jason. We weren't going to talk about this right now, but since you seem bent on pushing it today, why don't you come in and have a seat and we'll talk."

"Why don't I stand right here and we'll talk?"

"Jason—"

"I'll stand."

"You'll sit," his father said.

"I'll stand."

"I said you'll sit."

He turned his whole body toward his father. "I'll *fucking* stand."

His mother stepped around in front of him and slapped him hard. "You asked for that," she said when he stared at her, shock and pain still ringing.

"See you," he muttered when he could speak again, and stepped onto the walk.

"If you walk out of here," his father said behind him, "you'd better be prepared not to come back."

To what? he thought, and kept walking, though his tears blurred the sidewalk.

He had no money and nowhere to stay, but he was done backing down, maybe forever. It was five or six miles to school, so he went that way, cataloguing the details of breezes and textures but pretty well dead to anything on a larger scale.

At school, he found a loosely chained gate he could squeeze through. The building his locker was in was wide open, a janitor at work in there somewhere.

Crevices of locker and backpack gave up the last of their loose change, almost four dollars. He pulled on a crumpled sweatshirt and walked the twenty minutes, past the library and the park, to Denny's.

Standing in the dark, looking at his reflection in the glass double doors and fingering the coins in his pocket, he decided not to blow his money. It had been the most unrelenting day he'd ever experienced. The gold plastic clock over the cash register said—incredibly—two o'clock. Adults often said time sped up as you got older, and there it was. He certainly wasn't ready for it to be tomorrow.

By now, Roberto and Martin had to be back from wherever they'd gone. He could catch the 159 out to Sunland and
be there by, say, five o'clock, when it was just getting light. It
made sense to call first, but that would deplete his supply of
coins.

Maybe they were there at the Denny's, and he had only to
look carefully.

Knowing it was unlikely, he stepped up to the glass and
cupped his eyes, giving the yellow interior a cursory once-
over.

Of course they weren't there.

He'd come all this way only to rest too long and let his
momentum drain away. When he turned and headed around
the corner and randomly north, his feet hurt. Walking on the
flat sidewalk was like trudging uphill.

Just past the driveway to the parking lot, he stopped.
Where did he think he was going?

Running footsteps clapped up behind him. Startled, he
whirled.

"Are you blind *and* deaf?" Martin said, shivering in his
shirtsleeves. "Whoa, who slapped your face?"

"Roberto's watching the house?" he asked as he slid into the
booth lengthwise. The sketchbook was open on the table,
pen-and-ink supplies lined up next to it. Carter in his notch-
collared trenchcoat and fedora was gritting his teeth and
blasting through the open window of his speeding sedan.
Most of the drawing was in pencil; one corner had been inked
decisively black.

"I don't know," Martin said, picking up his pen and cleaning the nib with his napkin. In a casual tone, he said, "I take
it you haven't talked to him."

Jason shook his head, fatigue and the shakes starting to
hit him. "You know who I've talked to?" He listed them all on
one finger. "I've talked to parents, I've talked to cops, I've

talked to therapists, I've talked to counselors, and . . . I don't know. Somebody else." He tried to think, then jerked himself back from a little brownout in consciousness. Then, a little late, the obvious question: "What are you doing here?"

"Got no place to go again. You want something?"

"Uh . . . how much is the coffee here, again?"

"You're that tight on change, I'll buy you a cup of coffee." He signaled the waitress. "Hey there, sweetie," he said when she'd finished what she was doing and come over. "Whyn't you bring my friend Jason here a cup o' joe?"

"You got it, darlin'. Cream and sugar?"

"Yes," Jason said. "Thanks. How come you've got no place to go?"

"Well," Martin said, drawing short, blind strokes on his placemat until ink flowed from the nib. "I'll tell you. Roberto's dad came home. You know that brother of his that took off, Stuart?"

"Yeah."

"He showed up at some aunt's house or something like that in Texas, and the aunt called Roberto's dad, so he flew back to L.A. He showed up like an hour after you left."

"No way." Then there was a discontiguity and he realized he was asleep. Wrenching himself awake, he said, "What happened?"

"Well, let me think, 'cause I gots ta get this in the right order. Okay. First, Roberto says 'oh, shit,' 'cause he's at the window and sees the taxicab drop off his dad. Then his dad comes in and says, 'How long has Stuart been gone,' and Roberto says, 'A couple weeks.' Then his dad backhands him and orders me out. So *I'm* like, feet, do your duty, exit, stage left. So I'm out there on the porch, trying to figure out what to do next, and I hear him say to Roberto, 'What have I told you about letting people like that in the house?' Okay, dude. Fine; I see how it is. That's all I know. After that—" He shook his head. "Your guess is as good as mine, chief. That damn—"

He seemed to have trouble choosing a word. Marshaling himself, he said, "Well. I won't say what he is."

"Whoa." But fatigue had Jason on the mat now, and it was only a matter of waiting for the count. "So—" He yawned, kept yawning, spoke through it. "What'd you—what'd you—?"

He might have finished, and Martin might have answered, but the ref reached ten, and he was out.

"He paid for yours, honey. Do you want it now?"

The seat across from him was empty, the morning light outside the window weak, but getting stronger. He blinked blearily. "Did he leave?"

"Almost an hour ago."

"Oh, no!" He lurched out of the booth, still not quite awake, not yet sure why he was upset.

"You've still got a cup of coffee coming."

"Can I have it later?"

"I suppose that's fine, long as it's when I'm on duty."

Martin wasn't at any of the bus stops nearby, or hanging around in the quad at school, or in the parking lot, or near the library, or at the 7-Eleven, or anywhere in the park. Jason called information from a pay phone, but there were several dozen Altamiranos listed in Los Angeles, and he didn't know what city or what street. Or even, he realized as he waited for the 159, what name the phone would be under.

It was a chilly October morning full of pale light and nervous breezes. The "K.K.K." was gone from the station wagon's fender, morning dew beading on new polish. He went past it and up the Simonses' driveway onto their porch, and forced himself to knock without hesitating. Cardboard from a Pennzoil carton was taped over one of the four windowpanes. He managed not to look at it.

He knocked again, but this was an empty house. He closed his eyes for a moment, then opened them and forced himself to look at the damaged window.

Crossing the driveway and stepping over the low fence, he went around the station wagon and onto Roberto's porch. Two days ago, he'd have knocked perfunctorily and walked in; now he rang the bell and shivered on the porch. On the window's inside surface, straight segments of clear tape ran along the trapezoidal fractures, converging at a hole in the glass that was echoed a few inches back by a hole in the closed curtain.

The door was opened by a stranger, a wiry man of average height in a clean T-shirt and steel-rimmed glasses.

"You're Jason?"

"Yes. Is—"

The man backed into the house. "Come on in."

Roberto was sitting at the dining room table, which had two plates of eggs and sausage on it. His eyes were down.

"Hey," Jason said.

"Hey."

"Well, okay," his father said approvingly. His hand on the door edge was all knuckle and callus. "He said he knew you, and he does." He closed the door. "So now we know that much is true. Care for some coffee, Jason?"

"Um, no thanks."

"What brings you out here?"

"Well, I'm a friend of Roberto's, and—"

"Hold that thought," the man said. He turned toward the table. "That would be you?"

Eyes down, Roberto murmured something and shoveled food into his mouth.

"No, no," the man said. "Really. I want to understand." He turned toward Jason and nodded as though they'd agreed.

Jason said, "Mr. Goldstein, I—"

"Mr. Goldstein?" Addressing his son again: "So just to be sure I'm following, that would make you *Roberto* Goldstein?"

Something happened on Roberto's face as he chewed, a momentary writhing, and the tension in the room suddenly increased, erupting so tangibly that Jason felt his eyes widen and his feet take him a step back. Anger flashed on the man's face. He pounded the tabletop straight down with one hard fist, rattling the dishes, and Roberto took a huge gulp of orange juice, his eyes wide, flicking around as though he couldn't find anything safe to look at.

The man turned to Jason. "Then that would make you Roberto Goldstein's friend."

Unsure of the answer that would keep things sane, Jason nodded.

"Well, that's good." The man nodded. "Because you know, *Roberto* doesn't have any other friends, do you, Roberto?"

"I have friends."

"Oh, you do? Okay. I didn't know that. A lot of them?"

Roberto's glanced flicked up toward Jason and down again. "A couple," he murmured.

"A couple of good friends?"

A nod.

"Well, if they're good friends, you should tell them your right name."

Roberto shook his head, then froze in his seat as his father stepped toward him.

"What was that? I didn't hear it."

"Ro—"

Jason flinched as the man hit the table again, rattling the dishes.

"Careful how you answer, boy. What's your name?"

"His name's Roberto Goldstein," Jason said.

"Oh, it is?" The man turned again. "Tell him your name."

"Goldstein."

The fist hitting the table. Roberto jumped.

"As long as you live in my house, mister—"

"Yeah, right."

His father stepped toward him. "What was that?"

Roberto swallowed. "I said yeah, right."

"You'd better watch—"

Roberto smashed an open hand on the table and rose. "This is not just your house! *You* weren't even here! *I* protected this house!"

"You check yourself, mister, and sit your ass down."

Roberto took a step toward his father. He was almost a foot taller, and dark, and suddenly he didn't look at all gangly. Suddenly he looked dangerous.

"*I said sit down!*"

Jason's breath caught. Roberto's eyes narrowed.

"Think hard, mister."

Roberto turned toward Jason for a silent moment. The rims of his eyes were pink, the bags under them still dark. Unsure of what Roberto was looking for, Jason held his breath.

"Better be sure you're ready for the consequences, son."

Roberto wavered. Tiredness flooded his face. Then the rebellion drained out of his body and he looked gangly again.

He sat heavily.

"I apologize for challenging your authority, sir," he said, looking straight ahead at the dining room curtain. "It was insubordinate of me."

"That's better. Now tell your so-called friend, here, what your name is."

"Robert, sir."

The man gave Jason a smug look. Jason's stomach turned. "Go on. You're not done yet. Tell him your family name."

"My family name is Goldstein, sir."

The man flushed and his hands closed. "Your family name is *Summers*," he said. It sounded as though he were trying to match his previous bright tone, but he couldn't.

"Your family name is Summers, sir. I'm Elsa Goldstein's son."

"Your mother is dead."

"Maybe so, sir, but I love her, and this was her house."

His father stared at him as though paralyzed. He opened his mouth as though to speak. Roberto turned to regard him steadily. Summers made as to speak again, then wheeled and went into the kitchen. Back turned, he said, "It's time for you to go, Jason."

"He was protecting the house," Jason said.

"Oh," Summers said. His head jerked in a sort of nod, as though he were trying to swallow something jagged. "Well, then." He turned. Jason couldn't read his face. "In *that* case, I should shake your hand! Actually, you know what—" He came forward. "You're the one who should do that, *Roberto*. Stand up."

Roberto looked straight ahead.

"Get on your feet, mister."

Slowly, Roberto rose.

"Shake his hand."

Roberto extended a hand slowly. Jason took it.

"I want you both to remember," Summers said, "that the handshake of a liar is worthless. Understand that?" As the handshake ended awkwardly, he continued, "Now it's my turn," and put his own hand out. "Thank you, Jason, for helping my good son clean up what he did to his own house."

"What?"

"It was very nice of you to help him protect his dear, departed mother's house like that. I hope you both feel good about it."

"*What?*"

"When a man extends his hand to you, you shake it, Jason."

Bewildered—angry?—Jason looked at Roberto, then back at Summers, who angled his head toward his outstretched hand.

"What's it gonna be, Jason?"

Jason took a step back.

Roberto's head was down. "Pop—"

"What's it gonna be, Jason?"

Another step back. Jason shook his head slowly. "I'm not shaking that," he said.

Summers dropped his hand. "Suit yourself. You see that, Roberto? That's how a man stands up for himself." He nodded his approval and sat down to the remainder of his breakfast. "Remember what I said about the word of a liar, Jason," he said as he peppered his eggs. "You think about that."

"You better go," Robert said; but Jason was catching up now, and this felt anything but over.

He stepped forward.

"No," Robert said, looking up and seeing his face. "Don't. Please, just . . . just go. I'll see you at school."

Jason switched his gaze to Summers.

Summers shrugged. "Man says he wants you to go."

"He's not a liar."

"He's not? Oh, okay."

"Look, you—"

Robert cut in. "Jason! I'll just see you at school, okay?"

"Careful, there," Summers said.

Jason stood with clenched fists and no good options, in a house where he wasn't welcome.

Summers watched him now as he ate. "Better go," he said in a friendly voice.

Robert's eyebrows rose in reluctant agreement. Jason stood for a few long moments, then gave him a nod, unclenched his fists, and opened the door.

"Wait." Robert cleared his throat. "I, uh—I . . . I told the police where to find you."

"Well, duh." Why did everyone seem to care about this?

"*Thanks* for coming, Jason," Summers said.

Jason stopped and looked at him without speaking. "I owe you for the lesson," he said finally. Then the door closed behind him, and he was on the porch with nowhere to go.

57

A FTER the last note fell away to nothing, the silence
built until it was almost unbearable. Then Gary Warren accidentally kicked Zeb's Coleman lantern and
said, "Ow!" and the song was over. But there was still a mood.

"Let there be light," whispered the Inscrutable Whom
against the *shush* of lighted propane, and Zeb held the lantern
aloft in the unsealed space.

A few feet from the hole, a reel-to-reel tape machine reclined on a homemade wooden stand, staring blindly at the
ceiling like a bug-eyed monster. Near it was a tall stool and a
microphone stand with a microphone on it, the mike cable
going into the recorder. Behind it, two couches made an L
against two walls, with three little round tables at the ends
and angle. On the tables, milky vase-sized vials had once been
working lava lamps. To the right was a file cabinet.

But all that was underneath. On the surface—of everything—were mushrooms. Thousands, millions; they made a
thick, fungal carpet on the floor, hung from the fringe of the
swag lamp, sprouted radially from the tip of the microphone.

In thirty years, they'd carpeted every organic or porous surface: the couches, the walls, the end tables, the wooden stand. It was the recording studio from beyond the looking glass. The few surfaces without growth were metallic and corroded: the thick metal barrel of the microphone, the brushed metal face of the tape recorder, the painted metal doors of the filing cabinet.

And one other exception. Atop the file cabinet was a Buddha statuette made of plastic, painted to look like carved wood, a tiny blue light glimmering in its lap: the source of the blue glow. Jason looked at Robert; Robert was staring at it.

"Curiouser and curiouser," remarked the Inscrutable Whom.

"What is that," Zeb said in awe. "A blue LED?"

"It's the infernal light, man. The rhythm guitarist from Ill Wind spliced it off the building wiring."

"And it's still going?" Jason wondered.

Zeb put one leg through the hole, tested the ground, and grimaced. Another siren passed in the distance. "There probably wasn't power for about fifteen years while the place was empty."

"Still, that leaves another fifteen. I wish any of my gear would last like that." He looked at Robert, who was still staring at the statuette. "Hey, Robert, how you doing?"

Robert nodded to himself.

"Robert."

"Huh?"

"How you doing?"

"Could I—" Robert said, and stopped. "Zeb?"

"Yes?"

"And Gary Warren, of course, forgive me—both of you . . ." His expression was odd and searching. He took a deep breath. "Could I have that job?"

✦

The couches and carpet were caked with spores and rot; the eight-track recorder and the microphone were corroded beyond practical repair. The lamp was a wreck, its shade disintegrating at a touch, the varnish on its chain eaten by moisture.

The file cabinet held about a hundred flimsy, rotting cardboard boxes, ten inches square and three-quarters of an inch deep, standing on end, spines out. Thirty-year-old master tape reels, archived correctly: sealed in plastic bags inside their cardboard boxes, stored upright.

A few still had readable labels.

"Jesus Christ," Zeb exclaimed, head sideways as he browsed. "Do you know who— Whoa! Jesus Christ!"

Beyond the hole they'd entered through, the Inscrutable Whom erupted with laughter. "Hey!" he called from his spot on the stairs, and then almost couldn't get through what followed because he was laughing so hard he was crying: "Hey! Listen! You've—you've got to dig through a—a lot of crap to get—" He gasped raggedly. "—to—to get—to get to—*your old—tapes!*"

An explosive sound somewhere between a sneeze and a spit take was followed by a fresh round of near-asphyxiation. Standing at the hole with her hands in the front pockets of her jeans, a little smile on her lips, Peggy Stegner turned to watch her husband kill himself laughing on the stairs. Jason thought of Veronica the vicious werewolf and resolved to send her a card soon.

Moods have to fade, and after it sank in that Robert would be the night man and it was settled that he'd bunk on a cot in Zeb's office for a while, this mood ended. Zeb tapped a pen on the glass counter; Allan and Peggy Stegner gave each other the married *what do you think?* look.

"Well, now what?" Gary Warren said, and Jason, not yet

willing to give up the day and the company, said, "*Young Frankenstein.*"

There was a moment of six individual appraisals, and then Peggy's enthusiastic "Yeah!" was the rock that set the rest tumbling.

Zeb and Robert decided to talk more about their new arrangement, so it was Jason, going out with Zeb's video rental card and less-than-clear directions, who opened the door just as the girl—pale-pink skin, straight blonde hair flowing from the dome of a red knit cap—walked up to it and said, "Hi. I was here the other night to buy some cello strings?" She pointed at the door. "Is the tall cute guy here?"

58

HE was looking around her dim apartment when her phone rang.

"Sarah's house."

"You're there."

"I just came by to make sure I didn't forget anything. I'm on my way to the airport."

There was a long silence.

"Well," she said. There was something in her voice. "I didn't know where you were, and I couldn't find you, so I just called to see if you were there."

There was something in his, too. "I just got here."

More silence.

"All right," she said finally. "Well, I'm all checked out of the hotel and on my way too, so I guess I'll talk to you when you're back in L.A. and I'm back in New York."

"Okay, well—"

"Okay, bye," she said.

He looked at the handset as the click became silence and the silence became dial tone, was still looking at it as the dial tone became an off-hook alert, stood not hanging up until he noticed his feet starting to ache. He placed the deadbolt key gently on her coffee table and carefully double-checked the knob lock on his way out, feeling his aloneness as he watched himself go down her hallway, watched himself hail a cab, as he checked in at the gate, and as he watched the tarmac and the weird little airport trucks dwindle beneath him.

59

DECEMBER in Los Angeles.

It was getting down to forty degrees at night, and the ex-New Yorkers in cafés and coffeehouses along Washington were griping about the weather. This is nothing! This isn't a real December! What kind of Christmas doesn't have snow!?

Jason had not previously understood that they thought they were being ironic and witty when they did this.

He'd gotten into a new routine of bicycling in the cold mornings, taking Venice Boulevard to the deserted beach and following the bike path to the Santa Monica Pier and back, through fog so dense that sometimes he couldn't see anything but the broken yellow line directly under his bike. Sometimes he'd go as far as Will Rogers State Beach before turning around and taking the return trip at a moderate clip. There wasn't much going on with him: Some last-minute background music for an educational CD-ROM in November and nothing else probable until after the new year. A RollerBlading girl on the bike path had talked him into a date a couple of weeks previously, but he'd shown up just to cancel.

His regular stop after the bike path, before pedaling past the Firehouse on the remote contingency that Barry the Bouncer might be there, was a walk-up window on Windward Circle, where he eyed the wheatgrass suspiciously every morning and got a peach smoothie instead. It was a good place to watch the natives, and this morning, he had to wait in line behind a dozen wheezing, overweight, uniformed cycle cops wearing new helmets and perching awkwardly on mountain bikes.

"We're out of peach," the counter guy said when he finally rolled up to the window and ordered. "Banana or berry."

Tragedy.

He said thanks and wheeled around idly while he tried to cope. Finally he coasted within smelling distance of Joanie's Coffee Roaster, locked the bike to a street sign, and went in.

In addition to its primary function of making Venice smell like burnt cork at regular intervals through the day, Joanie's Coffee Roaster was one of the few restaurants that catered to bodybuilders and opened early on weekends. It was the kind of place where people greet each other, but most of them look like movie people, so you don't actually trust the greetings. Jason was messing around with the strap of his bike helmet when his smoothie order was called; and in the course of looking up to get it, he locked eyes with Barry at a table only half a room away, pink polo shirt, black watchband and shades, sitting across from a weasel in ugly sunglasses and an artsy-looking little poet's beard. The weasel's hair was slicked into dark runners over its bald spot.

Los Angeles is habitat to various species of weasel. This specimen was a movie weasel: air of importance, big talker, personality core that slithers around like mercury. Accent from somewhere East. Says it can get your project greenlighted. Be careful before you doubt this: since talent and integrity aren't required in the biz, discerning that the weasel has none doesn't tell you anything.

Jason collected his smoothie and moved to the sole vacant table, too far from Barry to eavesdrop. When the meeting ended, Barry looked at him on the way out, walked the weasel to its Corvette, and came back.

"Pitching a romantic comedy?" Jason said.

Barry looked at him and sat without speaking.

"I've been keeping an eye out for you at the Firehouse. You want to tell me what happened to my friend's music store?"

Barry watched him for a while and then said, "We have a deal."

"I've honored it. That makes me a better risk than the stoat you had breakfast with."

Barry watched him.

"Look," Jason said. "How about this. I'll tell you what I think, and we can go from there. You and Matthew are related somehow. He's your nephew, or you're his legal guardian, or he got you from Big Brothers of America, or you won him playing Yahtzee. Whatever. Doesn't matter. He didn't steal the theremin himself."

"Why not?"

"I don't know why not. Just the way you handled him. I've had time to mull."

Nothing. A blonde woman in her forties came in the door and squealed a *hello, darling!* at somebody.

"So if Matthew didn't steal it himself, he got it from the people who did steal it, which means you know who they are. I don't see you protecting a ring of adult hate crime perpetrators, so—"

He stopped. That had almost been a reaction.

Barry shifted. Jason waited.

"What hate crime?" Barry said.

"Are you asking me for information?"

The blonde woman was helloing other darlings.

"Tell me," Barry said. "I'll think about what to tell you."

They looked at each other. The blonde woman was making air kisses. A couple of busboys caromed between tables, sweeping dishes into plastic bins.

"All right," Jason said. "My friend who owns the music store is gay. Considering the amount of unnecessary damage done to his store, it seems reasonable that it might have been a bias crime."

"It wasn't a straight burglary?"

"No." When Barry didn't respond, he said, "Your turn."

"Was anything else stolen?"

"I didn't mean 'your turn for me to talk more.'"

Barry breathed silently once. "Was anything else stolen?"

"Plenty was written off. I don't know how much was damaged and how much was stolen." He tapped his fingers on the table. "Are you going to give me something now?"

After a shorter pause than Jason expected, Barry said, "They're kids. It wasn't a hate crime."

"So what was it?"

He watched Barry. Barry watched him.

"Pen," Jason said, pointing. Barry took it from his shirt pocket and handed it over. Jason wrote his number and that of the Magic Music Shop on a napkin. "Help me put my friend's mind at ease. I won't turn Matthew in."

Barry pushed his chair back, took the napkin, and left.

Nobody was usually up at eight on a Saturday morning, but as he carried his bike through the screen door and into the living room of their small back house, Leon came out of the kitchenette in gray sweatpants and uncombed black hair and said, "Yo, *tío*, Martin says we're going out for breakfast."

The Plymouth wouldn't start, even when he popped the hood and shorted the solenoid with a screwdriver, so they squeezed into Jason's little Ford pickup truck and went to the Denny's near the Santa Monica pier. A few tired-looking goth kids in black eye makeup were left over from last night, but mostly it was white hair and baseball caps.

"So . . ." Martin was toying with the sugar dispenser. "Wendy dumped me."

Jason, in mid-sip, blinked. He swallowed and put down his cup. "Ouch! I'm *really* sorry to hear that. What happened?"

Leon said, "She said he didn't have no ambition."

"Yeah, thanks, bro," Martin's shoulders twitched in a restrained shrug. "She said a lot of things, but that was the main one. I dunno. I always thought trying to be a good person and taking good care of your family was ambition enough, you know?"

Jason nodded. Each waited for the other to know what to say next.

"I'm sorry."

"Yeah, me too."

Neither of them said anything next. They drank their coffee.

Martin shrugged and shook his head. "I guess I can't blame her."

"Fuck Wendy," Leon blurted, and this made both of them choke on their coffees—which was unfortunate, because then there was no turning off the Leon Altamirano Comedy Experience.

When they'd eaten and Leon had calmed down, Jason said, "I've been thinking about back when we met."

"That makes two of us, chief. Hey, listen. Guess what we saw on DVD in the video store."

"You know they changed the ending."

"Like how, he doesn't find the kid?"

"I'm not sure. I never finished the book, but I know in the movie, he gets his eyesight and his girlfriend back and they all go off into the sunset. I don't know what else they changed."

"Well, we didn't rent it. Figured we'd wait for you to get back."

"You guys go ahead. I don't really want to see it."

"Yeah? Why not?"

"That whole time. You know?"

Martin nodded but didn't answer.

"You don't feel that way?" Jason asked after some silence.

Martin looked thoughtfully at the table. "Honestly?"

"Sure."

A little weighing gesture, a tilt of the head. "Until I took Leon in?" Martin nodded reluctantly, as though it were an admission. "I always felt like that whole time was the best thing I ever did. All the stuff I shouldn't have done after that . . . I always had that to look back on and say, yeah, okay, but I once did this really *good* thing."

Jason tried to understand as he drank his coffee, finally glimpsed just a flicker of it as the table conversation turned to soccer.

"Really?" he said.

"Hold that thought, Le. Yeah, really."

"Sorry, Leon. How come?"

Martin shrugged. "I just never knew people who stood up for each other before."

Jason nodded, which he seemed to be doing a lot lately.

Martin looked hard at him. "Why do you think when I came back down from up north, I came looking for *you* guys?"

When Jason took more than a couple of seconds to answer, Leon the opportunist said, "Bro—so anyway—" and the soccer discussion resumed. Jason sat and drank his coffee, sorting through shards of confusion and love, inclusion and loneliness, and the gentle conviction that he hadn't earned the great privilege of his friendships.

His cell phone was ringing on the bench seat of his pickup.

"National Association of National Associations," he said

after unlocking the door and snatching it up, half in the cab with the door against his leg. "Vice President in charge of Vice Presidents."

"Jason!"

"Hey, Zeb."

"Hey, Robert's right here—he's got something to tell you. Hold on—"

"—Jason?"

"Hey, what's up?"

"Uh, well. I had your DJ Coffeepot CD on in the shop last night, and this guy came in and heard it. He wants to give you twelve hundred dollars to do a rough music sketch for a TV commercial."

"A demo?"

"Yeah, that's what he called it."

"No kidding. What'd you tell him?"

"I told him you'd call him today. He gave me his card."

"Hold on . . ." He found a pen and an auto glass company notepad in the glove compartment and backed out of the cab, trapping the phone against his ear so he could put the pad on the hood and write. "Okay, shoot."

"His name's Ron Blakley." Robert spelled it and gave him the number. "I gave him the CD."

"Thanks. I'll give him a call."

"The company is Lindsay Tate Buckman Barrow."

"Oh yeah?"

"Is that good?"

"I don't know, but it's a major agency."

"There's . . . uh . . . there's one catch. He said he only works with local musicians."

Jason looked at the phone number he'd just written down. "So this is useless."

"Not exactly. I told him you were local."

"You did."

"It seemed important to him, so I said you were."

"Robert, how am I supposed—"

"Hold on. Zeb wants to talk to you."

"Hi, Jason.

"Uh, hi, Zeb."

"Look, these commercial guys like to be able to drop in on the session."

"Yeah, but—"

"You want the gig, right?"

"Zeb, I don't even know what the gig *is*."

"When he asks where you're located, tell him Brooklyn and give him the store number. Brooklyn's still farther than ad guys want to travel, but they'll do it if they think you're a secret weapon. He's also going to want some ridiculous turnaround time. Whatever he wants, tell him you can deliver it. Oh," he continued before Jason could interrupt. "He's probably going to want your fax number, too. Write this down."

Jason wrote it down. "Wait," he said. "How am I—"

"You worry about getting the gig," Zeb said, "and I'll worry about getting you here. All right?"

"Zeb, that'll cost as much as a demo's likely to pay."

"That's my problem. You helped me—now let me help you."

This was going too fast. "All right, but you take half."

"Your money's no good here," Zeb said. "Call the guy."

Standing in the sunny parking lot with Martin and Leon looking on, he called the guy. The phone was picked up before the first ring and an impatient male voice said, "Ron."

"This is Jason Keltner. You heard some of my music last night and wanted me to call about doing a demo."

The voice lost its impatience. "I'm in post hell right now, but I want to talk to you about that music. Is it available?"

"Sure."

"Besides the parts with the newscast, which I'm not interested in, are there any uncleared loops or samples?"

"Nope."

"Are you in the union?"

"Yup."

"Without going into details, we have some unusual problems with the music in this spot. We laid yours in this morning and it worked better than what we were going to use anyway, so we took a vote and yours is it. I'll give you ten thousand dollars to use thirty seconds of it, with some changes. That's half what I'd usually pay for a national, but as I said, I have problems with the spot, and underpaying you solves them. How's that sound?"

"What kind of changes?"

"Twelve seconds in, the client wants a rhythm track. Something tribal. Can you deliver that on CD by tomorrow at three o'clock P.M.?"

"Yes."

"Where's your studio?"

"Brooklyn. What's the commercial for?"

"For an office supply dotcom that'll be out of business inside of a year."

"Office supplies?"

"Hold on." Blakley turned from the phone and gave indistinct instructions to someone in his office. Returning, he said, "The spot's about the magic of freedom. It's all utopian imagery. Your music slugs right in. Hey, I'm sorry to push you, but this thing ships Monday afternoon. Do you want to sell?"

Did he have any anti-commercial feelings about that music?

No, he was pretty much done with it. And a rhythm track might be fun.

"Sure," he said.

"Great. What's your fax number?"

He gave Zeb's.

"Pleasure doing business with you, Jason. If that contract doesn't come by noon, call me. I'll be in touch."

"I'm flying back in from L.A. today," Jason said, looking at his hand as though it were his pocket calendar and trying to sound as though he were consulting it. "I'll be back late tonight, and I'll get on it then."

"Fine, as long as I have it by three. I may want to drop by the session. Let me give you my cell number. Do you have a company name?"

"Magic Music."

"Great name. Call me if the contract doesn't come."

"Sure," he said.

"Zeb, he wants changes by tomorrow."

"You told him you could do it?"

"Yes. Can I?"

"That depends. Can you be at the airport in an hour?"

"Yeah." He wrote down the flight information Zeb gave him. "He wants 'tribal.' I'm assuming he means what white people mean when they say it. Do you have a *djembe* and a nice, deep-sounding *shekere*?"

"No, but I will by the time you get here."

"Microphones—"

"It's all being taken care of. Just get here."

"Okay. Uh, thanks."

I think.

Eight hours later, he was stepping out of a taxicab in Brooklyn and standing under the streetlamp, looking at the shop as the cab drove away. Guitars and what looked like an *oud* hung in the window over a display of wind instruments and music books on red fabric. Then the door opened and out poured Zeb, Gary Warren, Robert and his girlfriend, all trying not to trip over a yapping Doberman the size of a large rabbit.

"Il Duce!" Gary Warren commanded. "Heel!"

Robert was standing behind his girlfriend with his hands

on her shoulders. "Jason," he said formally, "you remember Maryelizabeth Hart."

He nodded and tried to remember how to do a genuine smile. "Nice to see you again."

"Nice to see you again, too."

Robert beamed.

"Jeez, Jason," Zeb said, reaching for the duffel bag, which looked as though it were about to burst. "How much stuff did you bring?" Then, "Wow, it's light."

"I really hate to be rude," Jason said when Robert shot a glance at him and another at the duffel "but I've had eight hours to work up a good head of worry. Did you get the instruments?"

"Not to worry," Zeb said, carrying the duffel. "It's all here."

Il Duce shot ahead of them into the Magic Music Shop, which wasn't just back in order; it was back to being cluttered. On the back shelves, instruments fashioned from black PVC pipe were crammed in with the clay pots, and the area behind the counter was full of opened boxes and leftover nuts and broken strings.

"Walk this way . . ." said Zeb.

He'd seen restored cars before, and he'd seen restored furniture and restored instruments. He'd never seen a restored 1970s underground recording studio.

It had to have been a disagreeable job, scraping and shoveling the fungus, but all that was left was a mild, earthy odor, not unpleasant. Where the mushroomy couches had been, two new ones of the correct vintage sat, low and gold, and lava lamps oozed in red and yellow on two round walnut end tables. The theremin, about ready for another polishing, stood where the third end table had been. In the corner, the fungal swag lamp was gone and a bare hook poked from the ceiling.

Reclining on its wooden stand in the middle of the room, a shiny reel-to-reel eight-track recorder of late-sixties vintage waited. Indian rugs covered floor and walls for decoration and sound absorption. Off to the right, segregated, were concessions to digital technology: a computer, a couple of synthesizers, a couple of office-type swivel chairs. On the floor by the chairs, a tall, hourglass-shaped drum stood at the center of an ordered pile of percussion instruments.

"Does the eight-track work?"

"It does if you think of it as a seven-track."

"Cool. Let's use that, and then we'll bring it over onto the computer for editing. What do we have for mikes?"

"Whatever you want out of the display case. I tried a couple out on the djembe. It depends on whether you're going more for the slap or that big *bommm*, but the NT-2 sounded good to me."

"Okay. Did the contract come?"

"Right there on the computer table."

"How's it look?"

"It looks fine."

A look around the room. The staircase was its only ventilation. "I bet it gets warm down here."

"That's good!" Zeb said. "That's how you know you're getting to work."

"Okay," Jason said, relaxing a little now that the only thing left was the part he liked. "Let's."

Ron Blakley called when they were taking a break. The percussion tracks had only taken about an hour and a half, and the music was pretty much done.

"Two things," he said. "First, I'd like to drop by the session around ten."

"I'm not sure there's still going to be a session to drop by," Jason said. "We're just about finished tracking."

"That's the other thing," Blakley said. "No more tribal percussion. Now they want a didgeridoo."

"A didgeridoo." Jason looked at Zeb, who frowned intensely for about three seconds and then smiled.

"No problem," Jason said into the phone, giving up any fantasy he'd had of knowing what the hell was going on.

Zeb came back with a bass clarinet, twisting it near the top. "If you take the mouthpiece off and play it like a trumpet, it sounds like a didj." He put the mouthpiece on the computer table, took a deep breath, and turned pink as he demonstrated.

"When this is over," Jason said, adjusting the microphone stand, "I'm either not speaking to you again or buying you coffee."

Behind him, Maryelizabeth stuck her head in long enough to say, "Do you guys have a moose down there?"

They heard the door open and close at ten on the dot, and then Robert showed Ron Blakley down into the studio. He was about forty-five, in a leather bomber jacket, khakis, and a tan cap with a curved bill, and he was carrying his cell phone in his hand. At the bottom of the stairs, his jaw dropped, and he turned all the way around to take in the lava lamps and the rugs on the walls.

"This isn't the actual Magic Music Shop?"

Zeb stood. "The one and only."

"*Midnight at the Magic Music Shop?*"

"You've heard of it?" Jason said.

"I have an original pressing." He looked at the digital gear. "That's why I said it was a great name. I didn't have any idea it was actually the same place."

"It's the same place," Zeb said.

"Wow." Blakley came a few steps farther in. "This is a piece of musical history. What a find." He did another slow turn, then spun to face them and said in a hushed tone, "He's not here, is he?"

Zeb shook his head. "Not today. He's here sometimes, though." He pointed across the room.

Jason looked as Blakley did. Tucked into the corner by one of the couches was a pair of beaded moccasins.

"Wow," Blakley said reverently. "I almost don't want to talk about commercials in here." All thought of work was suspended as he gazed at the moccasins, then at the eight-track, then once more around the room. But he gathered himself back to business. "Almost."

Introductions were made. Blakley sat on one of the couches. "Play me what you've got."

Jason played it. "Great," Blakley said, standing. "Burn it on CD and consider it delivered."

"We were going to tweak—"

"Don't bother. We're going to tweak it in post no matter what you do. It sounds fine. It's done. Do you have a signed contract for me?"

As soon as they were up in the store again, Blakley's cell phone rang. He shook Jason's hand. "Thanks for the music. I'll put this through on Monday," he said, shaking Zeb's. "Five to six weeks for the check. This is Ron," he said into the phone as he shook Robert's and Maryelizabeth's and waved goodbye, and he was saying, "Yeah, I'm on my way back with it," as the door closed behind him.

"So how do you feel?" Zeb said when Blakley was gone.

Jason drummed his fingers on the countertop. "Want to do some more tracks?"

They stayed up recording banjo, synthesizer, and decapitated bass clarinet while Robert manned the store and occasionally came down to see what the hell they were doing.

"Remember what you told me about? That happened on the roof?" Zeb said around two o'clock, after they'd listened back to it again. "And I said I wanted to think about it?"

"Yes." He turned in his swivel chair to see Zeb regarding him soberly. "I figured you didn't have anything to say about it."

"I've been thinking. I didn't want to say anything unless I really had something to say. So now I want you to really listen to me, and really try to hear what I'm going to tell you."

"Okay." He breathed deeply once and tried to settle himself.

"Ready?"

Jason nodded.

"You tried."

He watched Jason try to absorb this, then said, "Oh! You know what this needs? A harmonium."

Robert came down the stairs with Jason's duffel bag, whispering, "Quick—Zeb's in the bathroom."

As they stood on the couches, hanging Robert's old gold rain lamp from the ceiling hook, Jason said, "Maryelizabeth left?"

"She said goodbye to you two hours ago."

"Oh. Sorry. We were kind of caught up in recording. I hope I didn't offend her."

"You didn't. Do you like her?"

"I don't know her well enough to say. Does she make you happy?"

Robert smiled. "Yes. So far."

Then Jason tried to think of a fast change of subject, but Robert was faster:

"Have you talked to Sarah lately?"

"Not since I got back to L.A."

"What happened to that?"

They stepped off the couches and Jason filled the reservoir from a bottle he'd brought in the duffel. Then Robert plugged it in, and as the pump started grinding, they stood and watched beads of glycerin begin to flow down the fishing line and into the plastic Pietà.

It was perfect.

"Martin sent you a gift," Jason said. From the collapsed duffel he withdrew a framed picture and handed it over.

"Wow," Robert said. "He still had it." He looked up. "For me, or for the studio?"

"For you. He made a point of saying that."

Fully inked now, the teeth gritted, the lines of wind blowing past the open window and the discharging pistol.

"Very cool."

Jason started toward the stairs. "I'm going to—"

Robert let him get halfway up before asking, "So what happened with Sarah?"

He could have pretended not to hear, but he sighed and came down slowly. "Well . . . if you'd asked me an hour ago, I would have said it was just one of those baffling relationship things. But . . ."

"But what?"

"Well, the truth is, I didn't try."

"Does she know you're here?"

"No."

"Why not?"

"It would be insulting if I suddenly called her when I was in town, after not calling her for two months."

Holding the picture of Tom Carter, Robert said, "So you're still not trying."

"But Tommy—oh, Tommy . . ." Fresh tears filled her eyes. "Why couldn't you save us?"

Suddenly, thoroughly sick of learning things, Jason snapped, "Look—!" But it was true, so he managed to rein in his retort.

"That's right," he said eventually.

Robert nodded.

"Carter's not the best model for relationships, Jason."

Until she answered, he didn't know what he was doing, but her sleepy "hello" seemed to spread through him and unlock something, and it didn't take any effort to say, without awkwardness, "It's me. I didn't try very hard and I'd like to do it better."

"I didn't try either," she said. He'd expected a pause while she caught her bearings, but there wasn't one, and when she spoke again, it sounded like she might have started to cry, which he envied. "Where are you?"

"At Zeb's store."

"You're here!" She sounded so suddenly, unadulteratedly happy that now he had to blink back a few tears of his own. "Will you be at the store for a while? Can I come out?"

"How about if I come out to you?"

"When?"

"Now."

"Okay."

"I love you."

"I love you too."

And that was pretty much that.

60

I T was eleven in the morning, and they weren't up.

"Don't ever do that again," she said.

"Do which?"

"Any of it. Well, not what you just did. Before that."

"Okay. You too."

"I'll try." She rolled toward the phone. "Who do you think called?"

He observed her bottom as she called for her messages.

"It's Robert . . . he says . . . he says . . ." She crossed her eyes as she listened. "I don't know what he says. You take it." Pressing a button on the keypad, she handed him the phone.

"Hi, both of you," Robert's voice said. "That is, assuming you didn't stop trying again all of a sudden, in which case, hi, Sarah—how are you? and I'm sorry Jason stopped trying all of a sudden, unless it was you who stopped trying, in which case I think you've made a mistake, not to say that he wouldn't have, had he been the one who stopped trying. But if neither of you has stopped trying, then hi both of you, and Jason, I thought I'd let you know that if one or both of you don't have plans, and preferably the 'one' would be you, which is not to say that I wouldn't want to see both of you, because I would, that is to say, I do, there's an interesting event tonight that I want to take you to. Both of you. If you haven't stopped trying. Call me at the store if you get this. Okay? Bye."

They spent the day doing nothing special; they went to a matinee, out for late lunch, and then back to her apartment for half an hour of privacy that turned into forty-five minutes and then into an hour and fifteen.

Since Jason knew where the 92nd Street YMCA was, they were meeting there, and then going wherever they were going. They tumbled out of the subway station onto a black street glossy with rain, and hurried a few blocks through a speckling drizzle to where Robert and Maryelizabeth waited on the corner. Robert looked odd.

"Sorry," Jason called when they were within hailing distance. Closer, he explained, "It was my fault. We didn't leave in time."

Robert waved it off. "No problem. We only got here a few minutes ago. We'll just have dinner after, instead of before."

"Hey," Jason exclaimed, realizing why Robert looked odd. "Nice shirt!"

"Thanks."

"Or should I say—" He turned to Maryelizabeth. "Hey! Nice shirt!"

"Thank you," she said, and hugged Robert.

"Yeah," Robert said. "Thanks."

"So where are we going?"

"Right here. It's already started, so we should hurry."

Inside, a hand-lettered sign by a closed set of doors said *Lester Kellogg Reading*.

Robert handed four tickets to the door person. "It was listed in the lobby when we stayed here before," he said to Jason's stunned expression. "I wasn't going to go tonight, but since you're in New York . . ."

"Well, I'll tell you," the trim, elderly man was saying onstage as they entered the darkened auditorium, "it was easier than I thought it would be. Once I said I wanted to reinstate the original ending, everything seemed to fall right into place."

"So just to be clear, you didn't threaten anybody," said the host, a concise woman in flowing black. They were in two chairs, with two microphones.

Kellogg chuckled. "Oh, no, there was no threatening. It was all very polite."

"I just want to ask a couple of brief questions. *Brief*," she reassured the audience, which laughed, "questions, and then we'll proceed directly to the reading, which is, after all, why we all came out on a rainy night. Ah . . . so is this the original ending, or an ending you wrote after the first publication, or—what?"

"No, this is the original ending. I was still early in my career when *The Night Men* was published. I knew it was a flawed book, and I felt insecure, so I rewrote the ending as my publisher requested, which was to climax with a showdown between Tom Carter and Borden Jarvis. In retrospect, I should possibly have caused a fuss, but I didn't feel, at the time, that this avenue was available to me. So when I was approached last year about what became this reissue, I jumped at the chance to reinstate what is, to me, the book's only true ending."

"Why didn't you want to write a showdown with Jarvis?"

"Well, it's a side issue, isn't it? The story isn't about beating up Jarvis. It's about saving a child. And as well, even if Carter wanted one, Jarvis would never allow such a showdown."

"He wouldn't," the host repeated.

"Quite right, it would make no sense. One doesn't become a successful evil ringleader by allowing one's nemeses that degree of access. Successful evil insulates itself and acts by proxy. It's very difficult to determine its true source; if one is looking for confrontation, an underling is the closest one's likely to get, and even then only if one is very lucky."

"You never get to fight the real bad guy."

"Yes, but more to the point: the desire for confrontation is an enticement to deviate from one's other goals."

"Such as saving the kid."

"Yes."

"And, of course, the movie had yet a third ending." The host glanced through her index cards. "Well, I had a question about symbolism, but—well, what do you think, audience? Do you want to hear about symbolism?"

The audience rustled. Jason and Robert glanced sharply at each other in the dark.

"Okay, that's what I thought. So what do you say we jump to the reading portion of the evening, and you and I can talk about symbolism later?"

"I'd be delighted."

"And this," she informed the audience pointedly, "will be the first public reading of this passage in . . . ever—is that right?"

Kellogg, licking his thumb and paging from the back of the book said, "Yes, the first time, that's right." He looked up. "And it's very short, a very short passage, so if you don't like it, your suffering will be short-lived."

As the audience chuckled politely, the host said, "And for those in the audience who may not have had a chance to read it—and you really should, because this is a *fabulous* book— Carter has . . . ?"

"Carter has been looking for a little boy who doesn't speak, and when he's tried to find this little boy, he's been stymied by various underworld characters of the sort we used to write about." His thumb was holding a place in the book. He looked inquiringly at the host, who nodded at him and said:

"Ladies and gentlemen, of three possible endings, here is the *true* ending of *The Night Men*."

61

H E didn't see Martin again until later in his life.

But about a week later, he happened to be walking past the soshes' tree during lunch as Robert came out of the cafeteria with his dumb tuxedo shirt half-untucked, and he heard Dan the rich asshole say, "Look at *that* loser," and all the soshes went heh-heh-heh.

He revised his trajectory and stepped in to stare Dan in the face.

"Hey, David," Trent said casually, off to the side. "What's the haps with your weird little *ex*-friend?"

David mumbled something unimportant. Jason said nothing and felt nothing. He watched without engagement as Dan said, "You got a problem?" and Trent said, "Still sleeping in the park, loser?"

Then Dan lost his nerve and dropped his gaze for the briefest moment, and as sparrows twittered in the trees in the quad, Jason turned his back and went to join his friend.

62

NOBODY was very hungry after the signing, so they headed back to the store to have coffee with Zeb instead of going out for dinner. On the train, Jason was unable to keep from looking happy about his signed book despite the fact that Sarah's expression said she thought this was adorable.

To Jason, it said on the title page. *Glad to have been of use. Maybe you'll help someone else— L. Kellogg.*

Maybe so, he thought. I hope so.

Zeb was out from behind the counter when they got there, and so was the young man who'd given Jason the rave tickets.

"Why don't you tell them what you just told me," Zeb said. His face was flushed.

"Yeah, okay." The young man turned. "Barry told us either come here and make good, or get out."

Zeb said, "John here is the only one who came."

"Get out of what?" Jason said to John.

"The halfway house. Barry runs it."

"Does Matthew live there too?"

John laughed. "Not anymore, bro."

They were all still in their coats. Jason lay his signed book on the counter. "What happened here two months ago?"

John shook his head. "That just got out of hand. We were up on the roof, and the skylight was unlocked. We just wanted to come in and see."

"On the roof, huh?"

"Yeah." John shrugged. "Somebody just lost it, man."

"Who?" Zeb demanded.

"I'm not here to rat anybody out. I'm just here to make good."

Robert said, "How exactly do you plan to do that?"

"You tell me, bro."

"Forget who," Zeb said. "Just tell me why."

John looked at his feet. "You know. Just one of those things."

"Uh-uh," Zeb said. "Was it because I'm gay?"

Looking up and blinking, John said, "Gay?" He searched the faces before him in apparent confusion. "No way, man. Because you're *white*."

"Uh," Jason said, after everyone was taken aback for a moment. "So are you."

"Yeah, but look. Somebody's dad isn't, right? and somebody's dad got beat up by some white cops, and then somebody sees this white dude sitting out in front pickin' and a-grinnin'. Get it?"

Jason's first visit to the shop. Zeb, outside in his sweater, posing with his banjo.

Zeb's face, already flushed, reddened. "They thought I was a fuckin' *redneck*?" he roared.

"And then," Robert said, "somebody finds himself in the redneck's peaceful music store at night and feels powerful."

"Oh, this is just—" Zeb said, struggled with the concluding word, and gave up.

"Oh . . ." John said. "Maybe something like that. But look. Here I am to make good."

Zeb was shaking his head now, and pacing. "You thought I was a racist, so you trashed my shop."

"Now, I'm not saying that! I just came here to make good. If you don't want me, I'll blow."

"Why the theremin?"

A shrug. "It was cool."

Zeb turned on him. "Siddown!" he bellowed, ramming a forefinger toward the chair in the keyboard section.

John went. Zeb followed. Jason said softly, "What's he going to do?"

"I don't know," Robert murmured.

Zeb paced in fury, then stopped, glared at John, and began to address him very, very quietly

"I can't watch this," Maryelizabeth said, covering her eyes, and both couples went downstairs and made a few abortive attempts at small talk. Then they just sat uneasily.

The front door opened and closed.

Coming down the stairs, Zeb grated, "I'm going to work his sorry ass off."

He glowered around the room. No one answered him at first. Then Sarah said, "Are you sure he's the one who did it?"

At the bottom of the staircase, Zeb shoved his hands into his pockets. "I doubt he did anything but go into an unlocked building and look around at night. But you know: The truth is, you never know who. It might've been him; it might not. I don't care. I'll take my pound of flesh from whoever offers it."

On the other couch with Maryelizabeth, Robert gave him a look of kindly tolerance. "And teach him a trade in the bargain."

Zeb's face colored. "Bite me, Robert," he muttered.

♦

Robert went with him to Newark Airport. Halfway to being a New Yorker already, he knew how to get a *car*, not a *cab*, for a ride to the airport, where to get the best Indian food in Queens, and he'd stopped waiting for the Walk signal.

They talked on the way in the back of the car, not about anything urgent: What Sarah was doing today (taking pictures of a gay male model and a gay female model—who despised each other—kissing with lots of tongue), how Maryelizabeth's classes were going this semester (just fine despite the Student Loan of Damocles), how Leon's were going (a little less shaky on the algebra), Zeb's nicknames for Il Duce ("Vermint," "K-none," "Doglet"), where Stuart might be (he'd never returned; India? Berkeley? Mars?), Allan Stegner's condition (no better, no worse, Peggy was cute) and weekend occupation (cosmic presence-in-residence under the Magic Music Shop).

"He brings brownies sometimes."

"How are they?"

"I really wouldn't know."

Traffic lunged and braked on the gray expressway. When the hired car finally pulled to the curb at the terminal, Robert said "Hold on" to the driver and got out with Jason.

On the sidewalk near the automatic doors, he said, "I'll come visit soon."

"You know where there's a couch you fit on."

The first clumsy silence he could remember having with Robert welled up from nowhere. He filled it awkwardly:

"Well. Take care of yourself."

"Tell Martin and Leon I said hi." They did the male embrace thing. "Also, I wanted to say. Thanks for saying that to my dad."

Before Jason could remember what this referred to,

Robert clasped his shoulder, said, "Bye," and was waving from the car as it pulled away.

Watching it recede, he remembered, and he stooped and hoisted his empty duffel bag and his new copy of *The Night Men*, and walked through the automatic doors, heading home.

63

I was sitting at my table when the bell rang. Jackie Boy was standing on the landing. Next to him the boy was dressed in clean serge, his eyes dark and opaque, Jackie Boy's big paw on his shoulder.

"Damaged goods for damaged goods," he sneered.

I looked down at the kid, whose eyes revealed nothing. "You'll be safe here," I said.

"Safe!" Jarvis' enforcer guffawed. The boy moved slightly away from him. "He ain't safe, Carter. He's dead. You both are."

My right snapped his head back, and he reeled into the railing. I stepped out of my doorway and slapped him hard. The door clicked shut behind me and I hit him again. He sagged, one hand on the railing, the other trying to stanch the flow of blood from his nose.

"You're dead, Carter! Dead!"

"Yeah," I said. I took another step toward him and he spun and stumbled down the stairs.

The kid was looking up at me in awe. I opened my door and stepped aside. Supper was on the table. I held the door. He went in

That's the rule.

Acknowledgments

Thanks to Michael Seidman as well as those at Walker who object when I try to thank them by name; to Ellen Geiger, Bob Ewen, Ken Cheney, Fred (Blake Arnold, Lori Snyder, Dawn Fratini, Lee Coltman, Gwen Lauterbach), Royal Huber, Shira Rozan, Jamie Scott, Barbara Martin, and Betsy Harding, the people on alt.support.mult-sclerosis (especially Stephen Baron), Joe Wallace, Lillian Roberts, Robyn Wolintz, Coyne Maloney, Bonnie Claeson and Joe Guglielmelli, John Pond, Richard Bugg, Richard Zvonar, Chris Meyer, Lucky Westfall, David Battino, Marty Cutler, and Paul Bishop; and to Mark Badger, to whom I should have tipped my hat two books ago but forgot.

The psychedelic folk music of Perry Leopold—a far better dresser than the Inscrutable Whom despite a shared predilection for flares, and from whom I lifted the resurrected-record story whole—is at www.christianlucifer.com. (Those who know Perry, don't worry—he doesn't have MS.)

The experience of one of *those* band moments is from my time with The Cosmic Debris, specifically the live cut "Siti's Dreamtime." (www.mp3.com/cosmicdebris)

Amazed thanks to Kathleen, Tom, Lori, and Blake, who took it upon themselves to ship me out of the country, and merci beaucoup to Kamel et Hassen at the Restaurant Miami in the 11de arrondissement and the baristas at the Austin Street Starbucks in Forest Hills. Caffeine is more crucial to the process than education or patronage.

I simplified the L.A. bus system of my youth. Someone had to.

www.woollymammoth.com/keith
nightmen@woollymammoth.com